A Summer
of
Surprises

AND

An Unexpected Affair

Jan Ellis

WAVERLEY
BOOKS

Dedication

For Dad, the original "Harold".

www.waverley-books.co.uk
info@waverley-books.co.uk

A Summer of Surprises and An Unexpected Affair
published 2017 by Waverley Books, an imprint of
The Gresham Publishing Company Ltd.,
Academy Park, Building 4000, Gower Street,
Glasgow, G51 1PR, Scotland, UK

First published in digital format in 2013
and 2015 by Endeavour Press Ltd.

ISBN: 978-1-84934-443-2

A catalogue record for this book is available from the British Library.

Printed and bound in the EU

Contents

An Unexpected Affair

Leading to

A Summer of Surprises

Chapter 1: The Bookshop

She carefully slipped the blade of the knife under the tape and cut. Peeling back the flaps, she lowered her face to the contents and inhaled deeply. Erika, her assistant, smiled conspiratorially.

"You've gone over to the dark side. You're definitely one of us now."

"You're right," said Eleanor as she lifted the pile of paperbacks from the box, sniffed them and set them on the counter. "My name is Eleanor Mace and I am addicted to books."

It was three years since Eleanor had bought the bookshop. Three years since she'd left her boring office job and caused her friends' collective jaws to drop by announcing that she was leaving London and moving to Devon. She might as well have said she'd got a new career as a yak herder for the consternation this had caused. They clearly thought she was deranged, though only her sister Jenna had told her so to her face.

"Just because you're divorced from Alan doesn't mean you have to lock yourself away from the world."

"Jen, I'm moving to the English countryside, not entering a convent."

"I can see it now," said Jenna, ignoring her. "In six months' time you'll have stopped shaving your legs, embraced tweed and discovered jam-making."

"Now you're being silly," said Eleanor, thinking that it had already been some time since her pins had seen a Gillette disposable. "It's not the end of the earth, Jen. There's a train station and you and Keith can come and stay any time you wish."

"I'd rather come on my own," said Jenna, wrinkling her nose as she tipped the last of the Chardonnay into Eleanor's glass. "You finish it. They probably don't run to white wine where you're heading. And what on earth will you *do* down there?"

That had been easy to answer: with the money from her divorce Eleanor could afford to buy a slightly crumbly bookshop with an adjoining cottage in a small, unfashionable seaside town. It had been a huge leap and scary at times, but running the shop made her happy and her enthusiasm for what she sold and her knowledge about the books and their authors was undoubtedly behind the small success she had managed to build for herself. She'd made sure the shop was a welcoming place with comfy sofas to sit on and coffee and homemade biscuits on offer. With help from her son Joe, she had built a kind of den at the back of the shop where children could read, and there was always an eclectic selection of new and second-hand books to browse through.

"Don't forget you've got that house clearance to go to this afternoon," said Erika, bearing coffee and biscuits.

"Nope, it's in the diary," said Eleanor, eyeing up a chocolate cookie. "Do you think you can control the rampaging hordes for an hour or two while I'm over there?" she asked, looking at her watch.

"Oh, I think we'll cope, won't we Bella?" said Erika,

addressing the spaniel who was stretched out in a patch of sunshine, wagging her tail. The dog was one of the draws of the shop and local school children would often drag their parents in off the street on their way home just to see her.

"I'll be back in time to lock up," said Eleanor, as she patted the dog, grabbed her bag and walked up the road to her van. It looked rather gaudy in the afternoon sun and she smiled at the recollection of that supper with her sister when she had laid out her plans for what would become The Reading Room.

It hadn't been until they were midway through the second bottle that Eleanor had admitted to swapping her sensible black Volvo for a lime-green campervan, or "hippy wagon" as Jenna had described it. Okay, it wasn't the easiest vehicle to manoeuvre around the vertiginous roads and narrow lanes of her new home, but the Combi had lots of room for boxes and she could also use it when she went to book fairs and local events, as she told herself. Aside from the practical considerations, it was fun and she loved driving it. She found the throaty rumble of the engine strangely comforting and every time she started it up she had the feeling that an adventure could be just around the corner. Driving the van gave her a sense of freedom, although she suspected people thought it was an inappropriate vehicle for a woman who was rapidly hurtling towards fifty. She might still have been a few years away from the big "Five O", but she was technically middle-aged.

As she drove along the town's narrow high street for her meeting, she took a peek at her neighbours to see who was busy and who was not. Passing some charity shops, the baker's and the fishmonger, she noticed that the hardware shop had already put out piles of brightly coloured buckets and spades and flimsy plastic windmills that whirred and spun in the brisk spring air.

The high street sloped down to the sea and Eleanor soon reached the road that scooped around the bay and gradually climbed up out of town, twisting and turning up onto the moorland that surrounded them. After twenty minutes, she had arrived at her destination – an Edwardian pile with extensive views of the coastline. It was a wonderful spot, but the big old family house was expensive to run so its owner, Malcolm Pearce, was downsizing: selling up and moving to a bungalow lower down the hill.

He had a lifetime's worth of books in the house and his children had told him firmly that he couldn't keep them all. Now, after several weeks of hard work, Mr Pearce had some bare shelves and Eleanor was about to acquire a motley selection of titles that she was moderately sure she could sell. One of the things people liked about her shop was the serendipitous nature of it: old and new books hugger-mugger on the shelves and in enticing heaps on a table in the back room.

As Eleanor pulled into the wide driveway, Malcolm came out of the house to greet her.

"Good afternoon, my dear. How kind of you to pop by."

"It's always a pleasure to come up here, Mr Pearce." She looked up at the big old stone house and the garden full of camellias and hoped the people who bought the place would love it as much as its current owner plainly did.

"Good, good," he said, smiling and leading her into a sunny sitting room where the boxes of books were stacked in neat piles. "I shall be very glad to wave farewell to this lot."

Eleanor had already helped him to take a load of books to the charity shop. What was left was for her to take away and – hopefully – sell. She looked at the boxes and hoped she could fit them all in the van. "Right. Let's get started!"

Malcolm insisted on helping and together they soon shifted everything out of the room. Eleanor brought the last box into the hallway and stepped outside into the spring sunshine. Later on, she would sort through the boxes again properly to see if there were any unexpected treasures among them. In the past, she had come across quite rare editions at similar house clearances, which she'd managed to sell to collectors over the internet.

She knew there were some early editions of local histories that would find ready buyers. Other boxes contained children's albums from the 1950s and 1960s: bumper storybooks for boys and girls, adventure stories and tales of derring-do with wonderfully evocative illustrations of swarthy foreigners in far-off lands.

"I'll go through everything back at the shop and let you have a cheque as soon as I've worked out the value."

"Splendid! Now let me see if my son's around to give you a hand loading these heavy boxes into your, er, vehicle. I think he's toiling in the garden somewhere." Malcolm opened the side gate and a small brown shape dashed towards them, closely followed by a tall dark-haired man in worn corduroys and a faded green sweater.

"Hello Crumpet," said Eleanor, bending down to greet the furry bundle at her feet. "Er, sorry, I don't know your name. I'm Eleanor Mace – Bella, Welsh spaniel."

"Daniel Pearce. Border terrier," he said, frowning as he removed a gardening glove to shake her hand. Eleanor recognised him as a peripheral member of the local dog-walking gang.

"Thanks for taking this lot away," he said, nodding at the heaps of cartons. "I can't imagine what you're going to do with Dad's junk."

Eleanor could feel herself prickle. "I wouldn't call it 'junk'. Your father has a very interesting library. Anyway, it's my idea of heaven to rummage among old books."

"You've come to the right place then. Is this your van?" He gave the Combi a pained look that she'd seen before in people who didn't get it. Probably drives a Saab, thought Eleanor, as she scratched Crumpet behind the ears. Shame your owner doesn't have your engaging personality, she said to herself.

"Be a good lad and help Mrs Mace to load up while I make us some tea."

Daniel Pearce gave his father a look that suggested he had much better things to do with his time, but he walked over to the boxes nonetheless. Eleanor got in the van and backed it right up to the porch so they wouldn't need to carry everything too far from the hallway. Opening the side door, she arranged the boxes on the floor as Daniel silently passed them up to her. Working together, it didn't take long to get the books moved and they had almost finished by the time Malcolm came out of the house with three mugs on a battered tea tray. "Really Father," said Daniel, taking his cup, "the rubbish you hang on to."

"This was a wedding present, I'll have you know. Your mother would never forgive me if I threw it away."

"I think it's charming," said Eleanor, helping herself crossly to a custard cream. This man really is an oaf. "They call it shabby chic, you know. In London it's all the rage."

"Hmm, no doubt. Well, I'd better get back to the garden." Daniel drained his mug and handed it back to his father. "Nice to meet you properly, Eleanor."

"Thanks for your help." She couldn't bring herself to say it had been nice to meet such a rude man.

"I apologise for my son," said Malcolm, sighing as Daniel left them. "He's a super chap normally, but he has been a grumpy so-and-so since Freya left him."

Freya! So that was the name of the rather glamorous woman she'd often seen striding over the hill with Crumpet. Looking down at her own ancient jeans and baggy jumper she suddenly felt a twinge of sympathy for young Mr P: what must it be like being married to a woman who wears full make-up to walk a small shaggy dog in the middle of nowhere at eight o'clock in the morning? No wonder he looked miserable.

"Oh dear. That must be difficult for him. For you all. Do you have grandchildren?"

He nodded sadly, "Yes, we have a granddaughter – I mean, I have a granddaughter. My wife passed away some years ago. Ah well," he said, brightening, "everything will sort itself out eventually, I'm sure. More tea?"

"Thanks Malcolm, but I'd better be off. We've got a big event happening tomorrow evening and I'm nowhere near ready." She brushed the last biscuit crumbs off her chest and climbed into the van. "We've got Lavinia Threlfall booked to do a signing session."

Malcolm Pearce frowned. "Lavinia ... ?"

"Oh, you may not have heard of her. She's a local author who writes rather sensational romantic fiction." Eleanor could see that Malcolm was not entirely won over. "Do come if you can – there'll be a reading, drinks and snacks."

"Thank you my dear. I may well join you."

"Great. I look forward to seeing you there." Eleanor started the engine and pulled out of the long driveway. The road took her back across the moor and down into town. Getting the boxes into the shop was going to be a team effort, so she decided to leave them in the van and sort everything out after the launch party.

Back at the shop, Erika had had a busy afternoon and was looking quite pleased with herself. "We've had a group of walkers in who bought maps and guidebooks, the primary school has placed a big order for next term, and Mrs Elliott came by and bought a stack of paperbacks for her grandchildren."

"Excellent," said Eleanor. "I can see I should leave you alone more often." Squinting at her watch, she saw it was home time. "Let's close the shop then Bella and I will go for a stroll."

Getting herself a dog had been one of Eleanor's major indulgences on leaving London. "You can't go for walks on your own," her new neighbours had told her. "People will think you're peculiar." To begin with, Eleanor had thought that was ridiculous but now, when she was out with Bella and saw a solitary walker on the moors in the rain, she too found herself wondering what they were doing there. When she'd mentioned this to Jenna, her sister had raised an eyebrow in a way that conveyed her increasing belief that all her predictions had been spot on and Eleanor was getting more eccentric by the day.

Collecting Bella and heading up onto the cliff top, she wondered which of them enjoyed these outings more. She especially loved their walks along the rocky paths that snaked around the headland. The view wasn't beautiful: on this side of the country the sea was generally the colour of weak cocoa, except when the sun shone on the water and turned it green or slate grey. Nonetheless, the area had a wildness that Eleanor found exhilarating. Some days she'd be entirely alone, but more often than not she'd encounter other dog-walkers, all bundled up against the wind that swirled in off the sea, summer and winter.

Striding along, hands stuffed in her pockets against the cool evening air, she nodded a greeting to an elderly gent with a whippet. Alfie, she thought it was called. One of the unexpected facts of dog ownership was that everyone knew the names of the dogs but not necessarily those of the owners. Eleanor smiled when she thought of some of the interesting conversations she'd overheard along the lines of, "You know who I mean – Mitzi (long-haired dachshund, yappy), she's split up from her husband and has taken up with Jaffa (golden retriever, dribbles a bit, but sweet natured)."

"I don't think much of Mr Crumpet, that's for sure,"

she murmured to herself, her feet crunching on the dry sand as she strode back down the path and along the beach. Bella rushed back and forth, nose and tail in feverish activity as she dashed from seaweed to driftwood to seagull. Eleanor smiled at the dog's evident joy and thought how lucky she was in her new life.

Chapter 2: The Launch Party

The next day, Eleanor tried to go about her work as normal, but she was excited by the prospect of that evening's launch. Persuading This Book Press to hold the party at her shop rather than the big chain store in the next town had been a real coup. She had worked hard at it mind, with promotions, window displays, a guess-the-author's weight competition – okay, she didn't actually do the last one, but she had managed to entice Lavinia Threlfall to The Reading Room for the launch of her latest novel. The books were a potent mix of historical fiction, romance and the occult set on their stretch of the Devon coast and they had a fervent local and national following.

All afternoon Eleanor and Erika had been busy decorating the room where the event was to be held. The publishers had stumped up some cash for drinks and Eleanor had done a deal with the bakery next door to get some special cheese straws. It was the sort of extravagance her accountant disapproved of, but Eleanor believed that people would be more inclined to buy something if they'd had a good time.

She brought an old-fashioned standard lamp from the cottage and arranged velvet shawls and paisley throws over the sofa, which lived by the back wall. With the lights dimmed, the space looked suitably Gothic and romantic.

"It looks like we're planning a séance," said Erika, as they stood back to admire their work.

Eleanor laughed. "So long as we only conjure up good spirits, I don't mind."

Right on cue, the door opened to reveal their author. Lavinia Threlfall turned out to be a rather dumpy woman, not in the first flush of youth, with bright copper hair and emerald nail polish. She was accompanied by her publicist, Georgie, a striking young woman with perfect teeth. Elegantly dressed in a black suit and wearing impossible heels, everything about her screamed "London". "Hello ladies. Where do you want us?"

Erika led them over to the area they had prepared for their visitor and Georgie set to work putting up posters and rearranging the piles of books that Eleanor had already put out. Later, Georgie shepherded customers over to the table where Lavinia sat in state and kept her charge supplied with wine and snacks throughout the evening.

They opened the doors to customers at 6pm and by 8pm the shop was packed with people wanting to meet Lavinia and to buy signed copies of her rather torrid fiction. Among them was Malcolm Pearce who seemed fascinated by her and even bought a copy of the book. He took it over to the cash desk, looking rather shifty.

"Don't tell my son – I'm supposed to be shedding books, not buying more!"

"Your secret's safe with me," said Erika, as she wrapped up his purchase.

Eleanor was circulating, chatting to regular customers and offering wine to those clutching books when she glimpsed Daniel Pearce across the room, scanning the gardening shelves. He caught her eye and nodded.

She weaved her way over to where he stood, a bottle of wine in her hand. "Hi! I didn't have you down as a fan of romantic fiction."

"I'm not."

"Oh. Well, is there anything else that catches your eye?" she indicated the shelves packed with glossy books.

"Not really," said Daniel, looking about the crowded room. "I've just come to give my father a lift home."

Right, she thought. I'm not going to make a sale here, but never mind.

"Can I top you up?"

"Better not, as I'm driving," he said, handing Eleanor his empty glass. "Thanks anyway." He wandered off to collect his father who gave Eleanor a cheery wave as they left the shop.

She waved back, then carried on where she'd left off, topping up glasses and smiling encouragingly at the people who were waiting to get their books signed by Lavinia. After a little while, she felt a tap on her arm.

"Hi, I'm Jim Rowe from the *Gazette*."

Eleanor turned around and smiled. "Gosh, you've turned up. I didn't think you'd come." Their paths had crossed before at other events and it had been Jim who had interviewed Eleanor three years before when she took over the shop from a Mr Williams, who had run it for nearly thirty years. She had been slightly embarrassed at Jim's treatment of her as a heroine, come to save the town's oldest bookshop from the clutches of wicked developers who hoped to open yet another coffee shop. However, apart from the hyperbole, he had done a good job – and taken quite a flattering photograph of her – and the interview was now framed and had pride of place on the wall behind the counter.

"Slow news day," he said, between mouthfuls of cheese straw. "A coachful of French tourists got jammed in a lane in North Yarnton, and we had an escaped sheep on the beach. Apart from that not much was happening, so I decided to swing by and see what our local celeb was up to."

"Well, I'm glad you did. Publicity is always welcome. I'll introduce you to our star."

"No need. 'Lavinia' and I went to secondary school together. She was plain Susan Green then."

At that moment, Georgie sprang into action and hurried over to where they stood chatting. "You must be Mr Rowe? We spoke earlier. Have you had the press pack? Lavinia can't wait to meet you," she said, turning towards her author. Lavinia, resplendent in ankle-length green velvet, swooped over to them wearing a smile that didn't quite reach her eyes.

"Sue, love," said Jim, shaking her hand, "how are things? Haven't seen you for ages."

"It's Lavinia to you. Still working for the local rag, I see."

"I certainly am, Sue, er, Lavinia. And you're still knocking out the old bodice rippers?"

Lavinia looked deeply unimpressed by this description of her work. "I prefer the term 'Gothic fiction'."

"Ouch," said Erika under her breath, "we'd better split these two up fast."

"I think this corner here would be perfect for your photograph," said Georgie, smoothly taking control and escorting Jim and Lavinia away.

Eleanor went back to topping up glasses and chatting to old and new customers. At the end of the evening when the few remaining books had been packed up and the promotional flyers all tidied away, Eleanor stepped outside to find Georgie and Erika sitting on a wall across from the shop each with a large glass of white wine.

"We're having a sneaky fag," said Erika. "Come and join us."

"When you write your memoirs, sweetie," said Georgie, patting Erika on the knee, "I insist on being your publicist. What a story!"

"Cheers to that!" said Erika, clinking glasses. Her slim figure and smart haircut made it hard to believe that Erika had actually started life as Eric. After twenty years in the Manchester Police Force, Eric had retired on a handsome pension and left the city to begin a new life as the person he had had to subdue for so long. Now Erika was officially female and Eleanor's one full-time member of staff and right-hand woman.

She had got the job at The Reading Room because she was very experienced, immensely thorough and good with the administrative tasks that Eleanor loathed. She was also well read and had an easy manner that customers soon warmed to. Another of her talents was an unerring ability to spot and deter potential shoplifters before they made away with the goods. It didn't happen often, but sometimes there would be a coachload of French school children in town bent on acquiring a few "free" souvenirs. Word would go from shop to shop that they were on their way and Erika would always be ready for them.

Now she shifted along to make room for her boss. "Eleanor, why don't you sit down and join us?"

"That is a very tempting offer, but it's freezing cold out here and I have to finish tidying up."

"Darling, let me help you," offered Georgie, slithering down from the wall.

"No, you stay there. You've both been brilliant and it won't take a minute."

"Oh well, if you insist."

"Actually, shouldn't you be looking after our author?"

"No need. Lavinia has gone to have dinner with an old flame, so I'm off the hook." Georgie rummaged around in her bag. "Okay, one last ciggy then I'm off to my B&B. This sea air is really quite exhausting."

"Don't leave tomorrow without coming in to say goodbye, will you?" said Erika.

"Wouldn't dream of it."

Eleanor couldn't help smiling as she went back into the shop. The launch party had been a great success: lots of books sold, new customers in the shop and nothing broken. She had made sure that highlights of the evening were pinged off into cyberspace and there would be photos in the local paper thanks to Jim Rowe.

"Need any help down there?"

Eleanor looked up from beneath the drinks table where she was putting empty glasses back into boxes to see Jim grinning down at her.

"No, everything's under control, thanks."

"Any chance of a drink? You're my final celebrity exclusive of the day."

"'Fraid not. Georgie and Erika have finished off the last bottle of Chardonnay." Eleanor frowned.

"Never mind – I'd actually prefer a pint anyway. Would you like to join me in the pub for a snifter?"

Eleanor hesitated for a moment then thought, why not? She didn't know Jim Rowe terribly well, but he seemed like a nice enough guy. "Okay. But only if you promise to spill the beans on 'Lavinia'."

"Deal. Now let me help you with those."

Together they carried the wineglasses and empty bottles into the office, then Eleanor turned off the lights and locked the shop door.

"Where to?" she asked.

"It has to be the King's Head," said Jim, leading the way down the high street to the harbour side.

The town had several pubs, but this was the one with the most character. The heavy oak door opened onto a narrow corridor then another door, beyond which was a stone-flagged room with a log fire in the inglenook. There was a group of locals at the bar and what looked like tourists at another table. As Jim went to the bar to get the drinks, Eleanor looked around the room. On the walls were photographs of the fishing boats that had once worked the seas along this coast, and the lifeboat crews who had pulled so many men out of the water. Weather-beaten men in heavy oilskins stared out from across the centuries. Another photograph showed the high street and the bookshop that was now hers. One of the things she loved about the town was its sense of history.

The pub was deliberately old-fashioned and completely unreconstructed – thank goodness. In a prominent spot behind the bar was a collection of mobile phones nailed to a board – Gerald, the landlord, insisted that customers should only speak to people in the same room, not somewhere else in the country. Quite right too, thought Eleanor as Jim joined her at the table bearing a pint, a large red wine and two packets of crisps. "Dinner," he said smiling.

Eleanor suddenly remembered that she'd not eaten since about 1pm and realised she was ravenous.

"Thanks and cheers!" The red wine on an empty stomach combined with the success of the evening made Eleanor feel giddy and bold. She couldn't help herself checking out Jim as he stood at the bar: stocky, and older than her with greying hair. What her mother Connie would refer to as a "silver fox". Oh, and quite a nice bum. The wine had gone straight to her head. She took a sip to cover her smile. "So tell me about Lavinia Threlfall."

Jim thought for a moment. "She was quite a looker when she was younger and determined to do well for herself. We worked alongside each other on the local paper for a few years, but she was always very ambitious and determined to go on to bigger and better things as a writer. Her father ran an abattoir, but you won't find that detail in any autobiography, I bet."

"Did you not want 'bigger and better things'?"

Jim shrugged. "Not really. I enjoy the job and I love this part of the world."

He sipped his beer and smiled across at Eleanor.

"So what's your story? I know about the shop, but not much else."

She took another gulp from her wine. "Oh, there's not much to tell really." *Not until I know you better,* she said to herself. "Got married, had kids, got unmarried, bought a bookshop. What about you?"

"Pretty similar, really – without the bit at the end. I was married to Margaret for twenty-odd years, and we have a son and a daughter. We split up a couple of years ago, but we're still good pals."

"That's nice," said Eleanor, peering into her wineglass. "I'm afraid Alan and I are not quite at the 'good pals' stage yet."

"Oh, I'm sure you'll get there. More crisps?"

Eleanor looked at the pile of crumbs on the table. "Sorry! I seem to have demolished most of those."

"That's okay. I think the fish-and-chip place is still open if you fancy something more substantial."

"Sounds great," she said, licking salt off her fingertips. "But I should probably go home. It has been a long day."

"Oh, that's a shame," said Jim, draining his glass. "I guess it's a microwave lasagne for me then."

As soon as she'd turned down the invitation, Eleanor felt a pang of regret. Why shouldn't she have a night out with Jim? She was a free woman, after all.

"Perhaps we could do it on Saturday?" she said at last. "If you like. I'll be ready for a night out by then."

Jim perked up immediately. "Okay. It's a date."

Chapter 3: A Hint of Romance

"A date?"

"That's what he said," said Eleanor, pouring water into the cafetiere, "but it's just a turn of phrase. There's no need to get excited."

Erika and Connie exchanged meaningful glances. "Love, this is the closest you've got to romance in two years, so we have every right to get excited." It was actually much longer than that, but Eleanor was not about to put her mother right on the details. The women were sitting in the office-cum-storeroom in the basement of the shop the morning after the launch party. Connie smiled at her daughter and held out her mug for coffee.

Eleanor's mother had been persuaded to move to a village five miles away on being widowed. She and Eleanor's father had had a long and happy marriage until Jack fell ill and died after a short illness. Afterwards, Connie had begun to shrink and fade as though grief was stretching her out, dragging her back to her deceased husband. She had moved to a new house but remained lost in herself, no longer willing to attend choir or enjoy her old pastimes. The girls had feared that they might lose their mother, too, when a minor miracle happened: Connie discovered internet dating. To be more precise, her neighbour had talked her into "having a look" during a "Getting to Know Your Computer" course at the village hall. She had had a couple of false starts but eight months and several dates later, Connie had recently returned from a Mediterranean cruise with Harold Greaves, a rather dapper eighty-something widower with a twinkle in his eye and love in his heart.

"I didn't think I would have to kiss quite so many frogs, not at my age," Connie had confessed to her startled daughters, "but my Harold was worth it."

Despite being all grown up, Eleanor's children had been shocked at their granny's behaviour, Phoebe rushing into the kitchen at Christmas to announce that she had seen Connie kissing Harold under the mistletoe, "Like properly – on the lips!"

"That is just gross," Joe had said, shaking his head in disbelief.

However, everyone had eventually grown used to the idea that Connie had a man in her life and Harold was now a much-loved addition to the family.

The only downside to Connie's new relationship was that she, like most converts, was bordering on the fanatical and had been urging her newly single daughter to go online and find true love. To keep her mother happy, Eleanor had succumbed and suffered a handful of excruciatingly bad dates with an assortment of oddballs. Now, the hint of a potential beau in the guise of Jim Rowe had set Connie off again.

"You aren't getting any younger, sweetheart, and you won't meet anyone stuck behind a bookcase."

"Thank you, Mother. I'm not quite ready for the knacker's yard yet."

"I want you to be happy, love."

"I am perfectly happy." And so she was, most of the

time. But sometimes she did think it might be nice to have someone to share things with again. Then she'd remember the last, dismal years of her marriage to Alan and shudder. Far better to be on her own and happy than be with someone simply because it had become a habit. And, anyway, it was not as if she was fighting them off with a stick.

Just then there was a knock at the door and Georgie walked in, looking relaxed and pretty in jeans and a white T-shirt, an overnight bag in her hands. She greeted them all warmly then plonked herself down on a pile of boxes.

"So, gals, what's happening?"

"We were discussing my daughter's love life," explained Connie, leaning over to introduce herself to Georgie.

"Ah, romance! My favourite topic," she said, helping herself to coffee. "I thought the journalist guy seemed really nice."

Eleanor gave her a sharp look. "Please don't encourage them," she sighed.

"He does seem keen on you, Eleanor," added Erika.

"He's a business associate. Now I think we all have work to do."

"Not me," said Georgie, grinning happily. "I've got the weekend off and my train back to London doesn't leave until mid-afternoon. Lunch anyone?"

Erika raised a hand. "Yup, count me in – as long as it's a quick one."

"If you don't mind spending your free time with a granny," said Connie, "I'd love to join you both for a bit of a gossip." Connie enjoyed her trips out with Erika, which were occasionally enlivened by a

24

little inside information about local members of the transgender community. ("Her, I mean him? The dentist? No, never!")

"Of course, Connie," said Erika. "It wouldn't be the same without you."

"Well, it's all right for some," said Eleanor, collecting the empty coffee things. "I've got books to sell."

Connie caught Erika's arm as Eleanor turned and walked back into the shop. "She definitely likes Jim," she whispered, with a smile.

"I heard that!"

Eleanor knew that her mother and friends meant well, but they really were infuriating sometimes. Feeling the need for a breath of air, she grabbed her bag and headed out. "Before you ladies disappear for lunch, I'm going to bring the van round and unload it."

"Shall I come?" asked Erika.

"No, you stay here. I've got a few other things to do along the high street and I could do with the exercise."

Stepping onto the sunny street, the wind whipped across her face, ruffling her hair as she stomped up the road. By the time she had been to the bank and the post office, and walked the short distance to the vehicle, she was completely dishevelled. She peered at her reflection in the wing mirror, unsuccessfully trying to dislodge strands of hair from her sunglasses as she dug in her bag for the keys. "Damn and blast it," she said to no one in particular. It was, she decided, one of the perils of approaching middle age that you spent a great deal of time talking to yourself.

She was crouched on the pavement, unpacking

the usual flotsam and jetsam that managed to accumulate in her handbag, when she saw a pair of slightly scruffy deck shoes appear at her side. Above them two tanned knees descended from a pair of khaki shorts.

"Are these what you're looking for?" Daniel Pearce stood there with the keys to her van in one hand and an old-fashioned string bag in the other. "You must have dropped them as you left the shop."

"Gosh, yes, thanks," said Eleanor, hastily stuffing the used tissues, old lipsticks, broken biros and dog chews back into the dark recesses of her bag where they belonged and rising to her feet. Daniel was standing between her and the sun, causing her to squint, despite the sunglasses.

"I've come down to get some fish for my father," he explained, waving the string bag in the air. "It's Friday. Fish day," he added with a frown.

Coming from London, Eleanor had initially found it odd that you could only buy certain products on certain days. Sure, the supermarkets stocked the usual range of prepackaged goods, but if you wanted the best local produce, you went to the weekly market behind the library.

"Mackerel," he added.

Eleanor smiled encouragingly. "How lovely."

They stood in uncomfortable silence for a moment or two as Eleanor unlocked the van door and climbed up into the driver's seat.

"My father enjoyed himself at your party last night."

"Glad to hear it."

"It seemed to go well."

"It did, yes," she said, pointedly closing the door.

"Well, it's nice to see you again, but I really must get back to the shop and unpack this lot," she said, nodding towards the boxes she had brought from his father's house. "I've not had time to do it because of the party."

"I can give you a hand, if you like."

"Oh, there's no need," she began to protest, before peering over her shoulder and realising how many cartons of books she had acquired. "Actually, that would be great. If you have the time."

"I have," he said, looking at his watch. "I'll meet you at the shop." With that Daniel strode off back up the high street, the string bag swinging rather incongruously by his side.

Back at The Reading Room, Erika came out to join them and, together with Georgie, they formed a chain gang and had the boxes unloaded in no time. Connie had offered to help, but was persuaded to wait on the sofa from where she called out encouraging remarks as the others trooped through the shop.

When all the boxes were in, Daniel wiped dust from his hands on his shorts and stood back to admire their work.

"Sorting out this lot should keep you busy for a while. When shall I come by for my father's cheque?"

He's keen to get his hands on Mr Pearce's money, thought Eleanor. "There's really no need to call in," she said with a smile. "I'll post it or drop it off myself once I've checked all the prices on the internet."

Daniel shrugged. "As you wish. Well, bye then," he said, retrieving his mackerel and leaving the shop.

"What a shame that such a handsome man has got

such knobbly knees," said Connie, rising from her spot on the sofa. "May we go for lunch now?"

Eleanor nodded, "Yes, you may, but don't keep my staff out too long."

Connie took Erika's arm and pulled a face. "Take no notice of my daughter. She's only miffed at being left out."

Eleanor ignored her, turning instead to Georgie.

"Thanks for all your efforts with Lavinia last night."

"No worries – it was fun."

"I'm glad to hear it," she said, giving the young woman a peck on the cheek. "Give my love to London."

She opened the door and ushered Georgie and the others out of the shop.

"Don't worry," said Erika, as she went past. "I won't let Connie lead us astray."

Eleanor couldn't help laughing. "Enjoy your lunch and I hope to see at least one of you back here later."

Chapter 4: Out on the Town

The next day it was business as usual in The Reading Room, and Eleanor found herself quite looking forward to fish and chips with Jim Rowe. It would make a nice change, she thought, to have some male company, surrounded as she was by women most of the time. Her brief sortie into internet dating had made her very nervous about meeting men, but at least she was pretty sure that Jim Rowe was not a nutcase.

Erika caught her looking at the clock at 5pm and smiled. "Not long to go, now," she said, cheerily.

Eleanor gave her a look. "I'm sure I don't know what you mean." Just then the phone rang.

"Hello, The Reading Room," said Erika. "Oh, hello Connie. Yes, yes it is tonight," she said, smiling across at Eleanor. "Oh, I don't know. I'll ask her." She held the phone away from her mouth for a moment. "Connie would like to know what you're planning on wearing this evening."

"Oh for heaven's sake," said Eleanor, getting up from the floor where she'd been restacking a shelf and going over to the counter. "I'll probably wear the same as I'm wearing now," she said, looking down at her admittedly dusty trousers.

Erika, who was always immaculately dressed, failed to hide a look of disappointment.

"I'm meeting a friend for fish and chips, not going to a ball."

Erika shrugged and held out the phone for her boss to take. "Don't shoot the messenger."

Eleanor sighed as she took it from her. "Hello Mum. Yes, 7pm. No, takeaway." She rolled her eyes as Erika "What? Oh, jeans and a T-shirt I suppose. Of course I'll let you know how it goes. Love you, too. Bye." She replaced the phone on the desk and went back to what she was doing.

"Ridiculous."

"I think it's nice that Connie cares so much about you." Erika's own relationship with her parents had been strained by the disappearance of Eric. Her mother had handled it surprisingly well, but her father had never fully come to terms with losing a son and gaining a daughter at the age of seventy-three.

Remembering this, Eleanor suddenly felt a bit rotten. "I know," she said, more gently. "But sometimes she treats me like I am still fifteen!"

"That's mothers for you."

Ten minutes later the phone rang again and it was Phoebe. "Hello Ma," she said, as Eleanor answered. "Gran says you've got a date."

Eleanor sighed as she ran through the details again with her daughter.

"Cool," said Phoebe. "You should go out more and enjoy yourself."

"Well, I'm glad you approve."

"I do, definitely. It's time you got over Dad and had some fun." Eleanor could hear a male voice in the background.

"Got to go, Josh is here. Love you, bye!"

Eleanor sighed as she put the phone down. Conversations with her daughter were always the same: a few words exchanged before Phoebe dashed off with Josh, Jason or whoever it was she was hanging out with that week.

Customers came and went and the next time Eleanor looked at the clock it was closing time. She cashed up and shut down the computer as Erika put away the coffee things and tidied up the books and toys in the children's corner.

"Bella and I will have a quick walk, then I'll prepare myself for this non-date that has the whole town talking." Hearing her name, the dog appeared from under one of the tables, yawning and stretching.

"See you both tomorrow, then," said Erika, as they left the shop. "Enjoy your evening!"

"I'll try," said Eleanor, as she turned the lock in the door and set off towards the sea front.

After a quick jog along the beach, Eleanor hurried back to the cottage to shower and change. The afternoon's conversations had made her think that perhaps she ought to make a little bit of an effort. Bookshops are dusty places, so Eleanor rarely bothered to wear anything terribly glamorous at work. Now she tossed aside her trousers and selected a pair of black jeans that she could wear with a smart sweater – it would be cold by the water.

She had arranged to meet Jim at the chippy at 7pm so they could eat their supper outside then retire to the pub. When she had shared this arrangement with Connie, her mother had been very unimpressed.

"Goodness. Harold would never expect me to meet him on the street like a common tart."

"This is not the 1950s," said Eleanor, the thought of her mother hanging around street corners in fishnet stockings coming unbidden into her head. "Women are allowed out on their own. Anyway, it was my suggestion. Fish and chips always taste better outside."

"That's as may be," said Connie, "but he could at least have come and called for you."

In fact, Jim had suggested coming to the cottage to collect her, but Eleanor was aware that the place was littered with books and she didn't have the energy to make it presentable for visitors.

Glancing at her watch she saw it was nearly time to go. After putting on some make-up and brushing her hair, she stepped back to admire her reflection in the bedroom mirror. "What do you think then, Bella? Will I do?" The dog raised its head and wagged as Eleanor twisted to check out her back view. Her midriff had never fully recovered from having the twins, but at least the daily dog walks helped keep her legs and bum in reasonable shape. "Hmm, not bad," she said, giving herself a quick squirt of perfume and grabbing her handbag.

When she got to the chippy, Jim was already waiting outside. He gave her a big grin as she approached. "You look nice."

"Thanks," she said, unsure whether to kiss him or not. They clashed noses as he bent towards her and she ended up kissing him on the jaw.

He smiled again and ushered her into the shop. "After you, madam."

They made small talk as they ordered their meals,

then walked down to the sea front, Jim holding the savoury bundles under his coat to keep them warm. When they got to the sea, they found a bench and eagerly unwrapped the layers of paper.

"Yum," said Eleanor, as she grabbed a chunk of fish with her fingers. "This is delicious."

Jim smiled and nodded between chips, "Glad you like it. There's nothing like eating in the fresh air, in my view."

They sat and ate contentedly as the wind whipped around them and seagulls squawked overhead. Jim was good company and, after the embarrassment of the half-kiss, Eleanor began to relax. Because he was local, Jim was able to fill her in on who was who in town and identify landmarks that were dimly visible across the bay. When they'd finished their meal, he suggested they go to the King's Head for a drink.

"That would be great."

Jim offered her his arm and Eleanor put her own through it as they walked around the harbour towards the inn. She insisted on buying the drinks this time, and carried them to a table in an alcove near the fire.

"Well cheers," she said, raising her glass to his.

Jim smiled and clinked glasses. "I'm glad you decided to come out. I seem to spend most evenings reviewing bad am-dram for the paper, attending council meetings or watching the local football team get hammered."

Eleanor smiled back at him. "Thanks for asking me. It's nice to get away from the paperwork."

"I thought your colleague handled that side of things."

"You mean Erika? Oh, we share it really." Eleanor hesitated for a moment, unsure whether or not Jim was aware of Erika's background. "Have you two met properly? I'm sorry, I should have introduced you the other evening."

"Oh, that's okay," said Jim, swirling the beer in his glass. "You were both very busy. Same again?"

"Yes please."

"Right," said Jim, standing and heading for the bar. "A pint of wallop and a large white wine coming up."

When he returned with the drinks, he had a small box tucked under his arm.

"Are you familiar with dominoes?"

"I am," said Eleanor, taking her wine, "but I probably haven't played since I was about ten."

"Which makes you the perfect opponent in my book," said Jim, as he tipped the pieces out onto the table.

Eleanor laughed as she arranged her dominoes in a row. "I'll give you a game if you remind me how to play."

Jim briefly ran through the rules and they had a practice match, which Eleanor won. She also won the next four.

"Sorry. It's obviously beginner's luck."

Jim raised an eyebrow. "Okay, best of seven."

When Eleanor won those games, too, she couldn't help laughing. "This is such fun, Jim. Can we do it again sometime?"

"I don't know whether I could bear the humiliation," he said, trying hard to look cross.

Eleanor made a disappointed face as Jim gathered up the pieces and slotted them back into their wooden box.

"Buy me a beer and I'll think about it," he said, grinning.

Eleanor bought another round and sat back down. She didn't know if it was the wine or the fire, but she was feeling all warm and fuzzy inside.

"Okay, I'm prepared to play again," said Jim.

"Great," said Eleanor, slapping the table enthusiastically. "Maybe I could bring Erika along, too? It might even things out a bit and give you a chance of winning."

"Hmm, that sounds like two against one to me. I think I need to get another friend along for a bit of support."

"Good idea," said Eleanor. "I may not be around much for the next couple of weeks, but let's fix something up for when I'm back."

Chapter 5: Memories of France

Sunday was bright and sunny, which Eleanor hoped would bring a few book-hungry day-trippers into town. She put her board out on the pavement and checked the window display before settling down behind the counter for a quick read of the papers. The shop had been open for about a quarter of an hour when Connie came in, accompanied by Harold.

"Good morning," said Connie, kissing Eleanor on the cheek.

"What are you doing in town so early on a Sunday morning?" she asked, knowing exactly what her mother's motives were but deciding to string her along a little.

"Oh, we were passing, weren't we Harold?"

"That's right, just passing." Harold nodded then slunk off to the back of the shop, officially to check out the latest history titles, as Connie pretended to peruse the poetry shelves.

"So," she said, sidling up to her daughter. "Did you have a lovely evening with Jim?"

"It was very nice, thank you."

Eleanor was nursing a teensy hangover and didn't feel like giving her mother a full exposition of her night out.

"Was there anything you needed, Mum?"

Connie smiled sweetly. "Just browsing, as they say."

Eleanor looked at the book her mother was pretending to study. "I didn't know you were keen on Persian love poetry. Shall I wrap it for you?"

Connie laughed and replaced the slim volume she had pulled at random from the shelf.

"Actually, I wanted to see how you were after your *date*," she said, flashing her best smile and putting the emphasis on the last word.

"I'm fine, as you can see," said Eleanor, refusing to play ball and moving out from behind the cash desk to greet a customer. "And busy."

"Good. As long as you're well." Realising there wasn't going to be any gossip that morning, Connie disappeared into the back room and reappeared with Harold.

"We'll be off then, love," she said.

Eleanor waved as the pair left the shop and walked, hand in hand, across the road to the tearooms.

Erika had Sunday mornings off so Eleanor had to manage a steady stream of visitors buying postcards and maps and even the occasional hardback book. Despite her love for paper and ink, Eleanor was no Luddite and had recently started offering e-readers to entice new customers into the shop. She had soon discovered that the keenest buyers of those sleek devices were often middle-aged women like herself.

"You know what they're doing, don't you Mum?" Phoebe had said, pursing her lips. "They're using them to read dirty books." Eleanor smiled at the recollection. The young were so prim these days. As she had told her daughter, "I don't care what people read, so long as they buy it from me."

There was no such excitement on Sunday morning,

but Eleanor was kept on her feet until lunchtime serving customers. It wasn't until the afternoon when the shop was closed that she managed to settle down in the office with her hoard from Malcolm Pearce's house.

She had a mug of tea, Radio 3 playing in the background and Bella snoring gently on her bed. Bliss! Sitting on the floor, Eleanor began opening the boxes and cataloguing the books, which she and Malcolm had packed together by subject. It was slow work, as she had to stop and read a little bit of each one. A couple of boxes contained travel guides used by Malcolm when he was living overseas. He had been a civil engineer in his younger days, working in Europe, Africa and the Middle East. Some of the older volumes were leather bound and contained beautiful prints and illustrations that she drooled over.

Eleanor lifted out two early Baedeker's guides to Northern and Southern France and carefully turned the pages, admiring the maps. She was a true Francophile and simply reading the place names gave her a thrill. Connie and Jack had taken their daughters to northern France on lots of bracing camping and walking holidays when they were young. Despite the sometimes unpredictable weather, those trips had given Eleanor a taste for the country and left her with a desire to see more. At university she had studied French, planning to become a teacher like her sister but, in the end, had decided teaching was not for her. Without a plan she had felt unsettled and been unwilling to go straight into any old job. After a few months of what Jenna described as "moping" she had persuaded her parents to let her go to France. She bought *The Lady* magazine for weeks and scoured it for exciting job opportunities but all it offered were positions as au pairs, so that is what she became.

Her friends were immensely jealous when she told them she had a job in France, imagining no doubt the warm sun and sandy beaches of the south. In fact, she ended up in a small town just across the Channel where the clouds were as low and the sky as grey as they had been in England.

She lived with the Junot family: Monsieur was a doctor while Madame entertained herself by running a shop selling "bric à brac" to Belgians who came across the border for a bargain, and the few enterprising Brits who ventured beyond Calais.

In between looking after the children, Eleanor practised her French and learnt to smoke Gitanes in what she hoped was a seductive manner.

After six months, she quit her job – much to Madame's annoyance – and headed south with another au pair, Marie from Switzerland. She and Marie had a blissful few weeks on the south coast flirting, visiting the sights and sunbathing. In the sun Eleanor's dark-brown hair developed a reddish tone and her skin tanned, making her hazel eyes stand out in a way that surprised her. She was amazed to discover that, for the first time in her young life, she was turning heads. In the grey north she had been as anonymous as at home, but here – glory be! – she was seen as exciting and different.

The girls hung around the beach until their money ran out. At the railway station they pooled their cash, caught a train as far north as their francs would take them and found themselves in a small town in the

Rhône-Alpes called Chevandier. Speaking French and English, Eleanor managed to blag her way into a job in a shop selling locally made pottery and gifts to tourists who made it inland from the coast. Marie got a job in a café run by another Swiss woman. How easy it had been, thought Eleanor, and how fearless they were back then. The girls had moved in with another escapee from the north, a skinny German blonde called Rosanne who made a living teaching English to local businessmen. She was older than the other two and intended to stay in France, whereas Marie and Eleanor had no plans and were happy to take every day as it came. All the girls worked hard but had a lot of fun, too.

Being young and foreign, the trio were irresistible to the local male population and Eleanor soon found herself a boyfriend. Christophe Vauban was tanned, strong and wiry with dark curly hair and what her gran would have referred to as "bedroom eyes". When, back in England, Eleanor had shown her best friends his photo, they were gratifyingly impressed.

"Oh my God, El. He is divine," said Lesley, who was already engaged to the boyfriend she had had since her first term at uni. "I knew I should have done French instead of Geography," she sighed. Her mate, Carole, who was still single, had initially stared open-mouthed at Christophe's photo, lost for words. "You are one lucky mare."

It was true, she thought smugly – she was. Christophe was gorgeous and being with him made Eleanor feel special, like she was in her own romantic film. The months they spent together also did wonders for her French and left her with a pretty good accent.

Rosanne's apartment was always jammed with people, so they spent lots of time in the park by the river, talking in whispers and kissing. Of course, being locked out occasionally only added to the excitement and they had lots of sex, often in peculiar places. Christophe had a thing about furniture and one weekend, when her flatmates were away, they had done it on the kitchen table and in her wardrobe. For years afterwards, she had been unable to look at French country furniture without an amused *frisson*.

In the evenings, Christophe was often working. His parents ran a traditional auberge in a shady street behind the Cathedral and he helped out there, either waiting at tables or in the kitchen. During the day, when Eleanor was in the shop, Christophe spent a lot of time hanging about with his friends in the square, smoking and looking cool on his Vespa, much to her boss's annoyance.

Eleanor loved him despite their having very little in common. And she adored looking at him: he was so perfect compared to the pale spotty boys she had grown up with. Her bedroom was high up at the back of the house and the moon would shine straight in through the window. After making love, when he had fallen asleep by her side, she would lie awake gently stroking his toned body, his skin silvery in the moonlight. As day broke, the sun would turn the fine hair on his bronzed arms golden.

They were quite captivated by each other: amazed and seduced by the love that enveloped them like a blessing. When Eleanor awoke she often found Christophe with his head propped up on one hand, smiling down at her.

"*Pourquoi tu me regardes comme ça?*" she asked, with her best pout.

"Because you are so beautiful."

"No, it is you who are beautiful!"

"I am a man! I cannot be 'beautiful'," he said, climbing on top of her. "I am – how do you say – 'handsome'."

"And so very modest!" she laughed, rolling into his embrace.

What would have happened if they had stayed together? It was she who had ended the relationship, although she had not intended to at the time. Marie had gone back to Lucerne to continue her studies and Rosanne needed to find another girl to share the flat with them. The replacement was incredibly loud and untidy and drove the other two mad. When the summer season came to an end, so did Eleanor's job. With the gift shop closed, it seemed like the perfect time for a break so she decided to return to London for a couple of months.

She had every intention of going back to France as soon as she had earned enough money for her and Christophe to rent a place together. To begin with, they had written to each other daily on crispy sheets of blue airmail paper and had even managed to speak on the telephone – at the time a huge extravagance that her father had frowned at. But gradually the love she had experienced felt more and more like a dream. Thinking about it later, she wondered if she had wanted it to end then, when it was most perfect. Shakespeare knew what he was doing when he killed off Romeo and his Juliet in their mid-teens: there's nothing sexy about middle-aged lovers.

The sound of Bella snoring broke Eleanor's reverie

as she sat there on the floor of her office with piles of books around her. "I wonder what he looks like now? Probably bald with a pot belly," she sighed. Or maybe not. Maybe he had turned into one of those incredibly attractive older men you sometimes see in French films. She closed the pages of the Baedeker and tidied away her lists. That was enough for one afternoon.

"Come, Bella. Walkies." The dog yawned then trotted over, her head down in readiness for Eleanor to slip the leash over her neck. "I think we'll have a wander along the big beach tonight, what do you reckon?" Bella wagged her tail in response. "After Easter you'll be *persona non grata* on the beach. Well, *doggy non grata*, actually." She chuckled at her own joke as she opened the creaky front door and went down the steps by the side of the shop that formed a handy cut-through to the next street and eventually the sea front.

At the beach, she slipped the leash from Bella's neck and let her run free. She smiled as the dog careered off across the shingle towards the sea, which was a good quarter of a mile out at that time of day. It meant there was a large expanse of sand to walk on, making it easy to avoid other dog-walkers if you weren't feeling particularly sociable. Which she wasn't. Eleanor's head was full of her own thoughts that evening – the what-ifs? What if she hadn't come back to London, met Alan and had the twins? Would she and Christophe have survived as a couple? They had had what people now call "chemistry", but did they really have much else in common? Thinking back, she couldn't remember what they'd talked about other than their own intense feelings for each other.

She quickened her pace as she approached the water then stood there, watching the foam dampen the toes of her shoes. Looking out to sea, she wondered whether Christophe ever thought about her. Unlikely, she decided, bending to pick up a piece of driftwood Bella had deposited at her feet.

She threw the stick and watched the dog race after it as it spun through the air and dropped into the sea. Bella retrieved it and shook herself vigorously.

Eleanor ducked as fat globules of wet sand flew off in every direction. "Home time," she said, turning and walking back towards her cottage.

Back from the walk, she towelled Bella down and fed her then made herself some supper. Afterwards, she sat down on the sofa with a glass of wine and opened her laptop. As the machine buzzed and bleeped into life, she told herself she was going to have a quick look to see what Malcolm's collection of early Baedekers was worth. She carefully checked the books' value (not bad) and jotted down the sums in her notebook.

She was going to turn off the machine, but something stopped her and her fingers hesitated over the keyboard. She had barely thought of Chevandier in twenty years, but now she had a sudden desire to see the place again. What harm could it do? She took a deep breath and opened up the town's tourist website, reading the promotional blurb.

"Beautiful medieval town ... riverside promenade ... art gallery, blah, blah," she read to herself. "Yup, that sounds like the place I knew," she said, taking a sip of wine.

Looking under "Food and Drink" she searched for

L'auberge du Sud, Chevandier, the restaurant owned by Christophe's parents. She was half-relieved and half-disappointed when the computer came back with no results. Well, that's that, she thought. How silly to think the place would still be in business after all this time.

"I wasn't very interested anyway," she said to the dog at her feet, before deciding to look at images, for old times' sake. A search for pictures brought up dozens of photos of the town she had once known like the back of her hand: the fortress and riverside park, the shady *place central* with its fountain and statue of a local dignitary who the girls had thought looked like Margaret Thatcher with a full beard. Eleanor smiled at the recollection and stroked Bella's soft ears.

Switching to "Street View" she discovered that Rosanne's apartment building looked much the same, although someone had replaced the creaky shutters and generally smartened it up. The gift shop she had worked in was still there, but it was now a store selling handmade soaps and toiletries. The wonders of technology, thought Eleanor, as she continued on her virtual tour of the girls' old stomping grounds. She found the Cathedral and the medieval alleyways around it. She clicked to move further along the street and there it was: Chez Christophe in big letters with "Auberge familiale du 18ième" in its familiar place below. She let out a startled yelp, her stomach lurched and she was sure her heart missed a beat.

She slammed the laptop closed, got up and walked around the room, went into the kitchen picking things up and putting them down again. Oh my goodness. Damn and blast it. She was amazed by the visceral effect that seeing the image of the restaurant had on her. It was like opening Pandora's box: she was pretty sure that if she searched further she would find a photograph of Christophe. Her Christophe, her first true love. "Yup, and the one I dumped for no reason at all," she said to no one in particular, attacking the dishwasher. Did she really want to find out about him, after all this time? What good would it do? If she wanted to she could probably find photographs of an unbearably chic wife and some adoring children, too. Bugger, bugger, bugger.

She had scrubbed every surface and was huddled in the kitchen door having an emergency cigarette (her seventeenth that year) when the phone rang. It was her sister. After chatting for a while Jenna asked if everything was okay.

"Yes, of course. Why do you ask?"

"Well, for one thing it sounds as though you're smoking," her sister had extraordinary powers of deduction. "Secondly, I know you very well and you sound agitated. So, tell all – what's up?"

Putting out the cigarette in a handy pot of geraniums, Eleanor breathed deeply and said, "I think I've found Christophe."

There was silence for a moment as Jenna dredged her memory for the name. "Christophe? The scrawny layabout you were shacked up with in France?"

"He wasn't a layabout, Jen. He worked at his parents' restaurant." With that Eleanor explained what she had found. "I think Christophe is still living in Chevandier and may have taken over the business."

"So, what are you going to do about it?"

"Do?" Eleanor, pulled a face. "Well, nothing. I don't intend to do anything, Jen."

"Hey, why not? You're a free woman with some holiday coming up and no plans. El, get yourself on a plane and go get him!"

Eleanor laughed out loud. "Is that really the sort of advice you should be handing out to your younger sister?"

"No, you're quite right," said Jenna, thoughtfully. "Eurostar would be more fun and probably cheaper. Now, shall I book or will you?"

Chapter 6: We're Off!

On Monday morning, Eleanor's head was still spinning with the discoveries of the day before. Jenna had been quite serious about the trip to France and she was right that Eleanor was due a holiday. She hadn't taken more than a day or two off since buying the shop, so determined had she been to make a success of the business for herself and the local community.

Thanks to events like the Lavinia Threlfall launch party, she felt much more confident and relaxed about the shop's prospects and had decided to take a whole fortnight off before summer. However, until the previous night's conversation she hadn't known where to spend the time. Now she was allowing herself to be carried along by the whirlwind that was her sister on a mission. Jenna found and booked the hotel and placed Eleanor in charge of the travel arrangements.

A week later the train tickets were booked, euros organised, undies chosen and legs shaved – she was off. Erika was left in charge of the shop with help from Connie, who had promised to tear herself away from Harold to house-sit and look after the dog.

As they drove to the station, Eleanor wondered what adventures the next couple of weeks held in store for them all. She was entrusting her beloved van to her son for a whole weekend. Joe shared her passion for the Combi and Eleanor just hoped that his passion would translate itself into driving carefully and not getting stuck in a hedge. Since his mother had moved to the coast, Joe had turned into a surfer dude and came to Devon at every opportunity.

"Look after the van, Joe."

"Of course I will. We're going to have some fun together, aren't we old girl?" he said patting the van's shiny green side.

"Hmm, not too much fun I hope."

"I won't do anything you wouldn't do, Ma."

"Well, I expect you to have a bit more fun than that!" she laughed, as he caught her in a bear hug.

"Oh, I'm sure you and Auntie J will have a brilliant time."

"Any problems, call me. Okay?"

"Will do."

"And make sure the van is back at the shop on Monday morning."

"Yes Mother."

"Bye love," she whispered, watching as Joe turned the van and drove it confidently away towards the south coast and the best beaches.

It was a long way from Devon to southern France, so Eleanor had arranged to spend the night with Jenna and Keith in Islington then catch an early train out of the international terminus at St Pancras. "It's all timed so we'll be in Chevandier in time for an aperitif in the square," she had explained to her sister. As soon as Jenna had suggested going with her, Eleanor's view of the trip changed completely. Her nerves were gone and she was determined to have a great time, visit some museums and galleries, do some shopping, eat excellent food and – just maybe – take a peek inside Chez Christophe.

Her sister lived in an imposing stuccoed terrace house in one of Islington's shady tree-lined streets. It was now worth a million, but Jenna and Keith had bought it in the early 1980s, well before the area became popular with City types. Keith was fond of telling people that "yuppies hadn't been invented" when they'd moved in. It was a big, rambling family home, full of noise and clutter. Exactly like a house should be, thought Eleanor, as she rang the doorbell.

Opening the door, Jenna kissed her sister then led her down the corridor and into the basement kitchen where Keith was busy with his casserole. Jenna loathed cooking but, fortunately for her, Keith was a great cook and enjoyed experimenting with food. He had retired early, Jenna said, because he had so many cookery books to work his way through.

Keith stopped chopping onions and wiped his hands on his pinny before giving Eleanor a peck on the cheek. "And how's my favourite sister-in-law?"

"I'm perfectly fine," she replied, hugging him back. "And how's my favourite chef?"

"Nervous – I'm not sure I should trust you two to go off on your own," he said, peering at them over the top of his glasses.

Jenna stopped laying the table to give him a kiss. "We'll be dandy, Kiff my love. Now, where's the cassis? El and I need to get into the spirit of things, and I think a kir royale might be the perfect thing."

She poured a little of the fragrant ruby red liquid into three champagne flutes and topped them up with fizz. "Cheers Sis and happy holidays!"

"Don't you mean *bonnes vacances*?" said Eleanor, as they all clinked glasses.

"You see? My little sister will look after the language side of things and I'll hang around looking glamorous."

"Hmm, that's what I'm afraid of," said Keith. "No holiday romances allowed, do you hear?"

Jenna winked at Eleanor, "Perish the thought!"

After supper, Eleanor had a luxurious bath and went to bed early, determined to get a good night's sleep. After a couple of hours, she awoke with a start, not sure where she was. She put on the light, drank some water then fell back into a deep sleep.

The next day dawned bright and clear: perfect travelling weather. Keith escorted them to the Eurostar terminal and hugged them both. "Have fun, you two."

"Oh, we will, Kiff, don't you worry."

"Bye Keith," said Eleanor, kissing her brother-in-law on the cheek. "Don't worry about Jenna. She's the sensible one, remember?"

"I wouldn't believe that for a minute. Now hurry up and get on your train."

Later, when they were in their seats and their bags safely stashed away, Eleanor smiled at her sister. "You are lucky, you know Jenna? Keith adores you."

"I wouldn't go that far, but he's not a bad old stick. Now, do they have trolley dollies on these trains? I could murder a coffee and croissant."

Chapter 7: Back to Chevandier

As the monotonous northern French countryside sped past, Eleanor looked over at her sister. Jenna had been reading a bodice ripper on her e-reader but had nodded off and was gently snoring. Now in her early fifties, she was still an attractive woman with white-blonde hair cropped short to emphasise her features. Jenna had always been naturally fair and slender like their father, whereas Eleanor had inherited her mother's colouring and build, which Connie liked to describe as "curvaceous".

On her return to London from Chevandier in the late 1980s, Eleanor had decided to shift some of the pounds she had put on in France. Like almost everyone else she knew at the time, she had started to attend aerobics classes to help "fight the flab". She had also taken up jogging, which she enjoyed more than the fitness classes, not least because they didn't involve wearing a skin-tight outfit and leaping around like an idiot. Reflected in the floor-to-ceiling mirrors, Eleanor thought that she and her fellow sufferers looked like so many Liquorice Allsorts in their multicoloured leotards, leggings and stripy legwarmers.

Running was different: dressed in comfy clothes with her Walkman clamped over her ears, she loved to pound around London's parks in the evening after work. When she had more time, she would go down to the South Bank, which was pretty empty of people in those far-off days. Sometimes she would pause to catch her breath and see what was on offer at the second-hand bookstalls under the bridge. One or two of the vendors had begun to recognise her and sometimes gave her a few pennies off, not that it was easy jogging with a bag full of paperbacks clutched in her hands, dry leaves and litter swirling around her feet.

One day, while running past the old London County Hall building, she tripped and fell. Sitting on the grass feeling dazed and slightly nauseous, she was joined by a tall young man with heavy rimmed glasses who stopped to see if she was okay. Her rescuer helped her to gather up her things and hobble to the nearest pub where, after a medicinal spritzer, she felt much better. The studious-looking young man was Alan and four months later they were engaged.

Alan was different to Christophe in every possible way. Whereas Christophe was skinny with dark curls, Alan was broad-shouldered with thick blond hair and a ruddy complexion. He was short-sighted but hated wearing his glasses, even though Eleanor said they were sexy and made him look like Clark Kent. Unlike the languorous Christophe, he was sporty and was prone to leaping out of bed at dawn to row on the Thames. Sex with Christophe had been fast and exciting, almost like a game. With Alan everything was slower and calmer, and Eleanor enjoyed the unfamiliar sensation of feeling quite small and strangely girlie in his rugby player's arms.

Perhaps the thing she liked most was that she could talk to Alan about all kinds of things because they had similar backgrounds. It had amused her trying to explain the mysteries of English culture, such as Marmite and Benny Hill, to Christophe, but it was even nicer to have shared interests and experiences with someone.

Alan had a robust sense of humour and they spent many Saturday evenings at comedy clubs or jammed inside smoky rooms above pubs. Having been away for so long, Eleanor saw the city through fresh eyes and quite ordinary things now seemed new and exciting. If she hadn't gone away, would she have found Alan attractive? He was certainly not "her type", whatever that was. Jenna had seemed surprised when the two of them had got together though, at the time, the sisters weren't particularly close and there was nothing said until many years later. Her parents were clearly relieved when Eleanor returned to England, yet she was aware that some of her friends were disappointed that she hadn't "lived the dream" and settled in France with her exotic lover.

Before they were married, Eleanor split her time between her parents' house and Alan's musty basement flat in south London. After the wedding, they managed to rent a one-bedroom flat at the top of a Victorian mansion opposite a park. It was noisy and expensive, but from their bedroom they could look out over the tops of trees. Eleanor loved the impression she had of living in a tree house and Alan would take advantage of their seclusion to wander around the flat completely naked on even the coldest of days.

He had a good job in the City doing something with computers – Alan had tried on many occasions to explain what, but Eleanor couldn't help glazing over when he got down to the nitty-gritty. She might not have understood exactly what Alan did, but she knew he was good at it and well respected by his bosses. Eventually he would earn enough for them to buy a large semi in a leafy part of town along the Thames where he could indulge his love of rowing, but in the early days they lived quite frugally.

Eleanor found a secretarial job in a legal firm and did some translating from French to English to bring in extra cash. They were happy in their eyrie above the park and life was good. They had never discussed having children – there was simply an understanding between them that one day it would happen. When they found out Eleanor was pregnant with twins, Alan cried and insisted on telling everyone he met, including comparative strangers. It got quite embarrassing when even the people in the corner shop and the guys from the Chinese takeaway were familiar with every stage of the twins' development.

They moved into the big house three weeks before the birth. After Joe and Phoebe were born, things were chaotic: Alan helped as much as he could before and after work, but they were both exhausted. Connie and Jack moved in for a couple of weeks to help, an experiment that came close to ending in tears all round. After many more tears, Eleanor was eventually persuaded they needed live-in help, so a trained nursery nurse moved in. She cost them a small fortune but Alan insisted on having her, saying that was what the money was for. Eleanor cried the first time she realised she had slept right through the night because someone else had fed her babies, but she accepted that the nurse was necessary for all their sanity, not least her own.

After six months, the babies went to nursery and Eleanor went back to work at the solicitors' office. She struggled to cope with motherhood and work and had a pretty miserable two years. Many years later she read an article about post-natal depression and was shocked when she recognised some of the signs.

Since deciding on the trip to France, Eleanor had found all kinds of memories were being stirred up, but, sitting on the train, she was surprised when an episode with the twins flooded back. It was something she had managed to push to the back of her mind, but now it came to her with a jolt. Eleanor closed her eyes, remembering that awful day. It had been a Sunday morning, the au pair had the day off and Alan was out rowing, so Eleanor was all alone.

Phoebe was grizzling, but Joe was screaming and there wasn't anything she could do to stop him. She couldn't bear his angry, screwed-up face and the noise that pierced her skull and made her brain throb.

She grabbed her coat, grabbed the keys, looked back once to where the twins stood in their playpen and left the house. Her head buzzing, she ran down the steps to the wide tree-lined street. She could still hear them. Could she? Or was it a radio somewhere? She didn't know, didn't care just walked, half running to the Underground station. She got on a train – where to? – she couldn't remember now. Not sure she even knew then. Got off. Walked and walked in the drizzle, sucking in the cool damp air, head down until her breathing settled.

Eleanor looked out at the French countryside streaming past the train window, her chest tight at the recollection. She had never told anyone: certainly not Alan. Not even her mother. How could she?

Returning to the house, flying up the stairs and into the bedroom the silence had sickened her. When she'd seen the twins curled up asleep she had wept, gulping for breath and not daring to believe they were okay.

It had never happened again and she never brought it up. Sometimes she wondered if the children remembered. Years later, Joe had a series of nightmares and refused to be comforted by her. She had felt desolate, but in some way it seemed only fair that Alan should be the one he turned to.

Eleanor sat up and took a gulp of water, wanting to clear her head.

Next to her, Jenna stretched and yawned.

"Are you okay, El? You look a bit pale?"

"I'm fine, Jenna, honest," said Eleanor. "This trip is rousing a few ghosts."

"Friendly ones?"

"Mostly friendly."

Jenna looked at her quizzically. "I hope so." She peered out of the window. "Where are we anyway?"

"Nearly at Lille where we can grab a coffee before catching our fast train south."

"Then lunch on the TGV? I'm starved."

Jenna had the good fortune to be able to eat constantly without ever gaining more than a few pounds.

"Why not," said Eleanor. "We are on our hols, after all."

Sitting in the station cafeteria later, Jenna caught her sister's hand. "You know this is the first time we've been away together, just the two of us, since you had the twins?"

"No, really?" said Eleanor, thinking that Phoebe and Joe had recently turned twenty-three. "It can't be so long, surely?"

"It's true – I've had to spend all my holidays with Kiff and those darned kids."

"Whom you adore."

"Maybe. But it's great to have a break from them once in a while."

Eleanor sipped her drink. "If we don't end up killing each other, perhaps we could organise another trip next year. Don't you have any ex-lovers we could track down?"

Jenna thought for a moment. "Well, there was Pete."

"And where do you think he might be?" asked Eleanor, warming to the idea.

"Last spotted in Watford."

"Hmm, not classic mini-break territory, it has to be said. Come on. Our train is due any minute."

As the TGV pulled into the station, Jenna had a huge grin on her face. "Wowee, El! This, as my pupils would say, is totally amaze balls."

When Eleanor had booked the fast train she hadn't realised it would be one with two floors. She couldn't help smiling as she followed her sister up the stairs to their seats on the upper deck.

As the train zapped along, they got fantastic views. "The scenery isn't very exciting, but at least we get to see lots of it."

"I'm having so much fun, El. Can we have lunch now?"

"Sure. Let's wander over to the café-bar and see what's on offer. It's bound to be better than nasty

British Rail sandwiches," said Eleanor, leading the way to the café.

They ordered their lunch from the counter and went to stand at one of the high tables where they could watch the French countryside roll by.

"Well, cheers Jenna," said Eleanor, clinking glasses and taking a sip of chilled white wine. "This is the life."

"It certainly is. Let's drink to Christophe, without whom we would not be having this break together."

"Amen to that. Ooh, and here's lunch."

They ate their *croques monsieur* – posh cheese-on-toast, according to Jenna – standing at the tables in the buffet like natives, looking out at the countryside. When they had finished their lunch, the sisters were happy to relax on the upper deck for the final couple of hours of the trip. Eleanor was fascinated by the buildings and scenery she had last seen so long ago, while Jenna was content to snooze by her side.

The train arrived in Chevandier right on time. As they stepped off the train and onto the platform, the heat enveloped them. Arriving from the coast with Marie in mid-July back in 1986, Eleanor remembered that it had been one of the hottest places she had ever been in her life. The heat sat around, heavy and ener-vating. Now, in the late afternoon of a spring day, the warmth was divine.

They gathered up their bags and Eleanor let Jenna persuade her to take a taxi to their hotel. It wasn't far and the cab soon pulled up outside a stone house behind the Cathedral.

Their room was huge; in fact it was a whole suite with high ceilings, two enormous beds and a separate sitting room. Best of all was the balcony, which looked over a shady square where some old gentlemen were playing *pétanque* and chatting. The muted clank of the heavy metal *boules* on the sand could just be heard from their rooms, where Jenna was laying out her things.

"Wow, look at the bathroom, El. This bathtub is huge. Bagsie the first soak."

"Sure, go for it. Then we should go for a promenade along the riverbank."

"Perfect," said Jenna, giving her sister a peck on the cheek, "I won't be long."

Eleanor unpacked her few belongings – unlike Jenna she wasn't particularly interested in clothes and travelled light. When she had finished, she went to sit on the balcony and waited for her turn in the big old bathtub.

Clean and fragrant from their ablutions, the women stepped out into Chevandier. Eleanor had copied one of the Baedeker maps and carried it with her along with a stash of more-recent guidebooks. They walked arm in arm through the park and along the riverbank. On benches, young people still sat kissing, just as she and Christophe had done all those years before.

"I bet they're not married," said Jenna, nodding towards an older man wrapped around a younger woman. "More like his secretary, I'd say."

"And what about the pair by the fountain?"

"Lovers. Been together a while. She's not happy with the situation."

They were giggling now, like a couple of teenagers. "It must be aperitif time, El. Let's find a bar for a drinkie before dinner."

Both the women were tired after their early start, so they decided to be sensible and have one teeny drink then an early meal. They found a simple bistro near the main square where they could sit outside and watch the world go by.

As they strolled to their hotel after dinner, Jenna yawned. "I want to be nice and fresh for all that lovely shopping tomorrow."

"I think you mean lovely sightseeing," said her sister. "Then, if there's time, I might let you explore the shops."

"Okay boss."

Back in their rooms, Eleanor curled up on the sofa to wait while Jenna went into the bathroom to remove her make-up and comb her hair. When it was Eleanor's turn and she reappeared wearing a pair of short pink pyjamas, her sister smiled.

"You look about twelve years old in those jimjams!"

Jenna was wearing a long silky nightgown and looked annoyingly elegant.

Eleanor glanced down at her outfit. "Don't worry, I shan't be going out in these."

"I think you should. They're cute."

"Very funny." Eleanor kissed her sister goodnight and crept between the crisp cotton sheets of her own bed. Getting to Chevandier had been fun. Now she wondered what their first full day in town would bring.

Chapter 8: Bonjour, Mon Ami!

Eleanor woke early the next day and read for a while before Jenna roused herself and they went down for breakfast in the hotel's inner courtyard.

"So, what's the plan?" asked Jenna, dissecting a *pain au chocolat*.

"Well," said Eleanor, scrutinising her map. "I'd like to visit the Cathedral and the medieval quarter. Oh, and there's the city art gallery and you mustn't miss the Victorian bandstand, which is unique."

"Sounds exhausting. When shall we have lunch?"

Eleanor frowned at her sister, who carried on munching.

"There'll be plenty of time for lunch. And did I mention the vineyard tours?"

"Ah, now we're talking," said Jenna, reaching for one of the brochures Eleanor had collected from the receptionist. "This looks great. Let's go."

"I was thinking we might do that tomorrow," said Eleanor, sipping her tea. "Oh, and I would like to see what some of the places of my youth look like now."

"*Mais oui, cherie,*" said Jenna, brushing crumbs from her lips and affecting an unconvincing French accent. "We must not be distracted from our mission to find *ze divine Christophe.*"

"Jenna, shush," said Eleanor, turning to look at the other guests.

"Good heavens, El. I do believe you are blushing at the very thought of seeing him."

"I'm not blushing, I'm hot. Shall we go?"

"Sure. I can't wait to discover what gems this place has to offer – other than lover boy, of course."

Eleanor handed Jenna a town map. "Here," she said. "You'll need it to find your way back to the hotel if I decide to abandon you."

"I'll be as good as gold, El, honest."

"I hope so. Now, shall we start with the Cathedral?"

Despite her protests, Jenna actually enjoyed visiting historical sites almost as much as her sister did. Because she knew the place so well, Eleanor was a well-informed and animated guide and the sisters had a busy day trekking around the town with plenty of coffee breaks along the way.

As evening fell, they wandered around for a little longer before choosing a busy café, with tables under trees decorated with sparkling white lights. Strolling down the high street and across the main square Eleanor had the oddest sensation. The last time she had been in Chevandier she was in her twenties. She was young, tanned, pretty – she now supposed – and constantly pestered by men. That was until she started going out with Christophe, after which it was as though some kind of secret signal had gone around and the local youths left her in peace. Now, it was almost as though she was invisible, which wasn't an unpleasant sensation. In fact it was quite liberating: she felt she could see without being seen.

When she mentioned this to Jenna, her sister sniffed. "Wait until you're the wrong side of fifty, like me. At 'a certain age' you start to disappear, your hair turns grey, your skin fades and it's as though you've become transparent. People look straight through you. Especially barmen," she said pointedly.

Not many people could ignore Jenna for long and, as if on cue, a handsome waiter with a tray and a crisp white cloth draped over his forearm hurried over to take their order.

"Cheers Sis," said Jenna, clinking glasses. "I'm pooped, but it has been a great day."

"*Santé*," replied Eleanor, with a smile. It had been a good day and there were several more to come. "So where shall we eat tonight?"

"Are you feeling brave enough to search out Chez Christophe?"

Eleanor looked serious for a moment. "You know, I'm really not sure that's a good idea." She helped herself to nuts from a chunky ceramic dish on the table, exactly like the ones she had sold in the gift shop all those years before. Was she mad even thinking of looking for someone she hadn't seen for more than twenty years? How would she react if she did find him? And what would her reception be like? She had pretty much abandoned Christophe, after all. "It wouldn't be fair to appear out of the blue."

"Why not? I'm sure he'd be delighted to see you."

Eleanor pulled a face. "Or maybe not," she said, grabbing a few more nuts. "Let's have another aperitif while I think about it."

Half an hour later and emboldened by their drinks, the sisters strolled off in search of dinner. After wandering around for a while they found themselves in the narrow streets behind the Cathedral. They squinted at menus and pressed their noses up against windows to see diners tucking into plates of mouth-watering food.

"I'm getting hungry, El. Which one shall we pick?"

"Gosh, I don't know. There are so many to choose from." Eleanor took a deep breath. "Actually, I think Chez Christophe should be around the corner. Shall we take a peek?"

"Absolutely," said Jenna, already setting off down the street, her heels unsteady on the cobbles.

"I want to see it, not go in."

"Of course not."

Eleanor caught up with her sister and they wandered arm in arm down narrow streets that began to climb gently towards the hills surrounding the city. After ten minutes of walking Jenna was starting to flag. "Is it much further, El?"

"No, it's definitely around here somewhere."

They turned a corner and Jenna whooped. "There it is!"

Eleanor caught her breath when she saw the familiar building, now with a new sign.

"Come on, let's see what they've got on offer."

"Wait!" said Eleanor, trying to grab Jenna's arm as she hurried over to the restaurant. "What if he sees me?"

Jenna stopped and turned towards her sister. "Okay. You wait there and I'll go and have a look."

Eleanor breathed a sign of relief and stepped back into the shadows as Jenna confidently walked over and perused the menu. After a second, the door opened and a young man came out and spoke to her, pointing at items on the menu. Eleanor couldn't hear what they were saying, but then Jenna turned and shouted across at her. "They've got a table," she said, waving. "Come on El, I'm starved."

Eleanor couldn't believe what was happening. "We were just supposed to be having a quick look at the place," she hissed under her breath as she rejoined her sister.

"Oops, I forgot," replied Jenna, disingenuously, as they entered the restaurant. "Don't worry. He probably won't be here anyway."

The door opened onto a dark room with scrubbed wooden floors and small tables covered in red or white linen cloths. On each table was a candle and a small posy of flowers in a deep blue vase. The place was almost full with what appeared to be locals, who smiled and nodded a welcome as the waiter led the two women to a table in an alcove at the back of the restaurant.

Eleanor took her place on the banquette, looking into the room. Her stomach felt tight with nerves. "I'm really not sure about this," she said again.

"El, it has been what – twenty years? You probably wouldn't even recognise each other." Jenna handed her the bread basket. "Relax. Eat something."

Eleanor took the bread reluctantly and spread the napkin on her lap. "You're right. I'm okay. I can do this." She lifted the menu and peered over it into the room. Apart from the young man who had lured them in, there was one other older waiter and a fair-haired girl behind the bar. Through the swing doors, a frenzy of activity could be seen going on in the kitchen. Her stomach lurched as she caught a glimpse of a small dark man in white ladling something onto a plate. Surely Christophe couldn't have got so, er, portly? No, she was being ridiculous. The man she had seen was much too short.

She took a gulp of water and looked up at the waiter who had appeared at their side. "*Bonsoir Mesdames*. Are you ready to order?"

"Could we have a couple more minutes, please?" said Jenna. "We are not quite ready."

"No problem," he said, bowing slightly. "I will bring the wine."

"What a dish," said Jenna, her eyes trained on the waiter's trim form. "If I was ten years younger …"

Eleanor laughed, "Ha! Twenty, maybe. You are a shocker."

The waiter returned with a carafe of red wine. "This is from my grandfather's vineyard," he said, pouring a little into each of their glasses. "I hope you like it."

Eleanor sipped the wine, which tasted of sunshine, long days and the baked earth of the Rhône Valley. "Um, this is really good."

As the waiter filled their glasses Eleanor began to relax. She settled back onto her velveteen seat enjoying the low hubbub of contented diners around her. Suddenly she felt hungry again. "Okay. Let's order."

Jenna waved at the waiter, who jotted down their choices on a small pad and flashed them a winning smile. "Excellent choices, *Mesdames*. I hope you enjoy your meal."

"I'm sure we shall," said Jenna, raising her glass. "What a smoothy he is."

Yes, thought Eleanor. "Actually, he reminds me of someone."

Jenna raised a quizzical eyebrow. "You mean Chri …"

"Shush!" Eleanor hissed. "Yes. He looks a bit like You Know Who."

"Do you think they could be related?"

"Gosh, no," said Eleanor, nibbling on an olive. "Of course not. All the young men in southern France look like him."

"You know how to make a girl jealous," said Jenna, looking around the room. "There I was trying to teach algebra to a classroom of horrible spotty teenagers and here you were living in sin with Mr You Know Who."

Eleanor smiled wistfully. "It was a special time for me."

"Yum, here comes supper," said Jenna, as the waiter reappeared with two plates: roast cod with lardons for Eleanor and a hearty casserole for Jenna.

They ate contentedly for a while, then Eleanor stopped and looked across at her sister. "I know this will sound crazy, but I think Alan was always jealous of Christophe, even though they never met."

Jenna dabbed her lips with her napkin and took a sip of water. "He wasn't jealous of Christophe, my love," she said. "He was jealous of all this." She swept her hand out and over the table, indicating the cosy room. "He never had the experiences you had. Never travelled, worked abroad or learned to speak French like you did."

Eleanor nodded. "You're right. Those were things that made me attractive to him but that he ultimately felt threatened by."

"Don't be sad, El!" said Jenna, squeezing her sister's hand. "It has all turned out for the best, really."

Has it? Alan was now in Toronto married to his

brand-new wife while she was here, getting tipsy, stalking someone she hadn't seen since Wham! were topping the charts.

"You have a great life with the shop, not to mention a new admirer, the lovely Jim."

"Who is just a friend," interrupted Eleanor.

"Okay, a lovely new *friend*," said Jenna, with emphasis. "And we've got several more days in France," she smiled. "And there's still pudding to come."

The waiter took their empty plates away and left a short list of desserts, which Jenna studied with interest.

"Jenna, where do you put it? You should be the size of a house, the amount of food you put away."

"You should see what I look like when I take my girdle off," she said, patting her flat stomach. "It's hideous."

Eleanor laughed and gave her a peck on the cheek. "Okay, dessert for you and coffee for me. I'm going to nip to the loo."

Down in the basement room, Eleanor studied herself in the mirror. She didn't look too bad, really. A couple of days in the sun had started to give her some colour, and her hair was still glossy and free of grey. "You'll do," she said to herself as she reapplied her lipstick.

Back at the table, she saw what looked like two glasses of cognac by their plates. "Jenna, I'm not sure cognac is a good idea! We've got to make our money last a few more days yet."

"It's okay," said Jenna, cupping a glass in her hands and nodding towards the bar. "They're on the house. The *patron* has just arrived and he brought them over."

And there he was: still tall and slender, his hair as dark and curly as she remembered it and with the tiniest hint of grey. Eleanor gasped and brought her hand to her mouth.

Seeing her, Christophe ran over. "Madame, are you unwell? Please sit down."

He pulled out a chair and gently ushered her into it as she stared silently up at him.

"Oh my word," said Jenna.

Clearly puzzled by the reaction, Christophe looked from one to the other for what seemed like an age.

"*Mon Dieu*," he said at last. "Ella? Is it you?"

All Eleanor could do was nod mutely.

"Ah, what a surprise! How wonderful to see you," he said, smiling and grasping her by the shoulders. "You look marvellous. Thomas, bring us some more coffee and cognac." He sat between them on the banquette, next to Jenna who stared at him open-mouthed. Composing herself at last, Eleanor introduced Christophe to her sister.

He bowed slightly and kissed her hand. "*Enchanté*, Madame."

"Likewise, I'm sure," said Jenna, quite won over by his old-fashioned manners.

"What brings you to Chevandier after all these years?" he asked, looking at the women.

"We're having a little holiday," said Eleanor, quietly.

"Why did you not tell me you were coming? Rosanne would love to see you again."

Eleanor looked puzzled. "Rosanne?"

"My wife! Don't you remember Rosanne? You shared a flat with her and Marie. Thomas, call your mother." So the handsome young waiter was

70

Christophe's son, after all. "I must introduce you to my boy." The young man bowed and shook their hands before dashing into the kitchen. "And here is my beautiful daughter, Elena." He stretched out his hand to the pretty girl they had seen working behind the bar.

Eleanor looked at Christophe. "Elena?"

He smiled sheepishly. "You know I always loved your name." As he looked at her from beneath his long lashes, she felt a jolt as her body remembered the thrill she had always felt when she was near him.

At that moment a tall blonde woman in chef's whites came out of the kitchen, looking slightly harassed and wiping her hands on a cloth. When she saw them a puzzled smile spread across her face. "Eleanor!" she exclaimed, extending her arms and giving both the sisters kisses. "This is a surprise. Your meal was good, I hope."

They both nodded and insisted that it had been delicious. After chatting for a while, Christophe rubbed his hands together and said "You must come to the vineyard for lunch on Monday when we close the restaurant."

"Love to," said Jenna, grinning broadly. "Wouldn't we, El?"

"Oh, I don't know ..."

"It would be our pleasure," added Rosanne.

"Please come," said Christophe, looking Eleanor straight in the eyes. "My parents would be so happy to see you again. After all this time."

Eleanor smiled weakly, completely overwhelmed by it all. "That's very kind," she said, eventually.

"I will send Thomas to collect you from your hotel at 2pm."

"Perfect," said Jenna. "We'll be ready and waiting."

"Excellent! I'm afraid I have to close up the restaurant now, but Thomas will walk you home." And despite their protests, that's what he did.

In the end, Eleanor was glad to have his company. Even though she knew where they were, her mind was in such turmoil she wasn't sure she would have been able to guide them back home.

When they arrived at the hotel, Jenna kicked off her shoes and collapsed on the bed. "Wow, what an evening."

Eleanor peeled back the shutters and went out onto the balcony where she sat with a shawl wrapped around her shoulders, gazing out over the square but not really seeing anything.

"Fancy the divine Christophe being married to the Teutonic maiden." Jenna had heard all about Eleanor's housemates over the years and was intrigued to meet Rosanne in the flesh. "What an amazing cook." She hauled herself upright, realising that there was no response from the balcony. "El, are you okay out there?"

Was she okay? She wasn't sure. "Yes, I'm fine," she called back into the room. "I just need some air."

She heard the pad of bare feet on the tiled floor as Jenna came out to join her, holding two glasses of chilled water. "Here, drink this."

Eleanor took hers gratefully.

"Oh Jenna, what have I done?"

Her sister sat down beside her, looking worried.

"What do you mean, El? You haven't done anything."

Eleanor recognised that she was a bit drunk, but

she knew cognac was not entirely to blame for the huge well of emotion now swirling inside her. She crossed her hands over her stomach, turning to her sister. "I feel, oh, I don't know," she looked out across the moonlit square, searching for the right word. "I've come all this way and now I feel ... unsettled. Yes, that's it: I feel unsettled." She stood and walked up and down the length of the balcony. "I saw someone tonight who I used to love and, and ..." She stopped her pacing and leant over the balcony. "And it seems like the ghost of that love is still here somehow."

Her sister was looking at her like she'd gone mad.

"Do you understand what I mean?"

Jenna shook her head. "No, El, I can't really say that I do. It has always been Kiff for me." Eleanor smiled. She envied her sister's constancy. Keith had been married before but had lost his wife to cancer when they were both quite young. He was older than Jenna who found herself with a two teenage stepchildren when they married. Together, they'd created a couple more of their own and now the whole brood lived in domestic, if chaotic, bliss in north London. "There are no exciting 'ghosts of boyfriends past' in my life."

"Except for Pete in Watford," said Eleanor.

"Ah yes, apart from him." She yawned extravagantly. "Can we go to bed now, El? All this excitement has quite worn me out."

"Yes of course. I'll be in in a minute."

Jenna gave her sister a hug. "Don't stay out here too long. You need your beauty sleep if you're going to see Christophe again on Monday!"

Chapter 9: Lunch at the Vineyard

The next day, fortified with several cups of *café au lait*, a heap of warm croissants and gallons of freshly squeezed orange juice, the sisters embarked on a full day of sightseeing. Since meeting Christophe at the restaurant the night before, everything seemed slightly surreal to Eleanor: the sights and sounds of the city were much the same as they had been in the late 1980s, but she had changed such a lot. Marriage, children and divorce had taken their toll and she was not the carefree twenty-something who had turned so many heads. But when Christophe had caught her hand and looked into her eyes last night, the thrill she felt had catapulted her back to her youth.

"You look miles away, El," said Jenna, pausing from examining an array of straw hats in the local market. "Is everything okay?"

"Yes, fine. I was just wondering how things were back at the shop."

Jenna peered at her from over her sunglasses. "You always were an unconvincing liar."

"All right – I was thinking about Christophe. And about my life ..."

"And what might have been if you hadn't married Alan the Android?"

It was an open secret that Jenna had never really

warmed to her brother-in-law and had not shed many tears when the marriage eventually broke up. Eleanor opened her mouth to protest, but Jenna held up her hands in submission.

"Okay, okay. I know he was a good husband, a devoted father, blah, blah, but he was bloody boring El, you have to admit. All that running around squash courts with the lads and traipsing across golf courses … "

"Keith plays golf!"

"Kiff may play golf," Jenna agreed, arranging a hat on her head, "but he doesn't actually enjoy it."

Eleanor couldn't help laughing.

"Alan was always so earnest," she added, handing over a handful of euros to the stallholder. "Anyway, you are a free woman and your ex-husband is in a much better place."

"You make it sound as though he's died!"

"He's in Canada with a dental hygienist, which I would say was much the same thing."

"You are, of course, right," said Eleanor, looping her arm through her sister's. "He's in the frozen north while I'm here in the sun with only twenty-four hours to go before I see my lost love again."

"Sounds like an excuse for a new outfit to me. Let's shop!"

"Oh, do we have to?" groaned Eleanor. "You know I can't abide shopping."

"I think that is pretty obvious from the contents of your suitcase," said Jenna, tartly. "There's certainly nothing in there that will do for lunch with the ex and his lovely wife."

Eleanor thought of the statuesque Rosanne, who

looked great even in her chef's whites with her hair casually piled on her head – and capitulated. "Okay then. But let's be quick."

"Absolutely," said Jenna. "I happened to notice a shop nearby which had some interesting things in the window."

"Lead the way."

Jenna had a good eye for a bargain and Eleanor soon found herself with a brand-new pair of linen trousers and a scoop-necked top. "I'm not sure about this," she said, tugging the neckline up over her cleavage. "It's not my usual style."

"That's because your usual style – if one could call it that – is 'dowdy bookseller'."

"Well, thanks a lot!"

"I'm trying to help you, El," said Jenna, turning her sister around to get a better view. "The pattern really suits you and the colours are great with your hair."

Studying herself in the mirror, Eleanor had to agree she looked rather good. "Hmm, maybe it's not too bad." The burnt orange fabric did bring out the highlights in her hair, she thought, and the turquoise details set off her newly acquired tan. She paid for the outfit and they left the shop.

Jenna turned to her sister. "Now we've sorted out your wardrobe, what shall we do next?"

"How do you fancy a river cruise this afternoon?"

"That sounds marvellous," said Jenna. "I especially enjoy sightseeing you can do sitting down."

"You'll like this bit, too," Eleanor said, pulling the brochure out of her handbag and peering at it. "It looks like we stop off at a couple of vineyards along the way."

Jenna clasped her hands together. "It gets better and better."

Eleanor led the way down to the riverside where they caught the boat and spent the rest of the afternoon on the water with occasional sallies onto dry land. After a couple of miles, they landed and were led to a kind of barn where smiling young people in smart black aprons offered them tiny samples of local wine. The sisters each bought some. At the next stop, they tasted some more and bought a couple of bottles.

Walking back to the hotel at the end of the trip, Eleanor tested the weight in her hands. "I think we may have overdone it with the wine," she said, wondering how she would fit it in her luggage.

"Nonsense," said Jenna. "It will make lovely gifts for Kiff and our new friends in Chevandier."

"True," said Eleanor. "And if our bags are too heavy to lift onto the train, we'll have to drink the wine first."

"That's the spirit," said Jenna, bursting into giggles. "No pun intended."

"I think we need coffee."

That evening, they had another early dinner at a pizzeria on the corner by their hotel. Eleanor had a restless night, wondering what the next day would bring. She awoke early and was up and ready by 7am. She left her sister sleeping and had a walk by the river before breakfast. Later, they both went for a wander around town, but all through the rest of the morning Eleanor felt as though they were killing time until lunch.

As promised, Thomas came to collect them from the hotel promptly at 2pm to drive them to the Vauban family home. Looking at him in daylight, Eleanor could see that he resembled his father around the mouth, but had the fine features and grey eyes of his mother. "He's going to break a few hearts," were Jenna's words of wisdom.

As the road climbed out of the city and wound up into the hills away from the river, the air grew hotter and stiller.

"Wow, look at those," said Jenna, as they drove past huge fields full of sunflowers.

Thomas smiled. "We are not far away now."

A little further up on the left, there was a modest wooden sign at the entrance to the vineyard with the family name decorated in vine leaves. They drove down a rough earth track past rows and rows of vines clinging to steep slopes. Thomas explained that they were mainly Syrah grapes from which his grandfather made the Côtes du Rhône they had sampled at Chez Christophe.

"Of course *grandpère* makes other wines, too. You will taste them later!"

He parked the car by an old barn and escorted the sisters to a stone farmhouse where a long table was set out on a shady veranda. Two dusty brown dogs of indeterminate breed lolloped over to greet Thomas, who wrestled with them enthusiastically.

Christophe came out of the house with a huge grin on his face. Beside him was Rosanne who looked cool and elegant in a green print dress. "Welcome to Château Vauban," she said, smiling and shooing chickens from beneath the table. "I hope you don't mind that we are a little rustic." She smiled again. "Can you excuse me while I finish lunch? Please have a drink and relax. It won't be long."

"Come, come and sit down," said Christophe. Thomas unseated a scrawny grey cat and dragged chairs over to the table. "Please, sit," said the young man. "I will tell my grandparents you are here."

"I feel like I'm in a commercial for olive oil," whispered Jenna, under her breath. "Do these people really live here?"

Eleanor smiled and nodded. "They come here at weekends and for holidays. It's the old family home. I believe that Christophe's father grew up in the farmhouse. I remember hearing about it, but I never came here."

They could hear pans crashing somewhere inside the house, then old Madame Vauban appeared in the doorway followed by her husband carrying two bottles of red wine. It had seemed unlikely they would remember her, so Eleanor was touched by the warm reception she received from the now-elderly pair whom she had not seen for so long.

Elena came out next, carrying a tray laden with crisp green salad, blocks of homemade paté, chunks of salami and fresh baguettes, which she set on the table. Monsieur Vauban spoke barely any English, so Eleanor translated for Jenna as he told them the history of the house and the vineyard, and explained how his wine was produced. Madame nodded and smiled, correcting her husband when he got something wrong.

In the background, Christophe flitted to and fro, bringing out plates and glasses. Although Eleanor tried to concentrate on Monsieur Vauban's story, she couldn't help glancing over at her former lover. She reddened as she framed the word in her head and Jenna caught her eye, making her feel even guiltier.

Thomas returned with a tray of ice-cold glasses on an enamel tray. "Ooh, this is lovely," said Jenna, sipping the pale pink liquid. "What is it?"

"It is called Pineau des Charentes," he said, "and it's strong, so take care!"

Just then, Rosanne appeared with a roast chicken on a pile of potatoes, all cooked in garlic and rosemary. "Please, dig in," she said, in immaculate English.

Christophe went around the table filling glasses with different types of wine which Jenna and Eleanor duly peered at, swirled around and sniffed before tasting as Monsieur Vauban looked on with evident amusement.

Lunch, which finished with juicy peaches and hunks of local cheese, was delicious and conversation flowed in a mixture of French, English and Franglais, much helped by the wine tasting. Rosanne and her husband told the sisters about the business and their hopes that Thomas and Elena would continue to run the restaurant and the vineyard as their grandparents had done. Eleanor told them about her children and the shop, and Jenna made them laugh by describing life with Keith and the extended family, including Connie and Harold.

"That was a fabulous lunch," said Jenna, rubbing her belly appreciatively. "Thank you so much for inviting us."

Rosanne waved her hand, as though it was nothing. "You are most welcome."

"Let me help you with those," said Eleanor, starting to collect assorted dishes.

"No, please. You are our guests," said Rosanne, taking the dessert plates from her hands. "You stay there and talk to Christophe," she said, shooting a look across at her husband. "I'm sure you have a lot of catching up to do. Jenna would you like to see the house?"

"Oh, I'd love to!" Jenna gave Eleanor a meaningful wink as she followed Rosanne into the shady kitchen. Monsieur and Madame Vauban also went into the house, miming that it was time for them to take a siesta. Elena excused herself, too, jumping on a moped and setting off to visit her boyfriend.

Sitting there alone with Christophe, Eleanor suddenly felt tongue-tied and shy. He grinned and pulled out a pack of Gitanes. "I don't suppose you smoke any more? All my English customers seem to have given up."

She laughed. "I've given up several times," she replied, taking a cigarette, "but this is a special occasion."

As Christophe lit her cigarette, then his own, she studied his face. He was still incredibly handsome. She blushed as he caught her looking at him. They sat in silence for a moment, smiling at each other, enjoying the moment.

"This is such a gorgeous spot."

"Yes, we are very lucky," he said, finishing his coffee and yawning. "I think I must take a walk or I will fall asleep. Would you like to come with me? I will show you the view."

"There's more to see?"

"Why yes, of course," said Christophe, as he stood and pulled back her chair. "Come." They left the veranda and he led the way along a path that went around the back of the farmhouse and through a small uncultivated area where the ground was scrubby and rough underfoot. The dogs ran alongside them, occasionally zigzagging off in search of lizards in the undergrowth. To begin with the way was hot and dusty and there wasn't much to see apart from the stony ground and a few ancient olive trees. From time to time as they climbed the hill, Christophe took Eleanor's hand to steady her. After ten minutes she was beginning to wonder whether he was joking about the view but, when they turned a corner, the vista opened up and she found herself gazing past the red-tiled roof of the farmhouse at rows of grapevines in neat, serried ranks. On either side were dark green fields that rolled down the hill to the river and the edge of Chevandier.

Christophe turned and smiled proprietarily, spreading his arms out towards the view. "*Et voilà!*" He led her to a rough wooden bench under a gnarled old tree and beckoned her to sit beside him. "It was worth the climb, I hope?"

Eleanor, dusty and slightly breathless from the walk, nodded in agreement. "Yes, it's stunning." And so it was. The late afternoon sun intensified the colours of the landscape that was spread out in front of them. There was no noise except for the "crick crick" of crickets in the long grass, the complaint of distant goats and a chatter of birdsong.

They sat there for a while then Christophe wandered off to look at the view, humming an old song and throwing sticks for the dogs. Eleanor closed her eyes and leant back against the tree trunk, luxuriating in the sensation of the warm breeze on her skin and the scent of pine trees in the air. The effects of the lunch and the wine had made her drowsy and she was about to nod off when she felt a sudden weight on her knee. She opened her eyes in surprise to see the dogs had thrown themselves down beside her in the shade and one of them had rested its big shaggy head on her lap. Christophe strode back towards her, his hands in the air in mock guilt.

"Orson, *bouge*! I'm sorry, but my dogs find you irresistible!"

"How flattering," she said, laughing.

He shooed the dog away. "They have very good taste."

"You are teasing me now," Eleanor said, laughing and trying to untangle her hair, which had suffered from the effects of the dusty walk. "I remember how mischievous you used to be."

He grasped her hands, suddenly serious. "I hope we can be friends, Eleanor."

"I hope so too," she said, though she wasn't sure what such a friendship would be like. They shared a past, but now they led such different lives and lived so far apart. They sat in silence, each lost in their own thoughts.

"I'm sorry I left you and went back to London," said Eleanor, surprised by the words that came from her.

Christophe stood and made a sound like "boff", shrugging his shoulders. "We were very young." He sat down beside her again and touched her cheek with the back of his hand. "But we were lucky to have such love in our lives, don't you think?"

She nodded her head. "Yes, we were," she said, putting on a pretend pout. "Do you forgive me for leaving you?"

"Of course," he said, hugging her. "If you had not gone, I would not have married Rosanne and had Thomas and Elena, and you would not have met your husband."

She wrinkled her nose at that. "Hmm, exactly."

Eleanor had shared the bare bones of her former marriage over lunch. Now, Christophe shook his head in disbelief. "I'm sorry to say this Ella, but the man is a fool."

She felt she should protest and outline Alan's good points, but before she could speak Christophe had leant over and pressed his lips gently but firmly on hers.

She put her hands to his face and closed her eyes, revelling in the moment, hoping to store the myriad sensations in her mind: the sweet pressure of his lips, the slight stubble under her fingertips, the wonderful scent of his skin. It was just one stolen kiss, but it was magical and forbidden and neither of them wanted to be the first to pull away because they each knew there could never be another one.

All too soon Christophe drew back, caressing her hair and smiling at her. "I should say sorry for kissing you, but that would not be true."

Eleanor felt the same, even though she knew it was wrong. She put a finger to his lips, partly to silence him and partly to stop him kissing her again, much as she longed for him to do it. She knew she should feel guilty, sitting there under the tree, kissing a married man, but she couldn't. At that moment, all she felt was happy. Seeing herself reflected in Christophe's eyes, she felt desirable again.

After a while, Christophe got to his feet and

stretched out his hand to her. "Come. Let's go back to the house. Everyone will wonder where we are."

Jenna will be intrigued to know what we've been up to, thought Eleanor, as she took Christophe's hand and they descended the path together, back to their families and their real lives.

After they had all said their goodbyes and promised to keep in touch, Thomas drove them back to the hotel. It wasn't until they were ensconced in their rooms that the sisters were able to talk about the events of the afternoon. By this time, Jenna was desperate to learn what had happened between Christophe and her sister.

"So, tell me all. You were gone for such a long time I was worried Rosanne would think you'd run off together."

Eleanor smiled enigmatically, she hoped. "Well, we had a lovely walk and a chat."

"A chat? Come on, El. Confess – did you have a snog?"

Eleanor tried her best to look offended. "A 'snog'? You can be so crude sometimes."

"Okay. A kiss, then?"

Eleanor was savouring the memory and gazed dreamily out across the balcony to where the elderly gents were playing *boules* and gossiping, as they did every evening. She was silent as Jenna grew increasingly frustrated. As an elder sister and a maths teacher, she was used to people giving her straight answers.

"Well?" she asked, after a moment.

Eleanor turned away from the balcony, suddenly serious. "Rosanne has no need to worry."

"Oh," said Jenna, who appeared quite deflated. "So nothing happened, then?"

"I wouldn't say *nothing* happened. I'm just not going to tell you about it."

"Now, that's not fair! You drag me all the way over here, make me drink my body weight in red wine, then refuse to share the juicy gossip."

"I had a lovely day and I hope Christophe and I can be friends, but that's all."

Jenna seemed disappointed. "Shame. I was looking forward to visiting you in your lovely French farmhouse."

"I'm no *femme fatale*," said Eleanor, laughing, "and certainly no home-breaker."

Jenna nodded in agreement. "I know."

"Which is not to say Christophe doesn't still fancy the pants off me."

"Woohoo! That's more like it."

"And we did have a kiss, but that's top secret!"

Jenna crossed herself. "Your sordid affair is safe with me."

Eleanor smiled and gave her a hug. "Thanks, Jenna. You're a pal."

That night Eleanor slept like a log, happy to have spent some time with Christophe and to know he found her attractive so many years after they had first met. She was also pleased to discover that by going back to London she had allowed him to create a happy life with Rosanne and the children. As she fell asleep, it was with a contented smile on her face.

Chapter 10: Confession Time

On Tuesday, the sisters had their final breakfast at the hotel, waved a fond farewell to their suite and lugged their suitcases into a taxi and back to the railway station. They both agreed it had been quite an adventure – and a successful one to boot.

Back in London, Keith was there to meet them at the Eurostar terminal and whisk them to the house in the evening.

"You're very quiet," he said to them once they were settled in the living room with mugs of tea. "Pleased with yourselves but quiet."

Eleanor and Jenna exchanged glances.

Keith stood there with his arms folded, waiting. "What have you been up to?"

"Sorry Kiff, I'm sworn to secrecy."

Keith looked suspiciously at his wife. "You must have had a very good time if you won't even tell me about it."

"It wasn't me, it was her," said Jenna, pointing at Eleanor.

"Thanks, Sis. Actually, Keith, I saw an old flame and ..."

"And?"

"And he was gorgeous," said Jenna, "but married and they had a kiss. Oops! And now Eleanor will kill me because I've told you."

"I didn't really expect you not to tell Keith," said Eleanor, smiling.

Keith sat down on the sofa, one arm draped over his wife's shoulders. "Kissing a married man, eh? I'm not sure I approve of this."

"It's not as bad as it sounds, honest."

"Okay, I'm all ears."

"Me too!" said Jenna.

Eleanor ran through the story of how they'd met Christophe and Rosanne in the restaurant and about the wonderful lunch at the vineyard with all the family.

"And then we went for a walk and he kissed me," she said, blushing. "But that was all and I really don't know if I'll ever see him again."

Keith looked serious for a moment. "It doesn't sound as if too much harm was done."

Eleanor felt a pang of guilt as she remembered the look on Rosanne's face when she and Christophe had arrived back at the house, obviously happy in each other's company. When they were all saying their goodbyes, Eleanor had squeezed Rosanne's hands and thanked her in a way which she hoped made clear that her husband was quite safe from her clutches. She had seen the tightness around Rosanne's mouth relax and recognised that Christophe was probably not the easiest man to be married to.

"I'm sorry to say it, El," said Jenna, "but I fear the divine Christophe is probably a bit of a love rat."

Eleanor laughed at the description, but had to agree. "Yup, you're probably right. He is lovely to look at, but I'm not sure I'd like to be in Rosanne's shoes."

"But it's great you know that now and can stop worrying about the 'what-ifs' and carry on with your life," said Jenna.

"Well, I'm glad everything has resolved itself," said Keith.

"I'll drink to that," said Eleanor, getting down on her knees and rummaging in her suitcase for one of their many bottles of wine.

When they had their glasses charged, Jenna stood and raised hers in a toast. "Here's to the people we love and the people we don't know we love because we haven't met them yet."

"How very philosophical you are, darling," said her husband, clinking his glass with hers and giving her a kiss.

"What a lovely speech," said Eleanor, laughing. "And please don't tell Mum about Christophe or I'll never hear the end of it."

Jenna rolled her eyes in mock outrage. "As if I would!"

Chapter 11: Time to Go Home

Eleanor spent the next couple of days in London visiting friends, going to exhibitions and having her first decent haircut in months. By Friday she was ready to head back to her home and the shop. When she had set off on holiday, it had been agreed Erika would only contact her if there was a problem she couldn't deal with. Given how competent Erika was, Eleanor was not surprised to have received no messages.

Arriving back at the station, Eleanor breathed in deeply. The salty tang of the sea never failed to thrill her. Even though she'd lived by the sea for over three years, it still felt like she was on holiday every time she got the first whiff of ozone.

She grabbed her suitcase and trundled out of the small station towards the car park where she had arranged for Erika to meet her and drive her home. The lime-green Combi was parked by the exit and through the window she could see Bella perched in her favourite spot on the front passenger seat, paws at the window and tail wagging furiously.

Eleanor smiled as she went around to the driver's side, wheeling her case behind her. As she approached the front door, it opened and an unfamiliar figure appeared. Eleanor was expecting to see her assistant, so she did a double take when she saw Daniel Pearce climb down from the cab.

"Hello Eleanor. Welcome home."

Eleanor really didn't know what to say. "Daniel? Good afternoon. Er, why are you in my van? Where's Erika?"

Daniel frowned as he bent to take her suitcase. "There's nothing to worry about. I'm only helping out."

He opened the side door to put her things in the van, allowing Bella to leap out and greet her owner enthusiastically, squeaking with joy and chasing her tail round and round. Once the dog had settled down a little bit, Daniel coaxed her into the back of the vehicle and helped Eleanor up into the passenger seat.

"Okay if I drive?"

"Sure, yes," said Eleanor, who was now genuinely alarmed. "Daniel, what has happened?"

"Oh, Erika had a bit of an accident."

Eleanor had visions of the shop burning to the ground. "What sort of accident?" she asked, immediately fearing the worst.

Daniel had started the engine and they were heading off up the hill. "I'm afraid she tripped over one of Dad's boxes a couple of days after you left and sprained an ankle quite badly. She can't stand, which makes driving and bookselling rather difficult."

Eleanor's heart sank at the thought of losing hard-won customers while the shop was closed. She groaned, running her hands through her hair.

"So how long has the shop been closed?"

"Oh, it isn't closed," he said cheerily. "Your mother is running the place."

"What?" Eleanor couldn't decide if Connie being in charge would be better or worse than the shop being closed altogether. "My mother?" Her mind boggled.

"But my mother has never worked in a bookshop before. And she's in there on her own?"

"Not entirely on her own. She's had help from Mr Greaves."

"Harold?" Eleanor had now convinced herself there would be complete chaos in the shop. "Why did no one tell me about this?"

Daniel shrugged. "I guess they didn't want to spoil your holiday."

"My mother and Harold have been running the shop alone for over a week?" She looked at Daniel in disbelief. "Neither of them is any good with computers." Apart from navigating dating sites, she thought to herself. She felt quite sick at the possibility that her complex accounting and stock control systems would be in total disarray.

"Oh well," said Daniel, "I've been assisting a little with that side of things."

Eleanor stared at him open-mouthed. "You've been helping? In my shop?" How had this happened, she wondered. She had been away for less than a fortnight and there'd been a coup. "It's very kind of you but, I mean – I don't mean to be rude, but how did you get involved?"

Daniel turned and smiled. "Well, I'd been out walking Bella." Eleanor's mouth opened to speak, but Daniel went on before she could frame the question. "Your son had gone back to London, Connie was busy in the shop and Erika couldn't walk the dog because of her ankle, so she asked if I could help. Actually I was happy to." He looked sombre for a moment before continuing. "Freya has finally moved out and taken everything with her, including our dog."

"I'm sorry to hear that." Crikey, what else had been happening while she'd been away? "You must miss her."

"I do. Despite the dog hair and fleas," he chuckled to himself.

Daniel Pearce had made a joke. Had she landed on an alien planet? Nothing was as it should be. Eleanor settled down in her seat with Bella's nose snuffling in her hair and closed her eyes. Maybe when she opened them again, everything would be back to normal.

Glancing around as they drove down the high street, things looked reassuringly normal. Daniel parked the campervan in the usual spot and wheeled Eleanor's suitcase down the pavement as she followed behind with the dog. Arriving at the shop, Eleanor found the place to be surprisingly ordered and calm.

"Hello love. Welcome back!" Connie came out from behind the counter to give her daughter a big hug.

"Hello Mum. What's been going on here?" She looked around the shop, noticing the neat pile of papers on the counter and a jug of fresh flowers on the central table from where a couple of her regular customers smiled at her and waved. "How are you managing?"

"We're coping fine. In fact, it has been rather fun!"

"But Mother, you've never worked in a shop before."

Connie pulled herself up to her full height of 5ft 3in, looking rather offended. "I ran London's only hedgehog rescue shop for eighteen months when you were first married."

It was true and Eleanor had completely forgotten.

"Sorry Mum. You are absolutely right, but that was donkey's years ago. There were barely any computers to worry about in those days."

"Well, that's where Daniel has been a godsend." She smiled over at him, where he sat stroking the dog and looking sheepish.

Before Eleanor could ask any more questions, she heard a murmur of laughter from the back of the shop. "What's going on there?"

"Oh, it's 'Storytime with Harold'." Connie pointed towards the back room where Eleanor could see an elderly gent in a grey sports jacket and yellow cravat in a comfy chair surrounded by small children and assorted mums all listening intently to *Guess How Much I Love You*. Harold caught Eleanor's eye and waved.

"I hope you don't mind, love. Harold has a way with children," said Connie, smiling indulgently. "We did it last week and the children loved it. Best of all, the mothers can't resist buying a storybook for their little ones," she added in a whisper. Eleanor was once again lost for words.

"Shall we have a cup of tea? Daniel, be a dear and put the kettle on. Harold is always gasping for a brew after he's been reading to the kiddies."

Daniel looked slightly uneasy. "Is it all right if I make the drinks?" he asked, glancing nervously at Eleanor.

"Sure, go ahead." As soon as he was out of earshot, Eleanor turned to her mother. "I'm still not entirely clear how Daniel Pearce came to be working in my shop," she hissed.

"It's perfectly simple. He came back from walking the dog one morning to find me in a terrible tangle on the computer. Harold had had a go, but it's not quite the same system as he's used to."

"You mean the dating site?"

"And other things," added Connie. "He's very good at shopping online and he checks my shares for me on there. Well, anyway, Daniel asked if he could help and he was so marvellous I asked him to pop in every day while you were away to keep an eye on things."

"But why did no one ring me?"

"We didn't want to telephone you in France because we thought it would be terribly expensive, didn't we, love?" said Connie.

"That's right," said Harold, who had finished his *Jackanory* session and now rejoined them at the front of the shop. "Your mother wanted you to have a lovely time without worrying about things here."

Eleanor looked at them both beaming with pride at how well they'd done and couldn't be cross.

"Three teas," said Daniel, handing out the drinks.

"Aren't you having one, dear?" asked Connie.

"No, I'd better get off because Father is expecting me. I'm going to check out another bungalow with him this afternoon."

"Well, thank you for all your help," said Connie, kissing him on the cheek.

"Yes, thanks young man," said Harold, clasping Daniel's hand in both of his and shaking it firmly. "I'm not sure how we would have managed without your technical expertise!"

"You're very welcome, Harold."

Eleanor stood there watching the mutual admiration society and felt quite left out.

On his way to the door, Daniel bent down to stroke the dog. "Bye Bella. I hope to see you again soon. And your owner, too, of course," he added.

Eleanor smiled weakly. "I think we'll manage from now on, but thanks for helping to keep everything afloat."

When he'd gone, they all sipped their tea thoughtfully.

"Well, we'll have this then leave you in peace," said Connie.

Harold nodded in agreement. "Yes, that's probably best."

How do mothers always know how to make you feel guilty, wondered Eleanor. "Actually, if you could stay and carry on doing what you're doing for an hour or so, it would give me time to take my case round to the house and check on Erika."

"I think we could do that, don't you?" said Harold, smiling down at Connie who nodded in agreement.

"Great," said Eleanor, emptying her mug and taking a quick peek at the computer screen, which seemed to be functioning normally. "I'm off. See you later," she said, as she trundled off towards the cottage, leaving Harold and Connie to chat up the customers.

After quickly emptying her suitcase and throwing a few things into the washing machine, Eleanor set out again to visit Erika in her flat on the top floor of a white 1930s block near the sea front. She had called ahead so Erika was expecting her. Her ankle was almost better and she planned to return to work the next day. They chatted about the shop and the holiday, and Eleanor filled her in on her encounter with

Christophe – she knew there was no point imagining it would remain secret for very long.

When Eleanor had finished talking, Erika looked thoughtful. "So you don't mind that Christophe isn't single and available?"

Eleanor laughed. "I can't say I hadn't fantasised about it when we were on our way to France, but no. Not really."

"So Jim is still in the running, then?"

"Jim Rowe? Oh, Jim and I are just friends. He's a lovely guy, but there's no romance there." She looked at her friend for a moment. "In fact, we thought you might like to join us in the pub next time we meet. He's going to invite another friend along, too. Fancy that?"

"Actually, Jim has already mentioned it," said Erika. "He saw me stumbling out of the GP's surgery on my brand new crutches and helped me upstairs to the flat."

Eleanor smiled. "He's such a nice chap."

Erika was looking decidedly shifty. "Yes, and then he made us both coffee and did some shopping for me because I couldn't manage the stairs."

Eleanor nodded as light slowly dawned. "Are you trying to tell me you and Jim are ..."

"Friends, yes," said Erika. "I hope you don't mind, but we've been getting to know each other while you've been away and I think maybe we might be something more than friends one day."

"Oh, but that's great," said Eleanor, genuinely happy for her. "And Jim knows about your, er, history?"

Erika smiled. "He does, yes, and he says he doesn't mind one bit. In fact, he says it makes me a more interesting person."

"Well, I'm really pleased," said Eleanor, giving Erika a hug. "And have you told Connie?"

"No, not yet."

"She likes a bit of romance – she'll be thrilled, too."

"I hope so," said Erika. "She was really hoping you and Jim might get it together."

Eleanor shrugged. "Don't worry about me. I'm fine on my own."

Chapter 12: New Beginnings

On Saturday, it was business as usual in the shop. Erika spent most of the day seated behind the cash desk while Eleanor dashed around, helping customers with their questions and unpacking new deliveries. Running the bookshop was much harder work than she had originally anticipated, but Eleanor loved the variety of it and enjoyed the relationships she managed to build up with her customers.

At the end of the day she received a call from Malcolm Pearce. After some chitchat about her holidays and his house move, he came to the point. "I don't mean to bother you, but I wondered whether perhaps you had a cheque for me yet?"

In the excitement of the trip to France, Eleanor had completely forgotten to send off the money. "I'm so sorry, Mr Pearce! Yes, I have your cheque here now," she said, digging it out from a drawer. She looked at the clock. "We'll be closing soon. Why don't I jump in the van and bring it over this evening?"

"Oh, you don't have to come all this way. Why don't you drop it in at my son's house next time you're passing, then he can bring it over."

Eleanor didn't know where Daniel Pearce lived, so she scribbled down the address on a notepad and promised to deliver the cheque in the morning.

"Great," she said to Erika as she put the phone

down. "Let's just hope Daniel's out. I don't think I could cope with Mr Crumpet first thing in the morning."

Erika laughed. "I think you're being a bit harsh. He was very kind to me and great with Connie and Harold when you were away."

"Hmm, so I gather. Maybe it's only me he's not keen on."

"That's nonsense, but if you're so worried about it why don't you go now and get it over with?"

"Good idea. Let's shut up shop and I'll walk over there with Bella."

Back at the cottage, Eleanor pulled out a map to check exactly where she was going. She could tell that Daniel's house was one of the swanky places facing the sea on the road that led out of town. She had driven by many times without realising it was where he and Freya lived. She decided to cut through the woods, so changed out of her work clothes into dog-walking trousers and wellies.

From the cottage, she walked down to the sea front then followed a footpath sign pointing the way up the cliff. It was a lovely walk along the rough path, twigs and fir cones crunching under her feet and sending up a fresh spicy scent. The dog chased back and forth investigating all the interesting smells.

After a short climb, the path reached the top road and Eleanor arrived at what she thought must be the address. She checked the number on her bit of paper then went through a wooden gate and down a gravel drive. The property at the end of the drive caught her completely by surprise. Although from the road it looked like a standard late-Victorian house, the side of the building facing the sea was one huge garden room. Here, the brick walls had been almost completely replaced with oak frames and tall panes of glass. From inside, anyone living there would have uninterrupted views of the coastline for miles on either side. It was obviously a modern development, but it was beautifully done.

"Wow," Eleanor whispered to herself. "Someone must be doing okay to be able to afford a place like this."

There was no car on the drive, so she was pretty sure Daniel was not at home. Plucking up her courage, she walked around the house, hoping to find something as humdrum as a letterbox. Eventually she spotted a modified milk churn by a side door. Above it, there was an engraved plaque on the wall that proclaimed "Pearce & Pearce, Architects".

So Daniel was an architect and it looked like Freya was one, too, judging by the names. She posted the envelope containing Malcolm's cheque into the milk churn, hoping it was indeed a letterbox and not a litter bin, and turned to leave.

As she did so, she caught sight of people in the garden room. She was going to wave or say hello when she realised the man she could see was Daniel Pearce and he had his arms wrapped around a much younger woman. Fearing she was looking at something she shouldn't be witness to, Eleanor ducked behind a large shrub. Was this the "other woman"? She didn't know why Daniel and Freya had split up, after all.

She was trapped: there was no way she could leave without being seen by the people in the house. She knew she shouldn't look but, from her post behind the bushes, she could spy on proceedings without being seen. The woman – girl really – was tall and fair, with long hair that fell in what could only be described as ringlets. She looked upset and Daniel appeared to be trying to comfort her.

At that moment, Eleanor became aware that Bella was no longer by her side. She looked around and realised to her horror that the dog had somehow recognised Daniel through the glass and was trotting over, tail wagging, to greet him.

She felt quite sick as she saw Daniel move away from the young woman and slide open one of the large glass doors. He knelt down to greet the dog, a look of puzzlement on his face. Just as Eleanor thought it couldn't get any worse, the dog turned around and ran back to where she was concealed behind the rhododendrons.

"Eleanor, is that you?" said Daniel, peering in her direction.

She smiled and waved as she came out from behind the shrubbery. "Hi, yes it's me," she said, a grin frozen on her face. "I came to drop off your father's cheque. Over there," she added, pointing towards the milk churn.

Daniel frowned. "Yes, quite a lot of people make that mistake."

The blonde girl, who had been crouching by the dog, scratching her behind the ears, now stood up and peered at Eleanor. "Aren't you going to invite your friend in?" she asked, turning to Daniel.

Eleanor was hovering midway between them and the bush.

"Yes, of course. Won't you take the weight off your wellies and come in?" he asked, obviously amused by her discomfort.

"Oh, I don't know," said Eleanor, shuffling from foot to foot, wishing the ground would open up and swallow her. "I should get back. It's Bella's teatime."

"Don't worry about that," said the girl. "We've got lots of dog food here, haven't we Dad? Or has Mum taken the Pedigree Chum, too?" With the last comment, the girl burst into tears.

Daniel hugged her to his chest. "Don't cry, sweetheart. You'll see Crumpet again soon, I'm sure. Emily is upset because Freya has taken the dog," he said, over his daughter's head.

"I'm so sorry," said Eleanor, patting the girl's arm. "You can take my dog for a walk any time you like!"

"That's really kind of you," sniffed Emily, disentangling herself from her father's embrace. "Especially as we've never met before."

Daniel smiled. "Let's go inside and I'll introduce you to each other."

"Well, if you're sure."

"Quite sure," he said. "And Bella, too."

After they had made their introductions, Daniel looked at his watch. "Tea? Or would you like something stronger? Wine perhaps?"

"Lovely," said Eleanor.

"Elderflower cordial for me, Dad, please."

"Okay love. And can you get the food out for the dog?"

Emily opened the cupboard under the sink and pulled out a dish and a selection of tins. "Rabbit, turkey or lamb?" she asked Bella, who sat at her feet.

Eleanor smiled and looked around the room.

Along the back wall were wall-to-ceiling shelves covered in glossy books on Eleanor's favourite subjects: art, architecture, history, gardening, travel. In between the books were intriguing artefacts, small prints and pieces of sculpture.

"Wow!" she said, moving towards them. "Can I have a look?"

"Sure, help yourself," said Daniel. "You can see why I didn't want to buy any more books from you the other evening."

She turned as he handed her a glass of chilled Sauvignon Blanc, feeling chastened. "I had no idea you were such a bookworm."

He raised an eyebrow. "Ah, there are lots of things you don't know about me yet."

He's right, thought Eleanor. What do I know about this man except that he likes books, has a beautiful daughter and an ex-wife who's a dog thief?

"Come and see this." Daniel walked to the end of the room and pressed a switch that lifted the blinds. It was sunset and the sun hovered like a pink tangerine on the edge of the water.

"How gorgeous," said Eleanor, admiring the view. "Whenever I see a sunset like this one, I think it's not surprising that in the past people thought you could fall off the edge of the world if you went too far west."

Daniel laughed and joined her on one of the big blue sofas. "Not if you were a sailor. Sailors knew from experience the world wasn't flat."

"Oh, don't get Dad started on sailing," said Emily.

Eleanor looked surprised. "You're a sailor?"

"There you are, you see," said Daniel, grinning. "Something else you didn't know about me."

He's teasing me, she thought. "Okay, okay. There are lots of things you don't know about me, either."

Daniel laughed, "I doubt it, having spent over a week in the shop with your mother."

Eleanor cringed. "What has she been saying?"

"Nothing bad, honest." Daniel was quiet for a moment, watching the sun as it fizzed on the water. "You know, I had a campervan like yours when I was younger. I loved it."

"Oh, what happened to it?"

Daniel looked over his shoulder to see whether his daughter was listening, but Emily had disappeared into the next room with the dog. "Freya made me get rid of it when we had Emily. Thought it was dangerous or impractical or something."

"What a shame. I bought mine precisely because we had one when the children were little. Being in the van brings back lots of happy memories for me." Eleanor looked out at the sea, remembering the blissful times they'd spent as a family camping on the beach. "My kids adored spending the whole day at the seaside, turning pink in the sun, eating gritty egg sandwiches and going to bed with their belly buttons and ears still full of sand." She laughed at the memory. "Oh dear, I was a terrible mother!"

Daniel smiled and looked at her. "It sounds like you were – you are – a great mother."

Eleanor laughed. "Ha! That's what Joe says when he wants to borrow the van and go surfing."

"Clever chap," said Daniel, topping up her glass of wine.

"So, tell me about this boat of yours."

"Oh, she's a classic wooden sailing boat with a small galley and sleeping area." He smiled, wistfully. "She's my pride and joy."

"She sounds perfect," said Eleanor, who had always fancied spending some time on the ocean waves.

"She is," said Daniel, "but I don't take her out as much as I would like."

"Why's that?"

"Freya was a bit of a landlubber and it's not the same being out on the water on your own."

"It sounds like me and the van. I don't get out in her as much as I should, though at least I've got the dog for company."

Daniel laughed. "You make me sound like a real loser!"

"Sorry, that's not what I meant," said Eleanor, worried she had offended him just as they were getting to know each other a little better. "Trust me to put my foot in it."

"You haven't put your foot in it at all," said Daniel, turning on the sofa to face her. "In fact, you've given me an idea."

"Oh yes? And what's that?" asked Eleanor, suddenly quite charmed by this man.

"Why don't we take your campervan to the beach and go sailing in my boat?"

"You mean, you and me? Together?"

"And Bella, of course."

Before the words had come out of her mouth she knew exactly what they would be. "I can't think of anything nicer."

"Great," said Daniel, smiling with pleasure and

clinking his glass against hers. "It's a date! And I hope it will be the first of many."

"Me too," said Eleanor.

And so it was.

THE END

(Or is it?)

A Summer of Surprises

Chapter 1: Lazy Sunday

Eleanor yawned and opened her eyes. Through the gap in the curtains she could see a strip of baby blue sky. She carefully eased her way out from under the bed cover and pottered over to the window, pulling back the curtains to let the early morning sun stream in. The seagulls were squabbling on the rooftops, and in the distance she could hear the lazy ebb and flow of waves on shingle. It was going to be another glorious day.

She climbed back into bed and watched the yellow fabric flap lazily in the breeze. Turning over, she smiled at the sight of Daniel's shoulder under the duvet beside her. Wrapping her arms around him, she folded her cool legs into the crook of his knees and nuzzled the base of his neck, breathing in his scent.

Waking, Daniel rolled over and hugged her to him. "Morning," he said, sleepily.

"Good morning to you, too."

"What time is it?"

"I'd say it was about eight o'clock."

"Far too early," he said, keeping his eyes firmly closed.

"But it's another lovely day and I don't want us to miss a second of it."

It had been one of those summers that come along

about once a decade and make even ordinary places look beautiful.

"Shame," said Daniel, gently running his hands up and down her back. "I was hoping for rain so we could have a lie-in." He kissed her cheek then her neck, making Eleanor squirm.

"That tickles!"

"Good," he said, gently grabbing her earlobe with his teeth.

She batted him away, laughing, and planted a kiss on his lips. "So, what are your plans for today?"

"Remind me what day it is?"

"Sunday all day, darling."

Daniel turned on his side, brushing his hair from his eyes and squinting into the sun. "Well, once you've had your wicked way with me, I thought I would rustle up a bit of breakfast while you make yourself even more delectable than you already are. Then we could take the hounds for a walk and maybe grab some lunch at the Bear. How does that sound?"

"That sounds okay to me," said Eleanor, rolling back into his embrace. "But don't fight me off for too long – I'm ravenous."

"And there I was thinking you only wanted me for my body."

"Your body is lovely, but you also make a mean breakfast."

"Let's just say that I know what you like."

"You certainly do, lover."

"Bacon sandwich ..."

"Yum."

"With crispy bits ..."

"Stop it, Dan."

"And brown sauce …"

Eleanor covered her ears, laughing. "No!"

"On crusty white bread …"

"That's enough," she said, wriggling out of his arms and pushing him away from her. "You are such a tease."

As it seemed that his lie-in was over, Daniel sat up and swung his long legs over the edge of the bed. "This wasn't exactly what I had in mind."

"It's your own fault. You've got me into a frenzy of anticipation and I can't wait any longer."

Daniel pulled a dressing gown over his naked body and gave Eleanor a crooked smile as he bent to kiss her. "I have that effect on women."

Eleanor lay back on the pillow hugging the duvet to her chest, feeling pampered and immensely lucky: there weren't many women fortunate enough to find the perfect man right on their doorstep as she had. "And Dan?"

He stopped at the door. "Yes darling?"

"Any chance of a cuppa to keep me going?"

He came back into the room and kissed her again. "For you, my love, anything."

"Thank you," she said, stroking his cheek. "I don't deserve you."

"What can I say?" He grasped her fingers and kissed her open palm, his slight stubble tickling the delicate skin. "You're one lucky woman. But then I don't deserve you either."

"That's true."

Daniel was grinning broadly as he padded down the stairs, doing his best not to knock over the piles of books along the side of the wall. Like most booksellers,

Eleanor loved her work and there were always stacks of chunky paperbacks in heaps all over the house. She claimed there was a system and that the higher up the staircase a book was, the more likely it was to be read next.

Opening the kitchen door, Daniel was greeted by Bella, Eleanor's Welsh spaniel, who rose from her bed to greet him. His own dog, Crumpet, had been fast asleep and snoring but she now yawned and stretched.

Daniel hummed tunelessly to himself as he filled the kettle and waited for it to boil. Bella nudged the back of his legs until he bent to scratch her behind the ears.

"Good morning, old girl."

She gave him a quick sniff and a lick of the ankles before heading over to the dresser where she stood staring fixedly at her empty bowl.

"Okay, I get the message."

After filling both dog bowls with biscuits, Daniel carried on making tea, grabbing a couple of red spotty mugs and putting them on a tray with the pot and a milk jug. Something was missing. Opening the back door, he stepped onto the patio, feeling the cool stone under his bare feet. Above him the sky already had the slight haze that often forms over the sea on hot days. He hopped gingerly across the gravel to the high wall where Eleanor had placed an array of terracotta pots and glazed planters that were barely visible under masses of foliage. Despite claiming not to be a gardener, she had managed to create a terrace packed with colour. Daniel picked a couple of roses, some sprigs of lavender and a small handful of bright yellow and orange flowers from the raised beds, then limped back into the kitchen.

After opening and closing a few cupboard doors, he eventually found an empty jam jar. Filling it with the flowers, he placed it on the tray next to the teapot and carried the lot upstairs to where Eleanor was dozing.

"Ta dah – tea and flowers."

Eleanor smiled. "Oh, you shouldn't have. These flowers must have cost you a fortune!"

"Less of the sarcasm, you. They are locally sourced, free-range roses and whatsits."

"Nasturtiums. My favourites." She picked up the jar, closed her eyes and breathed in deeply. "I love that peppery scent – it always reminds me of summer."

Daniel brushed her nose with his fingertip. "With greenfly at no extra cost."

"Ugh. I really must sort out the garden. Everything has gone to rack and ruin recently. There's just never enough time to do all the things that need doing around here."

"I hope you're not blaming me for that?"

"As if I would." She took his hand and pulled him down onto the bed so he was sitting beside her. "Although you are a very nice distraction."

Putting his mug on the bedside table, he turned to kiss her. "You say the sweetest things."

"And you do the sweetest things."

"Are we back on my bacon sandwiches again?"

"Of course." Eleanor laughed, snuggling herself into his arms.

"You know that flattery will get you everywhere."

"Actually I was thinking about last night. A film in town then an early night – what bliss."

He yawned. "I think it was the 'early night' that has done me in."

"Well, in that case, you had better lie down for a while longer ..." Eleanor threw back the duvet and Daniel let his robe drop to the floor and slipped in beside her. "Bacon sarnies can wait."

* * *

After breakfast, Eleanor looked up at the kitchen clock and frowned, thinking of the things she had to do. "You don't mind me abandoning you for a few hours this afternoon, do you?" As the owner of an independent bookshop in a small town she often had chores at weekends, as well as events to organise in the evenings. Putting in the extra hours was the only way to make the shop a success, but Eleanor sometimes worried that she wasn't giving Daniel enough of her time.

"I don't mind being abandoned at all." He knew that Eleanor always had reading to do before starting work on a Monday morning.

"If you're sure you don't mind. I just want to go through the book reviews in the papers and make a few notes." Eleanor smiled sheepishly. "And I might pop into the shop to make sure there are no problems."

Daniel laughed. "With Erika in charge? I think that's unlikely, don't you?"

"You're right, I know. She is more than capable of sorting out any problems. I'm a control freak with a serious book habit."

Erika was officially the assistant manager, but there weren't many things she couldn't take care of as well as her boss.

In the depth of winter, opening up the shop

wasn't much fun – especially when hardly anyone came through the door. But going into work for a few hours on a summer afternoon didn't seem like such a hardship, so Eleanor and her colleague took it in turns to do the Sunday shift. There would be plenty of walkers coming in to buy maps if the sun stayed out. If it was wet, people might wander in for a cup of coffee and a slice of cake in the new café area and hopefully pick up a book afterwards.

"Being totally devoted to the job is what makes you a good bookseller. Anyway, I have some important things to do myself later, like planning a particular treat."

They had been together for nearly two years and Daniel had decided to mark the occasion with a special outing.

"I wouldn't want to get in the way of exciting stuff like that. So what do you have in mind?" Eleanor was intrigued to know where they would be going, but Daniel was refusing to tell her.

"Let's just say I have one or two ideas." He smiled. "And you'll love it. Once I've decided what 'it' is, of course."

"I'm very happy to leave everything in your capable hands." Eleanor knew that Daniel had sussed out most of her likes and dislikes, but he could still surprise her. It was one of the unexpected joys of this partnership – the fact that Eleanor couldn't anticipate her man's every mood and move the way she could her ex-husband's.

Daniel swallowed the last mouthful of tea and patted his stomach. "That has set me up nicely for our walk. Shall we go?"

"Ready when you are."

They piled their walking boots and the dogs into Eleanor's campervan and headed off along the coastal road to an ancient woodland some miles from the town. Once there, they followed a shady path that ran alongside a stream, occasionally crossing from one side to another via rickety footbridges. In places they had to ford the water by hopping across smooth grey stones, which the dogs leaped over in easy bounds.

"I think we need to get a move on if we want a seat at the Bear."

Eleanor was slightly ahead of Daniel, throwing sticks for Bella whose long ears were sweeping the ground and collecting all kinds of foliage. "Are you hungry again already? We only seem to have been up here for ten minutes."

Daniel smiled and held out his watch for her to see. "Just over two hours, actually."

Eleanor sighed as she put her arms around Daniel's waist and he pulled her to his chest in a bear hug.

"We'd have had a longer walk if we'd left the house sooner," he said, gently brushing back her hair.

"And whose fault was that? I was the one trying to get us up and out early."

"Yes, but then it all went wrong when you jumped on me, so I would say that you are at least partly to blame."

"Fair point. But it was nice, wasn't it."

Daniel tilted her face up to his and kissed her. "Spending Sunday mornings together is always a treat."

Eleanor took his hand as they walked along. "Time with you flies by so quickly."

"Well, that's a good sign. When it starts to drag, you'll know it's time to trade me in for a younger model."

"No chance," she said, laughing. "I can barely keep up with you, never mind some twenty-year-old."

"You'll make me blush, woman."

"I was thinking of your general energy levels but, now you come to mention it, you are a lean, mean, loving machine!"

Daniel puffed out his chest, beating it with his fists and making Tarzan-style noises. "You bring out the he-man in me," he said, making her laugh.

They walked along in contented silence for a while, Daniel occasionally stopping to collect a stick for the dogs and send it spinning into the undergrowth where they competed to sniff it out and return with the prize.

The footpath twisted and turned, climbing up through the valley and away from the stream until it eventually came out of the woods and into bright sunshine. Dipping down, the path rejoined a track that ran into a village with a Norman church and a pub that did great lunches.

Daniel grabbed a spot in the garden that ran along the front of the Bear Inn and the dogs collapsed in a happy heap under the trestle table. They were used to the chickens that scratched about for crumbs and bits of pastry on the grass, and only shifted when the birds came a bit too close for comfort.

"I'm thinking cheese, some chutney and a wedge of crusty bread, all washed down with a pint of rough cider. How about it?"

"That sounds just perfect, Dan. Thank you." Eleanor leant back against the wall and tilted her face to the sun, feeling well and truly spoilt yet again.

Chapter 2: A Bolt from the Blue

They spent a happy hour at the pub watching the world go by, then walked back across the fields to the lime-green van that was Eleanor's pride and joy. Daniel took the wheel and drove them over the moor and down into Combemouth, the seaside town they called home. It was midsummer and the pavements were busy with pink-cheeked day-trippers in shorts and sandals devouring runny ice creams. It was an old-fashioned resort that appealed to young families, pensioners and walkers who enjoyed the combination of woodland, hill-top walks and broad sandy bays.

Daniel deposited Eleanor outside The Reading Room. "Don't work too hard. Even booksellers are allowed time off occasionally."

"Don't worry about me – I have plenty of time off. And you know I love it."

"Fancy meeting up later in the week for a drink after work?"

"That would be lovely," she said, bending to give him a kiss through the van's open window.

"I'll give you a call."

In the rear-view mirror, Daniel watched Eleanor smile and wave as he drove the short distance down the busy high street towards the sea front and his home. The house had once been a pair of terraced cottages belonging to two widows who had knocked down a dividing wall after they had each lost their fisherman husband and decided to live together. The arrangement had led to some fairly salacious gossip, which the pair had stoutly ignored before dying within hours of each other at a local nursing home.

Daniel had bought the house for a good price because it was a bit dilapidated and perilously close to the waves, but fortunately he was an architect who also knew a thing or two about old property. He had done his homework and satisfied himself that it was likely to see him out, despite what locals said about the next big storm probably sweeping it away.

Sometimes he wondered whether he and Eleanor might move in together one day. It was a possibility that he thought about but had never mentioned and she had never raised the issue. She was obviously enjoying her independence after years of marriage and Daniel wasn't a man to rush into anything: he wanted to be sure they had a future together before suggesting such a big leap. He was naturally cautious and – if he was honest – he recognised that he was still dealing with the fallout from his divorce from Freya.

His ex-wife was quite unsentimental about the area and had been more than happy to move to London after their split. Having grown up in Devon, Daniel was emotionally tied to the town and the lavish home they had created together on the cliffs in what was now a very expensive and desirable area. Freya, who was also an architect, had enjoyed the project – taking a Victorian villa and turning it into a state-of-the-art home with floor-to-ceiling glass walls that turned from clear to opaque at the touch of a button. She had loved being interviewed by lifestyle magazines about the sustainable nature of the building while Daniel hid in his office. But when the marriage ended, Freya was pleased to leave that chapter of her life behind and move on. Daniel had thought about buying her out and staying in the house, but had come to the conclusion that he couldn't bear to be there without her.

Turning the lock in his cottage's lumpy red door and entering the narrow hallway, he again wondered whether he had done the right thing to move down off the cliff to this small, dark place. It was undeniably cosy, but he sometimes missed the light and space of the big house. When he'd bought the cottage, he'd been in a dark place himself and had liked the way the rooms seemed to fold themselves around him. Best of all, there was nothing there to remind him of Freya.

His terrier dashed through the open doorway into the kitchen, making him smile. Crumpet had no doubts that this was now her home. Yes, he could have stayed put and pined for what he had lost or alternatively moved to a completely different town, but he loved being by the sea. Closing the door behind him, he glanced into the sitting room that Eleanor had helped to redecorate and filled with books and flowers. The place suited him fine.

To hell with Freya: it was the new woman in his life who would have all his attention today. He fed the dog, then made a cup of tea and carried it up three flights of stairs to his office in what used to be the attic space. From there he had a clear view right across the wide bay to the horizon. In the distance he sometimes saw huge tankers heading out to the other side of the world. Closer to home it was sailing dinghies that skittered across his window. Daniel loved to sail, so seeing all the activity could be a distraction, but generally he found that the constantly changing scene stimulated his imagination and helped him to work.

He had a clear mission this afternoon: to arrange something special to mark his and Eleanor's second year together. He just wasn't sure what that should be. Turning on the computer, he searched for "romantic breaks" then scrolled through pages of hotels showing identical couples with perfect teeth clinking champagne glasses in hot tubs. Grimacing, he decided to try a different tack.

He was beginning to enjoy his unexpected role as romantic hero: Freya hated anything verging on "soppiness" and Daniel had learned early on not to bother trying to woo her with hearts and flowers. Eleanor had never had that kind of attention from her ex-husband Alan, so it was a novel experience for both of them and something they had fun with.

What would Eleanor like to do? He'd thought about taking her to the theatre, but they'd done that the year before. This time he wanted to find something a bit different. When Eleanor wasn't in the shop she read voraciously and enjoyed everything from historical biographies and slashers to romcom. He tried to remember the books at the top of the pile, closest to her bedroom – they were mainly brand-new novels by authors who were unfamiliar to him, or slim volumes of poetry with textured covers in muted colours and elegant typefaces. She also loved Agatha Christie and JB Priestley and adored anything

Art Deco. Which reminded him of something he had seen at his father's house … He rubbed his chin thoughtfully then tapped in a few more search terms online.

After a while, he found just the thing. Scrolling down the web page he could see that this was the ideal venue: quirky and luxurious with a genuine literary connection and not too far away. "She will love it," he said, addressing Crumpet who had followed him upstairs and was curled up in a tidy ball at his feet.

Daniel looked at photos of the bedrooms, eventually choosing a suite that had a sitting room and its own private balcony opening onto the sea. Happy with his choice, he booked everything and printed out the confirmation, maps of the venue and directions. When the phone rang he was completely engrossed in the arrangements so the voice on the end of the phone caught him by surprise.

"Hi, it's me."

Freya's voice sent a bolt of electricity through him. It had a low timbre that would have made her a great radio presenter and had always been one of the things Daniel found most attractive about her.

It wasn't the first time that he had been thinking about Eleanor and Freya had called. The damn woman had a singular talent for catching him off-guard and he didn't respond at once.

"It's your ex-wife. Remember me?"

"Sure. Hello Freya. Sorry. I was in the middle of something."

She laughed, lightly. "Something good, I hope."

Daniel grimaced. He was careful not to share too much about his new single life. "Nothing bad."

"Well, that's nice to hear."

A few seconds of silence passed while Daniel gathered his thoughts. "So why are you ringing?"

"Do I need a reason to ring?"

"Yes, or at least you usually do. It's not as if we have that much to chat about any more." Since the divorce had finally gone through after many months of wrangling over money, their conversations had become far less frequent and were generally limited to arrangements over their daughter Emily who was at university in Scotland. "What was it you wanted, Freya?"

"Charming. Look, can you hold on for a sec. I can't hear a word here." It sounded as though Freya was in a café, the hubbub of voices busy in the background. "I'll move outside." Daniel could hear the clatter of high heels then traffic noises that never stopped in London, even on a Sunday afternoon. "Right, that's better."

He shut his eyes, picturing the city bustle around his ex-wife. They hadn't met for months and the thought of seeing Freya again filled Daniel with a kind of dull ache.

"I'm coming to Combemouth on Thursday for business and I thought you might like to take me out for lunch. If you're not busy with your librarian friend, that is."

Freya always knew how to wind him up and Daniel felt himself bridling. "Her name is Eleanor and she's a bookseller, as you know perfectly well."

"Oh that's right. I knew it was something to do with dusty paperbacks." As soon as e-readers were invented, Freya had embraced the new technology

125

and dumped all her paperbacks at the charity shop. She would have taken Daniel's books, too, if he hadn't stopped her. Now, when he noticed a treasured Penguin Classic missing from the shelves, he suspected that it had been thrown out during one of his wife's purges. "How about it?"

He quickly flicked through his diary. There wasn't anything in particular he needed to do that day and he knew Eleanor would be at the shop and not expecting to see him until the evening.

"Okay. Tell me when you're arriving and we'll go off somewhere."

"Out of town?" Freya laughed. "Is that because you don't want your girlfriend to see us together? Am I still such a threat?"

"Don't flatter yourself." It annoyed him immensely that she could always see right through him. He had never lied to Eleanor about seeing Freya, but it wasn't something he made a point of either. "Do you want me to pick you up or don't you?"

There was a moment's silence and Daniel knew Freya was marking up a point scored.

"That would be super. See you at the station at half past twelve?"

"Fine."

"I shall look forward to it."

He couldn't bring himself to respond in kind. Instead he grunted a farewell and replaced the phone. Sitting back down at his desk, he stared at the computer in a daze. The image of the hotel where he was taking Eleanor for the weekend was still up on the screen, but for a fraction of a second he couldn't remember what he'd been doing.

"Damn her," he said, running a hand through his hair as though brushing away thoughts of Freya. She had put him through the wringer over the divorce, both financially and emotionally, and it still hurt. Eleanor was the first woman he had been out with since then and he loved her, but sometimes he still found himself missing things he'd had with his wife. It wasn't that he was in love with her any more – far from it – but he couldn't completely tear her out of his heart and mind. He had a habit of rubbing a dark patch at the base of his thumb when he was agitated, and he found himself doing it now. The woman was still under his skin.

Chapter 3: A Daughter Calls

Eleanor stood on the pavement shielding her eyes from the sun, smiling as Daniel drove the campervan down the road towards the promenade. It was a delicious feeling to know she had the rest of the day and evening to herself but that she'd be seeing him again very soon.

She popped into the shop to make sure that everything was okay, then bought a stash of Sunday papers from the newsagent who gave Bella a gravy bone and told her she was a good girl. Back at the house, Eleanor collected all the magazines that had piled up over the previous couple of weeks, grabbed a notepad and pen and went out onto the patio. There she dumped everything on the table and sank into a creaky wicker chair that she thought of as her "thinking" chair.

Happily ensconced, she spent the next couple of hours poring over the review pages. It was something she enjoyed and had become quite adept at: making notes of what new books were available and trying to work out which ones would appeal to her loyal customers and which would catch the eye of casual visitors to The Reading Room. By going over the review pages, she could double-check that she hadn't missed any good books.

When she'd finished her task and had a nice neat

list ready for the morning, it was time to attack the garden. The weekend had been hot and the plants were looking parched and unloved so she pulled on her gloves and decided to see what she could salvage. Eleanor lacked the patience to be a great gardener, but she enjoyed weeding and creating order. As she moved around the terrace, deadheading roses and squishing greenfly between her fingers, she couldn't help smiling as she thought back over the last few months.

She had been divorced and – almost – celibate for several years before Daniel entered her life. Bullied into it by her mother Connie, she had flirted with internet dating for a while, but had hated the experience and come to the conclusion she would spend the rest of her days as a singleton. And that suited her fine: it was far better to be on her own than with an unsatisfactory partner just for the sake of it.

Daniel, on the other hand, had come out of a marriage he had thought would last a lifetime much more recently. But they had worked out a way to be together and were happy. And yet …

There was one tiny niggle in Eleanor's mind: they never discussed the future. She knew it was silly – she was fifty, for heaven's sake, and she had built a very nice life for herself in Devon after her divorce. She looked up from her work, brushing her auburn hair back from her face and leaving a streak of soil across her sweaty brow. So why wasn't she satisfied?

She loved her kids, the business, her cottage and she had great friends. Why should she want anything more than that? On the other hand, she was used to having people around her – she'd been married for two decades and when there was no one else in the house, she did feel a bit lonely.

What more did she want from Daniel? She tended to spend weekends with him and they saw each other most weeknights, but it wasn't like being with someone all the time. In other words, it wasn't quite the same as waking up next to them every day. Of being married. She laughed inwardly and pushed the thought from her mind.

"How ridiculous," she muttered, yanking handfuls of dead forget-me-nots out of the raised beds. It wasn't as if she would ever consider marrying again. And yet ...

"It would be nice to have the opportunity to say no, don't you think so, dog?" Bella padded over and lay in a patch of late-afternoon sun by Eleanor's side, panting dramatically. "I can tell you agree," she said, stroking the warm fur and wondering what lay ahead for her and Daniel.

She was at the sink scrubbing soil from under her nails when the phone rang in the pocket of her apron. Peering at the screen, she could see that it was a call from her daughter Phoebe who was spending two years with her father in Canada, working in a gym. It sometimes felt to Eleanor as though the mother–daughter relationship had been completely reversed, and this was one of those occasions. "Hello darling, how are things? How's work?"

After dutifully bringing Eleanor up to date with goings-on at the leisure centre, Phoebe directed her interest to her mother. "It's good. I think they really like me here, but never mind that. How are you?"

She knew and liked Daniel, and thought it was time that things moved on between him and Eleanor.

"Everything is absolutely fine."

"But has he asked you to move in with him yet?"

"Good grief, no. That's not going to happen." Not for the first time Eleanor was struck that Phoebe had inherited her father's directness as well as his athletic physique and fair hair.

"You say that, but I wouldn't be so sure. In my experience, men like to have their women safely tucked up at home where they can find them."

What Phoebe was basing this theory on at the great age of twenty-five was a mystery, but Eleanor had to laugh. It was typical of her daughter to be strong in her views despite an absence of evidence.

"Fortunately, Dan is independent and a bit solitary like me – we both need our space. We'd get on one another's nerves if we lived together."

Phoebe laughed. "You're not the least bit solitary. You always surround yourself with people. You're with Erika in the bookshop. Granny and Harold pop in nearly ever day – not to mention my waster brother – and you see Daniel most evenings. So anyway, if he asked you to sell up and elope with him, what would you say?"

"He's not going to ask me anything so silly, Phoebe. And don't be rude about Joe."

"Okay. Maybe not elope, but live with him?"

It was a question that Eleanor had been asking herself rather a lot lately, but she didn't yet have the answer. "He won't, so there's no point in even thinking about it."

"I'll take that as a 'yes', then."

"You can take it however you want because it isn't going to happen."

The line went quiet for a moment as Phoebe mulled over this disappointing response. "But you are still okay together, aren't you? I mean, nothing bad has happened between you guys?" Both the twins wanted Eleanor to have a settled home life, though it wasn't something that Phoebe's twin Joe was ever likely to raise with his mother.

"No, nothing bad has happened. Everything is fine. Anyway, how's Dad?"

"Dad and Leanne are still revoltingly happy."

"Well, that's nice because Dan and I are revoltingly happy too."

"I'm glad to hear it. Give him my love."

"Thanks, darling. I will."

Eleanor could hear noises in the background and could tell that Phoebe had been joined by friends.

"Sorry, I've got to go now, but I'll call you again soon."

"Make sure you do."

"I will, Mum, promise! Love you lots."

"And I love you too, sweetheart."

Finishing the all-too-brief call, Eleanor closed her eyes and held the phone to her lips for a moment, picturing Phoebe on the other side of the Atlantic. She missed her smart, beautiful daughter with her precocious wisdom.

Thinking about their conversation, Eleanor was aware of a teeny doubt, a doubt that had been pushed to the back of her mind, but which now came bouncing back: Daniel was sometimes distant from her. It was hard to pin down exactly what it was. He was

132

kind and loving, but now and again she felt as though there was an invisible barrier separating them.

If they were to have a future together, she needed to get under the barrier and find a place in his heart. She laughed at the phrase, thinking she sounded like a romantic heroine in one of those books with garish pink covers that she secretly devoured when no one was looking. Which reminded her that she needed to check the women's fiction shelves in the morning.

Chapter 4: The Reading Room

It was still a thrill for Eleanor to open up early on a Monday morning and walk around the shop before customers arrived, knowing that every book on every shelf was there because she had chosen it. She had grown in confidence over the years and knew she could sell some quite unusual stuff as well as the classics. She wandered up and down the shelves straightening things and making sure that the expensive art books were facing forwards so people would be sure to see them when they came in.

She was on her own because her assistant Erika had the day off to make up for doing Sunday duty. They worked together very happily, but both agreed that spending every day in the shop would be too much of a good thing.

Eleanor took a feather duster from under the counter and flicked at the wooden train set that ran along the wall in the children's book area. She had started stocking a few toys and gifts, which were proving to be popular with the punters – especially grandparents with birthday gift emergencies. There wasn't much tidying up to do because Erika had done most of it before closing up the day before.

The bookshop had been open for five years and Eleanor hoped that, having survived this long, she would be able to keep it going for many years to come.

She had worked hard to make it the hub of the community by hosting reading groups and storytelling sessions for the children, and putting on lots of events with local authors. The work wasn't always easy, but it was fun and she didn't regret abandoning her London life and nine-to-five office job to take on the shop.

At Easter, she had opened a café in the back room. It had been a tough decision to make because it meant cutting back on the children's area, but the "caff" was working well and brought in people who might not otherwise visit the shop. To begin with, Maureen – who ran Ye Olde Tea Shoppe across the road – was worried about the effect the café would have on her business, but they sorted things out one evening over a bottle of Merlot at the King's Head.

Looking through the shop window now, she could see Maureen in her floral pinny on the other side of the street arranging a display of freshly baked gingerbread people decorated with icing-sugar swimming costumes. Eleanor smiled and gave her a wave with the feather duster, which was acknowledged by a thumbs up. It had been a relief to settle what had threatened to turn into "Scone Wars": Eleanor would only offer tea, coffee and homemade cakes from the local baker and would send people across the road for hot meals. In return, Maureen would direct folk to The Reading Room for books and a cuppa. It was all about the high street shops working together to survive in a tough financial climate, but tourists were charmed by the sense of community.

Eleanor tidied the stacks of books on the oak table by the window. This was her selection of titles written by local authors, some of whom were quite ferocious and insisted on dropping by once a week to check on sales. Eleanor glanced at her watch and reckoned that she had twenty minutes or so for a quick read, so she settled down on the sofa with a pile of cookery books, hoping to check them out before any customers turned up. But it wasn't to be.

She had fixed a brass bell over the heavy wooden door to enhance the shop's period charm and it tinkled prettily when visitors came in. "Dingaling": at the sound of the bell, Eleanor frowned then composed her face into a smile. Any customer arriving so early in the day was clearly in need of a book and a card, so she jumped to her feet only to see her mother entering the shop.

Connie sometimes came in to help Eleanor with the café side of things on Mondays, a role she adored because she could spend time with her daughter and enjoy some gossip with the visitors. Eleanor had hesitated about employing her mother, but it had turned out to be a wise move because so many of Connie's friends would come in for a pot of tea and a mini Battenburg when they knew she was going to be serving.

"Hello love." Connie gave her daughter a hug and beamed at her. "You're looking perky this morning. Daniel is obviously treating you well." Connie no longer bothered to conceal how relieved she was that her middle-aged daughter was not "on the shelf" any more.

She disappeared into the office to leave her coat and put on a flowery apron, ready to do café duty. "I bumped into your young man and I gather there are plans afoot to celebrate a special day?"

136

Eleanor's upbeat mood meant that she was less annoyed by her mother's typically intrusive question than she might otherwise have been.

"If you mean that Daniel is organising something for our 'anniversary', you're right."

"So where are you off to this year?"

"No idea. It's going to be a surprise. Anyway, it's not for weeks yet, so I'm not sure he has even decided."

"He's such a nice boy," Connie said, dreamily. "It was obvious to me from the start that you were going to end up together. Just like that Jane Austen and Colin Firth."

Eleanor had heard her mother's theories many times and sighed. "I think you mean Elizabeth Bennet and Mr Darcy."

"Yes, that's the pair. I remember them on the telly, although your Daniel is much better-looking than that Colin Darcy with his big forehead and thin lips."

Sometimes, Eleanor wondered whether her mother was getting dementia, but had decided it was all an act and that she was actually no more dotty than the rest of the family. And much as Eleanor might have scoffed at the notion, secretly she rather liked being compared to two of her favourite literary characters and could see that there was a grain of truth in it.

She had initially jumped to conclusions about Daniel that turned out to be rather unfair. She had thought him rude and boorish, and they certainly hadn't hit it off right away. The first time they had met was when she had gone to buy a load of unwanted books from his father Malcolm Pearce who was downsizing to a bungalow and wanted to get rid of some stuff. The Reading Room was known for having a wide selection of second-hand titles as well as new, so Eleanor had offered to sell Malcolm's books in the shop or online to collectors.

Daniel had been very cool with her when Malcolm had asked him to lend a hand carrying the heavy boxes of books to Eleanor's van.

She hadn't understood why he was so unfriendly and wondered whether he thought she was taking advantage of his father. At least, that was how it had seemed then. She later discovered that Daniel had been dumped by Freya and was angry with the entire world, which made him prone to expect the worst of everyone.

Connie patted her daughter's hand. "Earth to Eleanor. You seem to have drifted off, love."

"Sorry Mum. I was just thinking about the second-hand shelves. What were you saying?"

"I was asking about your romantic break with Daniel. I did ask him myself when we met in the Co-op, but he said he wasn't at liberty to say anything at the moment." She chuckled to herself as she polished teaspoons on the bottom of her pinny. "He is ever so secretive."

Eleanor felt herself tense slightly. She didn't know what it was, but Connie sometimes had a way of hitting a nerve and making her hackles rise for no good reason. Theirs had been a fairly rocky relationship for a few years and they had only really become friends after Eleanor had had the twins. It was then that she had come to understand both her parents better.

"He's not 'secretive'. He's thorough and well organised and prefers to keep his plans to himself until everything has been properly sorted out."

"It's not a criticism. I think it's marvellous that Daniel plans surprises for you. Not that Alan didn't, of course," she added with a sigh.

Alan had always meant well, but Eleanor's ex-husband's surprises were sometimes a bit too much.

"True, but I could have thought of more romantic things to do on my fortieth birthday than go bungee jumping." Eleanor frowned as she remembered turning up at a charming country pub and being puzzled by the crane in the adjoining field. She shivered as she recalled the horror she had felt when Alan explained that hurtling headfirst into the car park in front of dozens of amused onlookers was her birthday gift. Alan had secretly arranged for her sister Jenna, husband Keith and their kids to be there, too, to witness her terror. However, Eleanor had to admit that once she'd been strapped in and pushed off the tower the experience had been amazing and had massively increased her "cool" factor with Joe, Phoebe and her nephews and nieces. "It took me a lot of champagne to recover from that particular surprise."

"It was rather thrilling to watch," added Connie, chuckling at the memory. "But, don't worry – I wouldn't put Daniel down as the bungee-jumping type."

Eleanor smiled. "I wouldn't have put him down as the skinny-dipping type either."

"The what, love?"

"Nothing. Anyway, as long as there's a nice meal and copious quantities of white wine involved,

I shall be happy wherever we go and whatever we do."

"Make sure you hang on to this one. He's quite a catch." Connie's biggest fear was that her daughter would end her days with only an elderly dog and some overfilled bookcases for company.

"There are people who would say that I'm quite a catch as well, you know: an independent business-woman with her own home and all her own teeth. I should be beating them off with a stick. As it is, I can't walk down the high street without admirers casting rose petals at my feet. Daniel needs to hang on to me."

"You are quite right, love, and you have some won-derful friends," said Connie, patting her hand. "But it's nice to have someone to warm your feet against on long winter nights. Or even cool summer nights, come to that," she added, coyly. She had been with her gentleman friend for nearly four years, but they still tended to behave like loved-up teenagers.

"And how is Harold?"

"He's just dandy, thank you."

Harold was a handsome eighty-something gent who Connie had met on a dating site for the over-sixties and together they were enjoying a brand-new life that had all their friends and family green with envy.

"Anyway, I can't stand here chatting all day. Those teacakes won't toast themselves." And with that, Connie turned her attention to the café.

Chapter 5: Thoughts of Alan

The rest of the day was busy with old and new customers popping in for books and cards and to enjoy cups of tea. Eleanor was grateful to have her mother's help and she had to admit that Connie was a whizz at persuading people to eat more cake than was strictly necessary and charming them into buying a book, greetings card or small gift on the way out.

At 5pm, Eleanor locked up the shop and walked down to the beach with Bella. Because it was summer, she had to go out beyond the end of the town beach to reach the "Dogs Allowed" area. It was no hardship being banned from the busy section by the promenade with its excitable children and youngsters playing loud music. She much preferred walking on the long stretch that curved under the cliffs.

Walking along with the sand crunching under her feet, Eleanor wondered what Daniel would come up with to mark their two full years together. She had discovered that he was one for surprises, but not in the way that Alan had been. Her ex-husband's outings would frequently involve jaunts to foreign cities, which could be enjoyable if you didn't mind taking in a football match along the way. Daniel's treats were actually focused on things that she liked to do.

Alan's idea of a good time was a morning session at the gym followed by an afternoon watching the rugby, preferably at Twickenham, not far from where they lived in southwest London. Eleanor had lost count of the number of Saturdays they had spent down there. She always enjoyed the crayfish and champers parties that followed a big game, but had found it difficult to get too excited about the matches themselves after the first few years. Because of Alan's job in the City, they often had company tickets which meant they were away from the action and the excitement of the crowds. Eventually, she had stopped going, choosing instead to visit a gallery or go for a walk with friends, leaving Alan to his own devices.

That's how their life had developed: separate interests meant they spent less and less time together. They shared the same house – and even the same bed – but gradually they grew apart without even noticing. There had been no fights and no big bust-up. It wasn't Alan's style: he had just begun to pay her less and less attention. Eleanor hated confrontation and Alan didn't see the point in arguing. A big, bluff man, Alan had never sulked or played emotional games in his life. Things were either good, not so good or terrible, and that was the extent of it.

Nonetheless, she honestly hadn't seen it coming. One day, he said he wanted to talk about something so they sat down over dinner for what Eleanor thought would be a discussion about changing the car or booking a holiday. What Alan came out with caught her completely off guard: their marriage was over and he wanted a divorce.

"The thing is," he had said to his stunned wife, "if we call it a day now we've both got a fair chance of finding someone else. Before we get too old, I mean."

That episode was typical of Alan, for whom it was a question of logic, not sentiment. It made being married to him remarkably easy in many ways. But when he decided they should call it a day, it was impossible to reason him out of it. Although insisting he still loved her and the twins very much, he had come to the conclusion they had outgrown each other, and that was that. She had been astonished and upset, arguing that he was talking nonsense and tearing them apart for no reason at all. She had spent months ricocheting between tears and feeling completely numb, but in the end she was reluctantly forced to admit that he might have a point.

The defining factor was when he'd asked her, "If we met now, would we find each other attractive?" She had laughed bitterly, hurt by the clear implication that he would not choose her. It was an impossible question to answer: okay, he was no George Clooney, but she loved him. On the other hand, she could see that by the time they hit their forties they would never have been paired up on a dating website because their interests, politics and attitudes to life were poles apart. Over the years, they had each developed in different directions and, although they got on well enough, the thrill had quite definitely gone from the marriage.

When Eleanor had told her sister that she and Alan were separating, Jenna had huffed and said Alan had all the sex appeal of a dead fish but he was probably having an affair anyway. He swore blind that there wasn't another woman and Eleanor believed him, but Jenna was exceedingly cynical. Despite – or perhaps because of – being happily married to Keith for her entire life, Jenna considered herself to be an expert on affairs of the heart. In fact, she thought she was an expert on most things, which probably went hand in hand with being an older sister and a maths teacher. Whatever the truth, a few months after their divorce Alan had found himself not only a job with a leading telecommunications company in Canada but also a brand-new girlfriend (now wife), Leanne.

One of the positive things about Alan's character was that there was no ill will, at least not on his side. He was an open, uncomplicated individual and had even invited Eleanor to his wedding. She had actually considered going for a moment, but really couldn't face it.

After some soul-searching, Joe and Phoebe had decided they would go. It had been tough for Eleanor, knowing that the twins were going to be at such a significant event without her, but she had done her best to hide her feelings. She didn't want either of her kids to miss out on an all-expenses-paid trip to North America because of her squeamishness. She had sold it to them as a fantastic opportunity to travel across the country and even visit the Rockies.

"If one positive thing has come out of this," Connie had said at the time, "the twins have now got very nice teeth."

It was true that Phoebe had come back from the trip with blindingly white teeth that winked at you from across the room. Leanne was a dental hygienist and had given the twins a serious going-over in a bid to win their affection and impress their father. Eleanor thought their pearly whites rather vulgar, but her daughter was thrilled with hers. Joe's made him look even more dashing and handsome. Sometimes she wondered how her and Alan's run-of-the-mill genes had managed to produce such attractive children: Phoebe was blonde and sporty like Alan, whereas Joe had her reddish-brown hair and hazel eyes.

The sharp call of a flock of gulls arguing over a discarded sandwich focused Eleanor's senses on where she was. She had reached the point on the beach where she liked to sit while Bella chased the birds and ran after the smooth grey pebbles that rolled backwards and forwards at the water's edge. She removed her shoes and sat on a rock, watching the water eddy around her feet.

It was funny, but she hadn't thought about Alan for ages. They'd been married for years and she had loved him dearly until he tore their marriage apart. She had been a different person then: an under-appreciated wife and overworked legal secretary in a city she found harder and harder to deal with. She had no regrets about leaving all that behind and opening her bookshop in a laid-back coastal town.

She sometimes felt guilty at the speed with which she had recovered from the break-up with Alan, despite the initial pain. They'd had a good life and he had been a caring father who always made time for the twins, but she had never felt an all-consuming passion for her husband. Over the years she had come to love him deeply, of course she had, but it was a gentle kind of love.

She knew it was ridiculous to try to compare them, but the feelings she'd had for Alan were not like those she had experienced with her first "proper" boyfriend – someone she had met in the south of

France after uni and who she had seen again briefly a couple of years ago. Crikey, she hadn't thought about Christophe Vauban for a while, either.

Sometimes it was hard to believe she was the same person who – aged twenty-one – had gone off to France with hardly any French and zero knowledge of the world. At the time, she had thought she was an expert in the language and in life, but it wasn't long before she discovered how much more there was to learn.

After a year or so working in a gift shop by day and spending nights entwined with Christophe, she had returned home to London and married Alan. When the twins were born she had put France out of her mind or, at least, out of her conscious mind. Married life and motherhood took up all her thoughts, but her time in the warm south was always there, like an intense dream that you couldn't quite recall but which left an impression of itself in your mind.

She wriggled her toes, which had grown brown over the summer, and lifted her face to the sun. She couldn't help smiling as she closed her eyes and let the memories wash over her. It would be hard to find a common denominator between the men in her life. The boisterous, sporty Alan had been nothing like the languorous Christophe and neither of them had anything in common with Daniel, who was sensitive and cool-headed.

She loved the fact that Daniel shared so many of her interests and enjoyed going to galleries and the theatre. Alan was intelligent, but he had never really understood her passion for the arts. Daniel was cerebral, without a doubt, and they could talk for hours about all kinds of things, as well as going for walks and mucking about on boats.

When they had first met, she'd thought he was going to be difficult and moody. Only much later did she realise that what she had taken for a lack of interest was actually a natural reserve. Daniel took his time weighing people up and had a thoughtful expression that could come across as forbidding if you didn't know him well. When you did get to know him, he was kind and funny and sexy and generous.

"And pretty gorgeous," she said to herself. So what if he was sometimes a bit distracted, as though his mind was on other things? It actually suited her quite well that he wasn't overbearing and possessive. That was the kind of thing she had liked in her twenties, but now she would feel swamped by someone who wanted to be glued to her side all the time. Their affair was just perfect.

Her feet were getting wrinkly in the water and tiny creatures were exploring the crevices between her toes. She dug them into the sand, enjoying the gritty sensation as the myriad tiny shells massaged her skin.

There was a woof as Bella, watching her with canine impatience, ran up with a piece of driftwood and dropped it by her side. Standing and paddling to the edge of the pool, Eleanor threw the damp stick so it spun through the air and landed in the waves with a splash.

"Time for dinner, let's go." At the sound of the magic word, the dog looped around and shot off in the direction of home. As they headed back along the beach, Eleanor's thoughts turned to the anniversary trip. Last year, Daniel had taken her to London and arranged for them to stay in a very smart hotel in Mayfair. As an ex-Londoner, Eleanor had found it slightly odd to be visiting the city as a tourist, but she'd rather enjoyed the novelty of the experience. Together they had done lots of those things that she would never have done when she lived there, like going to a musical, having tea at the Waldorf and watching the roller-bladers skate around Hyde Park. It had been fun, though she couldn't help noticing Daniel looking around every now and then as if expecting Freya to pop up from behind a bus.

Chapter 6: Hot Gossip

The next day, Eleanor had to call in at the bank first thing, so she left her colleague to open up. Erika greeted her with a smile as she entered the shop. "Morning boss. Connie's in 'Science Fiction'."

"She is? But she hates that kind of thing." Eleanor furrowed her brow. "She's not supposed to be working today, which means she must want something from me."

"You're very harsh on the old thing sometimes."

"Heavens – don't let Connie hear you use the 'O' word. She still thinks she's seventeen, you know."

"Good for her," said Erika, laughing. "I suspect that she's round there because it's nice and quiet and has the comfiest armchair."

"I'll find out soon enough, I'm sure." Eleanor dumped her bag in the office and ran a brush through her hair before going back into the shop to find out what her mother was up to.

"Good morning," said Eleanor, peering past Connie. "Are you on your own?"

"Don't sound so surprised. Harold and I don't go everywhere together."

"Yes you do, Gran," said Joe, who had wandered in and was now stretched out on the sofa by the shop window, playing with something on his mobile phone.

"Harold's gone to the library to change our books."

Eleanor winced. "I'd rather you didn't mention that place in here."

Connie chuckled. "Now, you don't mean that. You love libraries as much as we do."

"Past tense: I used to love libraries until I became a bookseller. Anyway, what have they got in there that I don't have here?"

"We finished our basic French course in June and we're moving on to intermediate in the autumn, so Harold thought we should prepare ourselves."

"Ahem ..." Eleanor turned and swept an arm in the direction of the shelf marked "Travel & Languages". "I think I might be able to help you."

"I know, love, but we can't keep on buying everything from you."

"Actually you could, but never mind."

"Are you planning another trip, Gran?" asked Joe.

"Oh, we might have a little run across to Wales."

"So you're not intending to trek through Europe again for a while?" asked her daughter.

"Oh, you never can tell where the fancy might take us. You know how adventurous Harold can be."

Eleanor furrowed her brow. "We certainly do." At Christmas she had agreed to let Connie borrow her vintage campervan for a trip to France, assuming that she and Harold would hop on the ferry and spend a few days in Brittany. In fact, the indomitable pair ended up driving all the way down to Provence, visiting Harold's daughter Rachel in the Rhône-Alpes on the way back and seeing in the New Year at the Eiffel Tower.

"As your dear father used to say, you only get one

turn on the great roundabout of life, so you might as well make it a good one."

An image of Connie and Jack giddily spinning around on an old-fashioned wooden roundabout always came into Eleanor's mind whenever she drove past the children's playground near the holiday camp on the coast road.

"You're so right, Connie," said Erika, "although I like to think that I've had two goes on the roundabout."

"I suppose you have, dear."

"Clockwise as an ugly bloke and anticlockwise as a gorgeous woman."

"That's not entirely true," said Eleanor. "I've seen the 'Before' photos and you were rather gorgeous then as well."

"On the outside maybe, but beneath the uniform I was a seething mass of bitterness and frustration that made me an ideal copper."

Erika's tone was light, but her friends knew she had experienced years of unhappiness living as a woman trapped in the body of a policeman. Thinking that it wasn't the time or the place to discuss Erika's complex life story, Eleanor swiftly changed the subject.

"So Mum, I don't mean to be rude, but what was it you wanted? Joe is here to help with cakes today."

"Can't a person pop in to see her daughter without needing a reason?"

Eleanor was looking at her suspiciously. "She can, but you were only in here yesterday, you aren't on cake duty and you've made it plain that you don't want to buy any of my books. Ergo the likelihood is you're here on a mission." The self-satisfied look that came over her mother's face whenever Connie had juicy gossip to impart was one that Eleanor knew well. "What's the news?"

"As it happens, there is something I wanted to tell you."

"Aha! I'm never wrong. So, come on. Spill the beans."

"I need to be comfy first. You can't expect me to talk standing up." Connie liked a little bit of prompting before she shared her information and Eleanor knew how to take a hint.

"Come and sit down on the sofa and Joe will put the kettle on. And bring your granny a bit of coffee and walnut cake."

"Make that carrot cake, will you love? Those walnuts play havoc with my dentures."

Eleanor sat drumming her fingers, watching as Connie slowly and deliberately ate the cake, chasing each scrap around her plate with a fork to make sure that not a single crumb or dab of buttercream topping escaped.

"Delicious," she said eventually, dabbing her fuchsia lips with a napkin and taking a sip of tea.

"You were saying, Mum?"

"Yes, what was it now?" Distracted by cake, Connie had started to think about the WI tea she was helping to run and had momentarily forgotten what she had come in for.

"You said you had some news."

"Ah, yes. That was it." Pausing for effect she made her announcement. "I have heard that a celebrity is moving into town."

"Is that all? I thought you were going to tell us that you and Harold were getting wed."

Connie came as close as a nicely brought-up lady in her seventies could get to snorting. "Now why would we want to do such a thing when 'living in sin' is so much more fun? Marriage is for youngsters like you and Daniel."

Erika had been listening to the conversation from the cash desk and now came to join them, trying her best not to laugh at her boss's pained expression.

"Spare us the gory details of your love life, please." Eleanor wanted to get her mother back onto the subject of celebs. They had held lots of bookshop events with well-known authors and actors, and Eleanor had a reasonable idea as to which of them lived in the area. "Celebs are good for business. Who is it? A writer? Or one of those film stars who have washed up on these shores? Johnny Depp? Nicholas Cage? Madonna?"

"Ah, now, I can't remember exactly." Connie looked up, as though searching for inspiration in the dark oak beams that ran across the ceiling, but actually rather enjoying dragging out the revelation.

Even the usually patient Erika was keen to hear the answer. "Is it anyone we should know? Have they been on the dancing or jungle shows?"

Connie shook her head. "The name wasn't familiar to me, I have to confess."

Eleanor rolled her eyes. "Okay, give us a clue: male or female?"

"Or trans?" added Erika, pointedly.

"It was a man. Definitely a man."

"Name?"

"Oh, I can't quite bring it to mind. It was an odd name, you see."

"How odd? Do you mean like Apple or Blanket?"

"No, that would be very silly indeed." She tapped her fingers against her temple. "It was something like Digit. Apparently he used to be terribly famous over here until he went off to live in America. They say that he's 'hot stuff'."

"Someone who is hot stuff is coming to live here?" Eleanor laughed. "That sounds most unlikely. Are you sure about this?"

Connie patted her neatly coiffed hair. "Absolutely. I got it from Deirdre at Zumba this morning. He's lead singer and guitarist in a rock band and quite a sex object, despite knocking on a bit."

Eleanor stopped herself from commenting on the age, given that Connie was seventy-four and her beau was in his eighties.

"But why on earth does Mr Digit want to live here?"

"He's been living in Los Angeles and is all burned out, so now he's looking for a quiet place to 'find himself' and get back to his English roots. Apparently he meditates and has been directed here by his guru."

"Are you sure you're not making this up?"

"I'm quite sure, Eleanor. Deirdre read it in a magazine at the hairdresser's yesterday."

"You shouldn't believe everything they print in those gossip magazines. I know this may come as a shock, but they have been known to invent things to sell copies."

Connie ignored her daughter and carried on. "Whatever his name, he's moving here which means there are going to be hoards of teenyboppers camped outside his house and paparazzi hiding in the trees."

"If he's a rock god, it's more likely to be leather-clad headbangers rather than teenyboppers." Eleanor frowned, calculating the effect on trade. "Not your average bookworms, though you never know. It might bring in new business." She was already thinking that she'd have to order in some more copies of Keith Richards' *Life* and source some decent guitar books.

At the mention of rock gods, Joe had taken the headphones out of one ear and was half-listening to the conversation. "Somebody Digit? You don't mean Bill 'Fingers' Widget of the band Tryll Spigot?"

"Yes, I think that was it. Well done, love."

"And he's moving here? Wow, that's awesome."

Eleanor smiled at her son. Despite being a fully fledged grown-up, Joe still spoke and acted like a young teen most of the time. He'd had a variety of jobs and was now doing occasional bar work and helping in a surf shop further along the coast. When he had time on his hands, he could sometimes be persuaded to help out at the bookshop, which he secretly rather enjoyed. He had a natural charm and was especially popular with the young children who visited the shop.

Eleanor had hoped that, by the age of twenty-five, Joe would have found a "proper" job like his twin Phoebe who worked at her father's local sports' centre where she was enjoying the challenge of transforming flabby middle-aged Canadians into sleek running machines.

Joe grinned. "So Fingers is coming here to meditate, Gran?"

"Well, they say he finds spiritual peace by the

sea. And I suppose it's cheaper in Devon than in California."

"It seems a bit odd to me," said Erika, whose professional background meant that she was always ready to smell a rat. "Combemouth isn't your typical rock god territory. It makes me wonder who or what he's hiding from."

Eleanor laughed. "You have a very suspicious mind."

"Thank you. That's how I ended up as Chief Superintendent."

"That's a very sensible point, dear. You wouldn't be much of a policeman if you weren't prepared to think the worst of everybody until you came to know them better."

"Thanks, Connie. I knew you would understand. Keep your ears to the ground and let us know if you hear any more about it."

"I certainly shall."

Chapter 7: Drinks at the Ship

The next evening Daniel collected Eleanor from the shop and they walked down the high street and along the bay to the Ship Inn. Despite its position at the edge of a quiet harbour, the Ship was still very much a locals' pub and one of their favourites. Daniel fetched the drinks and joined Eleanor at a table at the top of the terrace from where they could watch all the waterside activity.

Although it was nearly 7pm, the sun was still high in the sky and the air was warm and embracing. As usual, there were kids leaping into the water or paddling expertly up and down in bright yellow canoes while their parents kept half an eye on them, confident that their water-babies would come to no harm.

A young labrador plunged into the water after a toy, half-drenching the people closest to the sea who good-naturedly covered their pints and laughed.

Daniel turned to Eleanor. "Cheers darling."

"Cheers Dan. So how has your week been so far?"

"Pretty good, actually. My plans for the new school hall are coming on okay and I think I might be about to get a commission to develop a rather smart granny flat for some folk in Waterborough. And what about yours?"

"Not bad. The highlight was my mother coming in with some gossip about a rock star moving to town."

"Moving here? Really?"

"Yup. Connie heard about it from Deirdre, who had read it in some scandal sheet at Beryl's Hair, and you won't get more solid information than that."

Daniel laughed. "So where exactly is this celeb going to live? I can't see him in a sea-front bungalow."

"That's a very good question. I don't know." Eleanor wrinkled her nose. "Any ideas?"

"Well, there are a few nice villas on Cliff Road, but they aren't very grand."

"Apart from your old house."

A shadow crossed Daniel's face as he thought about the home he had created and lost. "Yes, but the new owners are doing very well with their luxury B&B, so I can't see them selling up. Anyway, it's not big enough for a rock star and his entourage."

"Maybe he'll build something from scratch."

"He might have to." Daniel looked thoughtful. "I can't think of anything along this bit of the coast fancy enough for a celeb."

"Perhaps you should get in touch – he could be in need of a skilled architect."

Daniel shrugged. "I'm sure he'll want someone higher profile than me."

Eleanor squeezed his arm then tenderly stroked the brown skin with her fingertips. "You're super talented, darling."

"Perhaps! But I'm not in the rock star league." Daniel took a sip from his pint. "He's bound to bring in someone from outside – London or the States, I would imagine. But never mind that, what are your plans for this evening?"

"I'm entirely in your hands."

"That's what I like to hear."

"Did you have something in mind?"

"Well, I thought that after a drink here I'd lure you back to my place for supper, get you tiddly, then try out a few new seduction methods."

"Sounds blissful. Lure away."

Daniel turned and kissed her. "You're such a pushover."

"True. A glass of wine and a packet of pork scratchings and I'm anybody's."

"You know how to make me feel special."

"I'm teasing." Eleanor hugged him tightly. "You are very special. And actually it takes two glasses before I let someone walk me home."

"I remember that from our first date," he said, kissing the end of her nose.

"I'm not sure whether that particular evening really counts as a date. I accidentally barged into your house and you had to see me off the premises."

"That's not quite the way I remember it," he said with a smile. "But this is important. Are you saying that last year we marked the wrong anniversary?"

"Not necessarily – but I don't see why we can't celebrate a different date each year."

Daniel rubbed his chin thoughtfully. "I think that's a highly original and quite splendid idea. Why should we celebrate the same date when we've had so many wonderful ones? I'll get us another drink while you have a think about it."

Eleanor frowned when she thought back to their initial encounters: none of them had been great. Their first meeting had been at Malcolm's house, but Daniel had been so distracted by the business with

Freya that he had hardly even registered Eleanor. She had found him rude and offhand, so it was not an encouraging start. So when it came to celebrating their anniversary, they had marked the time a few weeks later when Eleanor had dropped off a cheque at Daniel's and ended up staying for dinner and the two glasses of wine ...

Eleanor smiled as she watched Daniel duck to get his tall frame through the low door and emerge from the dark interior of the old pub carrying their drinks.

"I've had an idea," he said, placing the glasses on the table. "Why don't we celebrate the first time we went boating?"

"Gosh! Well, that was certainly memorable – for all the best reasons."

"In that case, boating day it will be."

"But, hang on – I thought you'd already booked something."

Daniel shrugged. "I have, but it's easily changed." He caught a strand of hair that the evening breeze had pulled loose and swept across Eleanor's face, carefully tucking it behind her ear. "I want it to be perfect for you, El."

The intensity of his expression surprised her and for a moment she couldn't think what to say. Instead, she kissed him and smiled as they sat looking out at the boats bobbing about in the harbour below them. "If it's anything like our original boating day, how could it be anything other than perfect?"

Chapter 8: Boating Day

Until that trip on Daniel's wooden sailing boat, *Zephyr*, they had been for walks and meals and shared a kiss or two, but nothing more.

They had prepared for the outing by visiting the farmers' market and stocking up with lots of picnic goodies: crusty bread, smelly cheeses, tomatoes fresh from the vine, some garlicky dips and a large scoop of olives. Driving off in Eleanor's campervan, they had enough food for an army.

Arriving at the dock, they transferred everything to the boat which Daniel steered out of its narrow mooring place and into the open water. Eleanor had been a bit worried about how Bella would take to sailing but, being a spaniel, she loved the water and had to be prevented from jumping into the sea at every opportunity.

After sailing up and down for an hour or so, they moored in a quiet bay with a tiny beach that was only accessible by a steep coastal path or from the sea. As a result, it was almost deserted. Squinting across from where Daniel had weighed anchor, Eleanor thought she could make out a handful of pinky-brown shapes on the sand. She screwed up her eyes, trying to focus on what they were. "There can't be sheep on the beach, can there?"

Daniel laughed. "If those are sheep, they've been shorn a little too close for comfort."

As Eleanor tried to make out what they were, a couple of the forms stood up and revealed themselves to be people – naked people in various shapes and sizes.

"It's a nudist beach!"

"Yup," said Daniel, extracting towels from the galley and setting them on the deck. "You don't mind do you?"

Eleanor was no prude, but she had never before been taken to a nudist beach on what was essentially a first date. It was certainly not what she had expected from Daniel Pearce. He really was a dark horse.

"No, of course I don't mind. I'm just a little surprised, that's all."

"So, do you fancy a swim before lunch?" He was already pulling the T-shirt over his head and kicking off his shoes. "There's nothing like it for sharpening your appetite." He smiled encouragingly. "Can I tempt you?"

She mentally scanned her body and decided that it was not in any condition to be presented to the general public.

"Sure. As long as I can keep my cossie on."

"Whatever makes you happy," he said, with a smile. "You don't mind if I take my things off, do you?"

When was the last time a man had asked her that? She shook her head in what she hoped was a casual manner. "Of course not. Go ahead."

"Okay. But you had better avert your eyes!"

She suspected that Daniel was teasing, but she did look away until his clothes were all in a heap on the bench next to her. She looked up in time to see his lithe form disappear under the water. He really was a surprising man and she liked him more and more.

Surfacing with a splash, Daniel brushed his dark hair back from his face and laughed.

"Come on in, the water's lovely. A bit chilly, but lovely."

She gingerly stepped out of the loose cotton dress she was wearing and stood there in her sensible blue and white dotty one-piece. Daniel was a strong swimmer and was already several metres away. Bella was sitting in the boat, looking up at her mistress and eager for a swim.

"What do you think, dog? Shall we go for it?" Bella tipped her head to one side and wagged her tail. "Perhaps you're right." What harm could it do for Daniel to see her naked and bedraggled? Would he admire her adventurous spirit or be put off by her saggy bits? There was only one way to find out.

"Let's do it!" Gritting her teeth, Eleanor rolled her swimming costume down to her ankles and climbed onto the edge of the boat. "In for a penny, in for a pound." And with that she screwed up her eyes, pinched her nose and jumped, squealing as the cold water broke around her. "I must be mad," she muttered to herself, as she began to move her arms and legs in a jerky breaststroke and swim towards Daniel.

As she reached him, he turned and gave her the widest of grins. He was genuinely surprised and impressed that she had – literally – taken the plunge.

"Hey, good for you!"

"It's freezing out here!"

"Not if you swim fast. Come on. Twice to that rock and back, then we can eat."

As she gasped her way through the cool, clear water Eleanor found that sensation was gradually coming back to her limbs, and her chest didn't feel as constricted as it had done when the cold first hit. So they swam to the rock, had a race, then went twice around the boat, where Bella joined them.

By now, Eleanor had adjusted to the temperature of the water, which felt delicious as it caressed her every pore.

"I can't believe I've reached this grand old age and have never been skinny dipping before!"

"Never? Really?"

Eleanor frowned and tried to remember if she had ever swum naked in the past. "Well, maybe in my twenties." Had she once swum naked in France with Christophe or was that a dream? It was the kind of thing she would expect to remember, but so much of what they had done together had been exciting that it was quite possible she'd forgotten. It was the time in her life that was the most vivid and also the most unreal.

"Well, we must do it more often. If you'd like to."

Eleanor felt a thrill at the word "we". "I would. I'm definitely a convert."

"Excellent." Daniel lay back and floated, his eyes half-shut against the sun. Eleanor had a peek at his body and decided it was very nice indeed. He was a runner, and had the trim form and taut muscles of a much younger man. Lying there she made a mental note to herself to look into the cost of gym membership.

Closing her eyes, too, she tipped her face up, spread her arms wide and let herself drift, enjoying the sensation of the breeze on her bare skin. The beach here was shingle, so the water was crystal clear. After a while, Daniel caught her hand and they drifted together, enjoying the sensation as the water went from warm in shallow areas to quite chilly where there was a dip in the seabed.

"This is delightful, but I have no feeling in my legs and I think my toes have turned blue."

"Ah, that's the sign it's lunchtime."

"Great. I'm starving."

Daniel was very gentlemanly and swam away while Eleanor hauled herself back on board and slipped on her sundress. She made sure that she had a towel over her head and was vigorously drying her hair when Daniel emerged naked and glistening from the water.

Bella was pulled on deck and wrapped in a towel before she could soak them again with a shake of her long fur.

"Okay," said Daniel. "You have a choice of lunch venues: we can go onto the beach or eat here."

Eleanor weighed up the attractions of eating on sand surrounded by naked strangers or dining in comfort on the boat with one desirable man. There was no contest. "Here, please."

"Splendid choice!" Daniel fitted the table on its slot between the benches and began fetching plates and glasses from the galley area.

Leaning against the side of the boat with the sun on her back, Eleanor felt like purring, she was so happy.

"This is definitely a very pleasant way to spend an afternoon," she said, reaching out as Daniel handed her the contents of their picnic basket and a bottle of chilled white wine.

"To my mind, there's nothing better than messing about on boats." Daniel stopped and smiled at her. "Well, I guess there are a few other things, but this is pretty near the top of my list."

He's thinking of sex. Eleanor was aware of every inch of her body as the soft breeze licked across her salty skin. Or is that just me? She felt tingly and alive, ridiculously proud of herself for daring to swim naked with a man she barely knew.

"I'll drink to that," she said, raising her glass to his. "Cheers. Now, let's eat."

They were both ravenous after their exercise and everything tasted especially delicious in the fresh air. So they ate and chatted as the sun dipped lower in the summer sky. When the picnic was finished, they stretched out on either side of the table to doze in the sun. The combination of a brisk swim and two glasses of wine made them sleepy, and the gentle rocking motion of the boat was soporific.

After a while, Eleanor stretched and yawned. "One last swim before home?"

"Good idea," said Daniel, rubbing his eyes. "Otherwise I might fall asleep right here."

"Last one in's a sissy."

Eleanor was already on her feet and had wriggled out of her dress. Daniel laughed as he tugged off his clothes then plunged hand in hand with Eleanor into the waves.

* * *

Thinking back, it had been quite an amazing day. Eleanor was not the kind of person to rip off her clothes and frolic naked. And yet it had seemed quite normal to be swimming around starkers with a man

166

she had only known for a matter of weeks. It had been liberating and rather wonderful. She had gone into the water as a rather staid middle-aged woman and come out feeling invigorated and daring.

As evening fell and cool air began to sweep in off the sea, they packed up their things and headed back to Combemouth in the campervan. Daniel sat gazing out of the window as Eleanor manoeuvred the creaky vehicle along the steep-sided lanes, the foliage sometimes interlocking like fingers over their heads so it felt like driving underwater.

They picked up two enormous portions of fish and chips to eat back at Daniel's house, sitting in the kitchen looking out to sea. Eleanor had intended to drop him off then go home alone, but when he invited her to stay the night it seemed like the most natural thing in the world. It's hard to be shy when you've spent most of the day together naked, and they tumbled into bed together with delicious ease.

Chapter 9: A Blast from the Past

After drinks at the Ship, they had gone back to Daniel's cottage and barbecued some chicken in the garden before falling into bed. They awoke blissfully entangled under the duvet. Now it was Thursday, the day that Daniel had arranged to have lunch with his ex-wife, but somehow he hadn't yet got around to telling Eleanor.

She had her own cupboard in Daniel's bedroom, and riffled through it for some clean clothes. It was going to be another warm day, so she chose a pair of cut-off trousers and a loose cotton top. Combing her hair, she saw Daniel studying her in the mirror, a slight frown on his handsome face.

"What's wrong? Do I look all right?"

"You look lovely, El," he said, walking over and kissing her gently on the tip of her shoulder.

"Well that's okay then. For a minute I thought you'd gone off me," she said, smiling. "What are you up to today?"

Daniel had fully intended to mention lunch with Freya the night before, but the subject just hadn't come up. Was it too late and did it really matter, anyway?

"Oh nothing much." There was no reason not to be honest but, for some reason, he felt reluctant to share his plans. "I've got some drawings to finish, then I have a meeting." He stopped, waiting for Eleanor to ask him who the meeting was with. If she asked him, he would tell her it was Freya, the way he had always told her in the past. But she was busy gathering up her belongings and didn't ask – so he bottled it. "And you?"

"My plans? Sell some books, rearrange the window, stop Joe from eating all the cakes and Erika from slapping the school kids. The usual."

"Is Erika okay? She seems rather bad-tempered at the moment." He felt a bit sneaky for avoiding the subject of his meeting, but it didn't seem like the moment to bring Freya into the conversation. He'd tell Eleanor all about lunch later.

"I don't think she has recovered from the break-up with Jim yet. It really dented her confidence, you know?"

Daniel nodded, but actually it was hard to sympathise with someone's predicament when you didn't fully understand it. Why, he wondered, would a man want to be a woman in the first place? And why would an ordinary bloke like Jim Rowe want to go out with a trans woman? Jim was a reporter on the local newspaper and a friend of Eleanor. He was one of those people who were always around and who knew everyone because of his job. He had come to know Erika after covering events at the bookshop and been fascinated by her despite – or maybe because of – her background. Daniel didn't know which. Eleanor and Erika were close friends as well as boss and employee, so he had never felt able to ask his girlfriend too many questions in case she thought he was prejudiced rather than just perplexed. He smiled encouragingly. "I'm sure she'll get over it eventually."

"I don't know. She's tough, but the break-up hit her hard, poor thing." Eleanor looked at her watch. "I've got time to make us a cuppa then I must fly."

Daniel kissed her. "I'll put the kettle on. You take your time."

"Thanks, love. And shove a bit of bread in the toaster, will you?"

"If you're lucky there may be some Nutella left."

"That sounds like the ideal emergency breakfast."

* * *

After Eleanor had left, Daniel spent the rest of the morning moving bits of paper around and trying to concentrate on a couple of new proposals that he needed to finalise, but his mind was on Freya. Since the divorce had gone through, he hadn't had much cause to see his ex. As a result, they hadn't yet negotiated a new way to behave – or at least, he hadn't. Daniel was pretty sure he only ever entered Freya's mind when she needed something from him.

Unable to sit around any longer, he jumped in the car and arrived at the station early. Looking at his watch he saw there were still twenty minutes to go before the London train arrived. He sometimes wondered how many hours of his life he'd spent waiting around for trains, planes and people to turn up. He smiled when he thought about Eleanor. Her view was that life was too short to waste it hanging around waiting for things to happen. He was gradually getting used to her screeching up at the last possible minute to see a film or catch a train. It used to give him palpitations, but he had learned that she did always turn up eventually, even if it was with only seconds to spare.

Being punctual was a trait he shared with his ex-wife. In better days, they used to laugh and say that was why they were together. They were both twenty minutes early for their first lesson at Sheffield where they had signed up to study architecture.

Daniel was modelling himself on Robert Smith of the Cure at the time and was dressed in skinny black jeans with his hair in soft spikes. He had recently come up from Devon and was feeling overwhelmed by the experience of life in a northern city.

He was sitting in the stairwell trying to look mean and moody when Freya turned up. He heard the metal tap, tap of her boots on the shiny grey floor before he saw her. She was remarkable even then for not following any particular fashion trend. He remembered her walking towards him in Doc Martens, wearing animal-print leggings in burnt orange under a black and silver tunic. Her hair was cropped short and dyed the same orange as her legs.

Freya swore afterwards she had never possessed such hideous garments and that Daniel must have been confusing her with someone else. But there had been no one else. The vulnerability of those skinny legs striding along the empty corridor in the outsize boots completely bowled him over and the sound and vision of their first encounter was burned into his memory forever.

By the time someone turned up to unlock the classroom, they'd had a dense conversation about Frank Gehry and Mies van der Rohe and it seemed only natural that they should sit at adjacent desks. Daniel was aware of his heart beating in his chest and he found it difficult to concentrate on the "concepts and practice of drawing" because all the time he was wondering what would happen after the lesson. Would they go for a coffee? Or back to his room for a smoke? In fact, neither happened.

He hadn't anticipated that Freya would clank off with some other friends with barely a glance in his direction. Daniel had retreated to the library, theoretically to do some reading for their end-of-term assignment, but in fact to sit and stab himself in the hand with a biro for being so useless and not asking her out.

Sitting in the car, he realised that he was staring at the dark blue mark at the spot where his thumb met his index finger. The ink had seeped under his skin and remained there as a constant reminder of that day.

He drummed the steering wheel and looked up at the station clock. Five minutes had gone by while he was in his reverie. He turned on the radio, fiddling with the buttons until he found a classical station without adverts. They were playing the heart-rending melody by Albinoni – Freya's favourite piece, damn it – that they had listened to endlessly when they were first in love.

She had introduced him to it when – eventually – he had worked his way from classmate to boyfriend, which had taken most of the first two terms. He had looked out for her over the next few weeks, hoping to continue their conversation, but his heart sank as he saw her get swept away by other groups. When they met in class, she barely acknowledged him. She wasn't rude; it was worse than that. It was as though she'd forgotten they'd ever met.

He started to think he'd imagined the whole

conversation. Or had she mistaken him for someone else that October morning? Had she thought he was one of the tough Cornish lads who hung around together at Sheffield and got into fights with the local kids?

"Pathetic." The memory of those long desperate weeks still rankled with him. The chamber orchestra had finished playing and the clock showed that the train was due in eight minutes. Daniel decided to get out of the car and wait in the station.

Looking back at himself aged eighteen, Daniel couldn't believe how innocent he'd been. When he compared himself to Eleanor's children or his own daughter Emily, they were so much more sophisticated when it came to boy-meets-girl stuff. He had simply hung around the student bar getting drunk with his mates, rehearsing what he would say if the happy day came when he found himself alone with Freya. And that day did come – or evening, actually.

They bumped into each other in the kitchen at somebody's party and ended up walking back down the hill to her shared house. He thought they would have sex, but in the end they just talked all night then slept until 2pm and went to the pub. Afterwards, she invited him to stay again and that was that. What she saw in him, he wasn't sure. But the desire in her eyes was real and it blew him away.

In turn, Daniel loved Freya with all his being and was dazzled by her confidence and raw ability. No one had ever looked at him the way she did – as though she wanted to eat him up. It made him strut around with a confidence he had never known before.

She also helped him with his work. By their second year at uni he was on his way to being a good draughtsman with a strong practical sense, but Freya had brilliance. She started to win prizes and it wasn't long before she became the star of the department.

She was also gorgeous and clever and had no shortage of admirers. Daniel was flattered and amazed that she chose him over some of the other young men who hovered around her.

His shyness had come across as playing hard to get, which Freya found intriguing. And she had grown to love him, too. In the summer holidays they hitchhiked all the way across France to see Le Corbusier's Cité Radieuse housing development in Marseille. After they were married, they travelled further afield, visiting architectural classics like the Crystal Cathedral in California and the Guggenheim Museum in Bilbao. Freya would take hundreds of photos while Daniel made precise sketches in black ink on thick pads of creamy white paper.

Cheesy as it sounded even to his ears, she was the love of his life, his best friend and his business partner. They had a great time together until Freya – to Daniel's huge shock – became bored with her "small" life. That's what she had called it in their last, vicious argument when Daniel knew it really was over between them: her small boring life. And, by implication, boring husband and daughter. "Damn her," he muttered to himself, getting agitated again as he paced up and down.

Before too long, the train drew into the station. The locals said it had escaped Beeching's cuts because it was so insignificant that no one had even noticed it was there: a tiny blip on what was the main south-west coastal line. Today the platform had a 1950s charm that the tourist office kept up by filling the tubs and hanging baskets with petunias and gaudy begonias. There were only two lines – one up and one down – so it was easy to spot Freya as she stepped down from the first class carriage onto the platform and walked towards him.

She was wearing oversize sunglasses, barely there sandals and one of her favourite baggy dresses – what Daniel used to refer to as her "sacks". He knew that on most women – including on Eleanor, he thought unloyally – they would look terrible. On Freya's slender figure the dress looked understated and expensive.

"Well hello." She tipped her dark glasses onto her head and brushed her cheek against his. Her skin smelt floral and his senses lurched as he recognised the cologne she had bought him for Christmas a decade ago then stolen for herself and worn ever since. How could he find her so exasperating and yet still so damned appealing? The things she had said and done had cut him to the core, but when he saw her again his heart beat faster. It was partly aggravation and partly the habit of old love.

Taking her bag, Daniel walked ahead to the car. "I thought we'd go up to the Lighthouse. It'll be quiet there."

The Lighthouse was a new restaurant that was getting decent reviews for its cooking. Freya smiled. "Fine by me."

He threw her bag onto the back seat then jumped into the driver's seat without looking over, despite feeling her eyes on him.

"You're looking well," she said. "You've put some weight back on."

He turned and looked at her, not sure whether she meant that as a compliment or not. After they'd split, he'd lost a couple of stone and grown gaunt with the sheer misery of it all. In the last year, and thanks to Eleanor, he'd filled out again and the dark shadows around his eyes had faded away and were now concealed under his summer tan.

"Thanks."

Heading out of town, they passed the roundabout that used to make them laugh, but which now caused Freya to grimace. Grandly named the "Gateway to the Sun", it was sponsored by the local undertakers, who tried to downplay the lugubrious side of their business by festooning the traffic island every summer with outsize windmills in bright primary colours.

"God, I'd forgotten how grim this place is."

Daniel tensed. "I happen to like it."

"Unattractive and sad."

"The roundabout has been that way for years, Freya, and you've been around it a thousand times. Don't pretend you haven't."

"Maybe." She shrugged. "Everything looks different when you've been away for a while. I guess I'm used to a more sophisticated environment now."

With the money from the divorce, Freya had purchased a dockside flat in one of those parts of London where the only boats that docked were million-pound pleasure yachts.

Daniel laughed. "You live in Tower Hamlets. It's hardly Knightsbridge."

"Limehouse Reach, actually."

"And how's the waiter? Still around, or have you upgraded?"

"Ted is running his own cocktail bar now, actually."

"With your money, no doubt."

Freya looked at him sourly. "Don't be pathetic."

"I just wondered how someone who is barely out of his teens has had time to save up enough to buy his own bar."

"He's managing it for a friend. Not that it's any of your damned business."

Daniel shrugged and smiled, pleased to have scored the first hit. "Well, isn't that nice?"

They travelled on in stony silence for a while. Daniel took the road inland that climbed in tight zigzags through patches of woodland, crossing and recrossing the valley until they eventually came out on top of the moor. Once they had driven over the second cattle grid, the road gave them an unhindered view of the wide bay and the open sea beyond. It was a sight that Daniel had seen thousands of times in his lifetime, but it never failed to lift his mood. It was also a stunning location for a restaurant and he heard Freya almost purr as she caught sight of the chalky white building against the deep blue of the sea.

"Good choice," she said, turning to him.

He nodded, unwilling to show how much her approval still mattered to him.

Chapter 10: Table for Two

An elegantly dressed woman greeted them at the front desk and ushered them to their table by the window. Daniel looked at Freya as she sat opposite him in her charcoal linen dress, her eyes scanning the room while her fingers played with a packet of grissini.

They ordered their meal from the short but expensive menu – scallop tempura starters followed by grilled plaice for her and veal for him – and sipped fizzy water. Freya was still sulking slightly after Daniel's dig about her boyfriend, Ted.

"So what's the news from London? Are you happy there? Has it worked out the way you wanted? Was it worth giving up all of this for?" He nodded towards the view. It was one of those days when the sun caught the sea at such an angle that it looked almost turquoise with deep green patches rather than the usual muddy grey. They both knew what Daniel really wanted to ask: was her new life worth abandoning her husband for?

She swivelled her head sharply towards him. "Not that again." There was a note of exasperation in her voice and Daniel suddenly felt angry with himself for asking the question. "How many times do I have to explain it before you understand?" Freya's cool grey eyes fixed on his as she adopted the tone she used for difficult clients. "If you're a male architect who happens to be married with kids, clients think of you as an architect. If you're a married woman with children, you're a mother first and foremost. People don't take you seriously or value what you do to the same extent."

Daniel put down his glass of wine and tried not to sound too aggravated. "For an intelligent woman you do talk crap sometimes. Being divorced and operating on your own won't make one iota of difference to your career."

"Is that so? And what the hell would you know about it? As it happens, I'm starting to get much better commissions now than I ever did when I was with you."

"Sorry." Daniel tried to control his emotions, which were in a turmoil. "I'm sorry, okay? You'll be a huge success, you know you will. You'll be the next Zaha Hadid, designing opera houses and government buildings. Not creating dull apartments with your ex-husband."

Freya patted her lips, leaving a crimson smudge on the heavy linen. "Perhaps, perhaps not," she said with a shrug. "But I have to try. Can't you understand that?"

Daniel nodded, exasperated. "Of course I do. What I don't understand is why you felt you needed a divorce in order to do it."

"I'm bored with this topic of conversation." Rolling her eyes to the ceiling, Freya brushed away a strand of dark hair from her cheek. "Can we change the subject now, please?"

"Okay, here's a subject for you." Daniel leant across the table, his voice an urgent angry whisper. "I can't stop caring about you, just like that." He snapped his fingers, causing a waiter to turn and start towards them until Daniel waved him away. "My feelings can't be turned on and off like a tap, Freya. We were together – in love – for a long time."

She pulled away from him and made a show of folding the napkin. "I know that." She squirmed, embarrassed by the emotion welling up between them. "And I do still love you. In a way. But I need to do something different now, while I can."

He dropped his head, defeated again. Of course she was right. Anyone who knew them put their separation down to a gap in ambition: Daniel was happy with his life and his work in a small country town, whereas Freya felt there was so much more to see and so many things to achieve.

A low cloud had covered the sun, flattening the light. Looking out, Daniel found that he could no longer see where the sea ended and the sky began. The view, the pale oak floors and sage walls, Freya in her "sack" – everything was grey or pinky-pearl. The restaurant was nearly empty – even the few discreet staff had disappeared – the gulls had fallen silent, and he had the oddest sensation that they were alone and adrift midway between sea and sky.

He took a sip of water and blinked, bringing everything back into focus. There was no point endlessly going over why Freya had left him. What was done was done, and he had to accept it and get on with things as well as he could. He knew that.

The tension was broken by a smiling young waitress bringing their desserts. "So, where are you having your meeting?" asked Daniel, suddenly remembering why they were there.

"The client's coming over to the hotel in the morning."

"Are you going to tell me what the job involves?"

Freya laughed and scooped a spoonful of dark-chocolate mousse from its tiny pot. "Sorry, client confidentiality."

"Really?"

"That and the fact that I have a couple of options to present and I'm not one hundred per cent sure which of them the client will go for yet." She tapped the slim briefcase by her side. "I'm hoping we'll final-ise the plans tomorrow, but you know what it's like."

"Sure. Big ideas meet lack of money."

"Money won't be a problem in this case." She wrinkled her nose. "But there could be other consid-erations to do with environmental sustainability and that type of thing."

Daniel knew Freya well enough to suspect that she really wanted to discuss the job with him. "It sounds like a major project. And if there are environmental considerations I'm guessing it involves the cliff. Or possibly the waterfront?"

"Stop fishing – if you'll pardon the pun."

It was a poor joke, but they both laughed, relieved to be off the tricky subject of emotions and back onto safer ground.

Daniel rubbed his chin, thoughtfully. "So it's a big expensive commission, perhaps for a cliff-top or a sea-front development. Now, who might have the wherewithal to finance that?"

"I'm not going to tell you, so you can stop asking."

"I'm not asking, I'm speculating." He leant towards her and smiled. "I can't think of anyone local, so I'm guessing it's someone from outside town."

"No shit, Sherlock."

He caught the sarcasm in her voice, enjoying the game. "My money would be on a certain musical has-been."

"He's not a has-been," she hissed. "He's taking a break and plans to make some sensible investments."

"Ha, got you!"

"Don't you dare breathe a word of this to anyone, do you hear?"

"Wow, would I?" He patted her hand, which she withdrew a fraction too slowly. "I'm only winding you up. Of course I won't mention it to anyone."

"Not even to your lady friend?"

"No, not even to Eleanor." He smiled now. "So, come on. Spill the beans."

"Buy me another glass of this delicious Viognier and I'll consider it."

Freya was proud of her work and Daniel knew she would be eager to show the plans to someone who knew the terrain. She handed him her iPad and let him scroll through the drawings.

"I think we've got the sustainability issues covered with the solar panels, the choice of local materials and the rainwater tanks." She relaxed back in her seat and looked at him steadily across her wineglass. "So. Do you think we'll get it through?"

Daniel scratched his chin thoughtfully. "Hard to say. If you can convince the planners that the building is energy-neutral that's one thing, but I can't see the council giving you the go-ahead for the theme park bit."

"It's not a theme park. Don't you dare use that phrase! It's a meditation zone with a water park at sea level."

"Okay, water park. The bit with the jet skis."

"And they aren't jet skis. They're like mini hover-craft – they don't have propellers or moving parts, so they will cause minimum disruption to the sea life."

"If you say so." Daniel smiled. He couldn't help being impressed with Freya's inventiveness when it came to getting around regulations.

"You'll write in support when the planning permission comes out, of course?" Although it was phrased as a question, it was clear from Freya's tone and the way she eyeballed her ex that it was more of an order.

Daniel leaned back in his chair, nodding slowly. "If I think the design is appropriate for the setting and that there aren't going to be any issues with local transport, etc. ... then, yes, I'll support it."

Freya beamed at him. "I knew I could rely on you, darling."

Daniel flinched at the use of the endearment that had once meant so much to him. "I'll approve it if I think it's right for Combemouth. Not for any other reason."

"And because it will help my reputation, I hope?"

"That as well," he nodded. "Yes."

"And if your lady friend disagrees?"

He shrugged. "I don't see why she should, if it's a decent proposal." Not that what Eleanor thought had any bearing on his decision, he thought grumpily. "And anyway, it could bring more people to town, which will be good for the high street and for her business."

"Well, that's all right then. I wouldn't want to cause any friction between you lovebirds."

"Don't worry. There's no chance of that happening."

Freya smiled her sweetest smile. "Shall we get coffee?"

* * *

After the meal, Freya refused the offer of a walk – "In these shoes?" – so Daniel drove her the short distance along the top road to her hotel.

"Thanks for lunch."

"You're welcome. I look forward to seeing how the plans develop. Let me know if I can help." Why had he said that? He didn't know and regretted it almost immediately. As if Freya would need any help from him, anyway.

She looked at him coolly then a flicker of warmth lit up her eyes as they both remembered the years they had worked side by side, wrestling with problems of space and unrealistic budgets until – inevitably it seemed – they would alight on the same solution at the same instant. "I will." And with that, she picked up her bag and walked into the hotel.

Back in his house, Daniel's head was buzzing. Freya's plans for Bill Widget's development were inventive and daring: they would inevitably ruffle a few feathers locally, but he loved what Freya was trying to do. Her ideas were innovative and fun – and nothing like his own designs. He leafed through the drawings for the school extension he'd been trying to finalise that morning, then threw them back on the desk in disgust. Without Freya to stimulate him and bounce ideas off, he could see that his work was becoming dull and pedestrian. He still landed commissions and people liked what he did, but he was beginning to hate his own ideas.

"Boring crap." Compared to what Freya was capable of, his own work was unimaginative and predictable.

Throwing off his clothes, he donned his jogging gear and went back downstairs.

"Come on, Crumpet." The dog looked surprised but pleased by the prospect of an unexpected outing in the middle of the afternoon and followed Daniel as he slammed the front door behind them and pounded off towards the beach. He needed a long run to clear his head.

Chapter 11: Hold the Front Page!

Over at the bookshop, Eleanor had had a busy morning and was just finishing lunch when Connie bustled in brandishing a copy of the *Combemouth Chronicle* in the air like a weapon. "Have you seen the local paper?"

"Good afternoon, Mother, and how are you?"

Ignoring her greeting, Connie opened the paper with a flourish. "It's all here. Everything about the rock star coming to town."

"So Deirdre was right?"

"My sources are never wrong, Eleanor." Connie slapped the paper onto the counter. "You should appreciate that by now."

"Don't get into a huff."

"I'm not getting into a 'huff'. Although it would make a nice change to be taken seriously now and again."

Eleanor gave her a hug. "I take you very seriously. Now show us the story."

"It's on page seventeen."

Erika stopped what she was doing and came over to the counter as Connie turned over page after page of "news" about stolen wheelie bins, lost cats, scout group fundraisers, etc., until reaching the article about "Fingers" Widget.

Popping on her glasses, Erika ran a slender finger

down the column of type. "It says here that Bill Widget's plans include not only a brand-new house and meditation zone on the cliff top but some kind of water park at the end of the bay."

"A water park? Surely not." Eleanor looked up in alarm. "If that's true, it would mean redeveloping a whole swathe of land close to the coastal path, and maybe cutting off public access to the beach. What is he thinking of?"

"That will never get planning permission," said Connie.

Erika snorted. "It depends who he knows and how many favours can be called in."

"But Widget isn't local, so how could he influence the decision-makers?"

"Ways and means," said Erika, tapping the side of her nose. "Ways and means."

"Well really," said Connie. "We can't have people coming into town and damaging our seaside. I don't like the sound of this at all."

"Quite right, Mum. But hopefully it won't come to that."

Connie leafed through the rest of the paper then threw it into the bin marked "Recycling". "That's about all there is of interest in there. So," she said, turning back to her daughter, "what about your news?"

Eleanor looked surprised. "Mine? Why would I have any news?"

Connie gave her a look as though she was being deliberately dim. "Has Daniel told you where you're going for your trip yet?"

"No, he hasn't." And I'm not sure I'd tell you

anyway, she thought. "He has said that I should pack an overnight bag, but not what to take," she added with a frown.

"That should be easy," said Connie. "All you own are trousers."

"Ha, ha. That's not true. I have skirts and dresses, too – I just don't wear them as often as you'd like me to." Eleanor's interest in clothes was almost zero and she considered the process of buying them as only marginally less tedious than cleaning the kitchen floor with a toothbrush.

Her mother was unimpressed. "Don't you want to look nice, love? I'm sure Daniel will be making an effort."

Erika folded her arms across her chest, looking pensive. "Connie has a point. Maybe we need a trip to the shops."

Eleanor rolled her eyes in horror.

"What a super idea," said Connie. "It would only take you an hour or so to pop into Waterborough and buy something decent."

Eleanor could tell she was being ganged up against. "But I can't spare an hour to go shopping. It's the end of the month and there are payments to sort out and books to order. And I don't even know what I need for this jaunt."

"I'm sure you've got some decent clothes tucked away and forgotten at home," said Erika. "If you like, I could pop round and see what we can extract from your wardrobe. Then we'll have a better idea of what you need."

"That sounds like a very kind offer, doesn't it, love?"

Eleanor hesitated, not because she doubted Erika's

taste but because of the untidy state of her house. Now she spent half her time at Daniel's and half in the cottage, her belongings were scattered everywhere and she had an odd assortment of clothes in both places.

"Well, if you wouldn't mind wading through the debris to get to the cupboards."

"Happy to help." Erika had made a study of women's clothing during the long years when she was still living as a man and had developed a shrewd sense of which combinations worked and which didn't. Eleanor suspected that Erika must have been a snappy dresser in her masculine years, because she certainly had excellent taste now.

"Okay," said Eleanor, feigning an enthusiasm for the task that she didn't feel. "I'll collect my stuff from Daniel's and we can sort through the lot in one go. Why don't I let you loose on my wardrobe tomorrow and I'll knock up some supper?"

"Good plan," said Erika.

After work, Eleanor drove over to Daniel's place and was not surprised to find the house empty: he quite often went for a run in the early evening after a long day working on drawings at his desk. She was on her knees on the bedroom floor, emptying drawers and throwing clothes into a bin liner when he came into the room, hot and sweaty from his run. At the sight of Eleanor packing her things away, his face fell.

"Christ, you're not leaving me are you?" Daniel's head spun and he felt sick at the thought that he was about to lose her.

Seeing his traumatised expression, Eleanor leapt

to her feet and ran over to hug him. "No, darling. Of course not!" Beneath her cheek, she could feel Daniel's heart pounding – whether from his run or the emotion she didn't know. "Erika has offered to help me sort out my clothes tomorrow evening, so I thought I'd better add these things to the heap."

"Thank goodness. You gave me such a fright." He lifted her face to his and kissed her lips more urgently than he had ever done before, his blue-grey eyes fixed on hers. He kissed her again, more gently now, overwhelmed by how much he had come to love her and how much he desired her. She was physically so different to his ex – all curves and softness against his wife's boyish, athletic figure. Damn Freya. Suddenly what he wanted more than anything was to hold Eleanor's body next to his, to run his hands over the soft skin of her thighs and lose himself inside her.

Eleanor's own heart began to beat faster, but from desire rather than fear as Daniel gently caught the hem of her top and lifted it over her head.

"Wow. Remind me to give you a fright more often."

"Please don't," he said, gently tipping her back onto the bed.

Chapter 12: Getting Organised

After an evening of unexpected passion, Eleanor drove home in the morning with the clothes she had collected from Daniel's house. These were now in a neat pile on her chest of drawers, ready for inspection.

After work, she pulled the rest of her clothes out of the wardrobe and passed them to Erika, who arranged them in a line across the bed.

"We need to see exactly what you've got, so let's put tops here and bottoms over there."

"Whatever you say, boss."

"This wardrobe could do with a radical overhaul, but this is a short-term emergency." Pursing her lips Erika swapped garments around, pairing them up in ways Eleanor would never have imagined.

After an hour, they had several workable combinations and a heap of clothes for the charity shop.

"You know, it's really not that bad." Erika had arranged the clothes by colour, making it much easier to see their potential.

"Goodness, I didn't realise I had so much black."

"Too much. It's really not flattering on the older skin – if you don't mind me saying so."

"Course not." Eleanor smiled and shook her head. She had known Erika for years and was familiar with her blunt way of talking. "I can tell you've watched too much Trinny and Susannah."

"Do you know what? Those girls were a great help to me in the days when I didn't know if I was a pear or an apple. In the end I decided that a stick of celery was the closest match."

Eleanor frowned. "I think I'm more pumpkin."

Erika laughed. "Rubbish. You're a classic hourglass shape just like Connie: curvy in all the right places."

"I wish!" Eleanor twisted from side to side, looking at herself in the mirror. "I think the top part of the hourglass is fast collapsing onto the bottom half and taking everything in between with it."

"That's because you don't hold yourself properly." Erika came over and tapped her on the top of the head. "Imagine a piece of string coming up through here and I'm tugging on it. Now straighten your back, pull in your stomach and tuck your tail under."

Eleanor lifted her head and pulled her shoulders back. "Coo, you're right. I must be at least an inch taller – and I can see my waist again."

"You may laugh, but it works. Either think 'string' or you could walk about with a book on your head."

"Now where am I going to find one of those around here?" Eleanor laughed at Erika's expression. "Sorry, I know you're trying to help but my sister was given the good figure and I inherited the brains. Actually, Jenna got those as well."

"You're too hard on yourself, Eleanor. Daniel obviously likes the way you look, so you should, too."

"He does, doesn't he? I am very lucky."

Remembering the enthusiasm with which Daniel had pounced on her the evening before, she made a show of studying a pair of trousers so as to avoid her friend's eyes.

"Which brings us back to the matter in hand." Erika grabbed a dusky pink dress, a dove grey tunic, a pair of white linen trousers, a deep blue sweater and a blue and white striped top. "So for dinner, these would go well together. And this will be suitable for a stroll and, if you take those jeans you've bought but never worn, you can mix and match."

Eleanor stood back in amazement. "You should have your own TV show, Erika!"

"True. I could be the new Gok Wan. Now what about shoes?"

"Shoes? You mean I can't wear these?" Eleanor lifted up one foot on which she wore a battered sandal.

"Absolutely definitely not. What else do you have?"

Eleanor chewed her lip. "I think there are some in a cupboard on the landing. If not, we'll have to raid Phoebe's room."

Out in the hallway, Eleanor went down on her knees and pulled out three boxes with new pairs of shoes in them. "I'd forgotten about these," she said, returning to the bedroom with her stash. "Which ones shall I take?"

Erika barely hesitated. "All of them."

"You're joking, right?" Eleanor laughed as Erika shook her head. "I'd better find a bigger case, then." She climbed onto the bed and extracted a soft canvas bag from the top of the wardrobe. "This should do," she said, brushing off a cobweb. "And you'll be impressed to hear that I've got a brand-new nightie and some decent underwear I've been saving for 'best'." She rummaged through the dresser by her bed and pulled out a selection of lacy frillies in pink and black. "They're a bit girlie for everyday wear, but just the thing for a romantic mini-break." She threw them onto the neat pile of clothes and grinned at Erika. "That'll do, don't you think?"

Erika nodded. "I'm happy with that."

Eleanor put an arm around her shoulder. "You're a star," she said, embracing her friend. "I don't know what I'd do without you."

"It's my pleasure. I do enjoy a clothing emergency. It gives me a chance to put into practice my years of undercover work in Marks and Spencer's lingerie department."

Eleanor had only ever known her friend as Erika and sometimes she forgot that Eric had ever existed.

"Can I ask you something?"

Erika put down a cardigan she was folding and looked at her. "You know you can ask me anything you like. In fact, now that I've seen the contents of your knicker drawer, I'm not sure we can have any secrets from each other."

"How did you – that is 'Eric' – manage to buy women's clothes in the early days?"

"You mean when I was still a big hairy bloke? Oh, I had a few entertaining moments in C&A over the years, believe me. You just have to be thick-skinned and devious." Erika laughed. "I suppose I did what everyone used to do and pretended to be looking for things for my girlfriend, who just happened to be 6ft 2in with size 11 feet and my waist measurement. Trannies have it easy nowadays because you can get everything over the internet and avoid face-to-face encounters with snotty-nosed sales assistants. It was no laughing matter trying on man-sized slingbacks at

Freeman, Hardy & Willis in Chorlton-cum-Hardy in the 1990s, I can tell you."

Eleanor shook her head, smiling. Erika was such a strong, confident person that it was easy to forget the years of struggle she had gone through to arrive at this point. "I think you're amazing."

"Not really."

"Well, I think you are. Anyway," said Eleanor, looking at the clock, "it's time for fish pie and Chardonnay."

"Sounds good to me. Lead the way."

* * *

In the kitchen, Eleanor put the pie on the table then opened a bottle of wine and handed Erika a glass. "Cheers and thanks for all your help."

Erika clinked her glass against Eleanor's. "You're welcome. I like a challenge, as you know."

The meal was delicious and the women fell silent for a moment as they concentrated on not burning their mouths on piping-hot mouthfuls of creamy sauce. Eventually, Eleanor spoke. "Now my clothes are sorted out, I have another mission for you."

"Really? What's that?"

"I want to contact the council about Widget's plans and I thought you could help me with a list of questions. It might be worth sending a letter to the paper, as well."

At the mention of the paper, Erika's face clouded over.

"Sorry …"

Erika's affair with Jim Rowe, the lead reporter, had come to a sad end some months before but it was still a sore point. She had insisted it was no big thing, but Eleanor knew how important it had been for Erika to have someone in her life who loved her just the way she was. She had hardly dared to hope that she could beat the odds and find a man who wanted to have a proper relationship with her, a trans woman. Finally it had happened and they had been happy together for over a year, but eventually Jim had found the pressure too much and called the whole thing off.

"That's okay. It was a 'conscious uncoupling', as they say nowadays, and we're still friends. Or at least we were until he got together with Chris."

Eleanor squeezed her hand. "Bloody men. They're more trouble than they're worth sometimes."

"Except for Daniel. He's a good one."

Eleanor couldn't look directly at Erika, the memory of the previous night's intense session fresh in her mind. "I'll drink to that," she said, sure she was blushing as she pushed her empty plate to one side. "Let's make our list."

They had finished their meal and cleared the table when there was a knock and Daniel's face appeared around the kitchen door.

"Hi ladies. I let myself in," he said, giving Eleanor a proper kiss and Erika a peck on the cheek. "I hope I'm not interrupting anything." He sniffed the air, which smelt enticingly of smoked fish. "Something smells good in here."

"It's Eleanor's fish pie – it's the best."

"So good, in fact, that it has all gone." Noticing Daniel's look of disappointment, Eleanor went to the dresser and grabbed some plates. "You can join us for cheese and biscuits if you're starving." She looked at the clock, which showed it to be 9pm. "How come you haven't already eaten?"

Daniel pulled up a chair opposite Erika and winked as she handed him a glass of white wine. "I did have a very small bit of chicken salad after my run with Crumpet, but that seems like ages ago now."

Eleanor just smiled, thinking of some indoor pursuits that helped Daniel to burn off the calories. Although he was her age, he seemed to eat as much as her son and stay almost as skinny. His wiry frame was one of the many things she loved about him.

"Cheers," said Daniel, taking a sip of wine and grabbing an olive. "So what have you two been plotting? This doesn't look like a wardrobe rejig."

"My wardrobe has been rejigged magnificently, thank you. And why should we be 'plotting' anything?"

"Oh, I don't know. It could be something to do with your laptop being open and Erika having a notebook by her plate."

"There are no flies on you," said Eleanor, as she unwrapped a selection of cheeses and placed them on a wooden platter in the middle of the table.

"Okay," said Daniel, pinching off a chunk of Shropshire Blue and popping it straight into his mouth. "Let me guess. A book launch?"

"Nope. Our events are all in hand for the rest of the summer. We are very well organised, you know. Have another go."

"You're not reorganising the shop again are you?"

"Ugh, no chance. I'm only just recovering from the latest change when we moved the caff around. You wouldn't believe how heavy those children's books are."

"I would because I helped, remember?"

"Of course you did, darling. Guess again."

"You're coming up with recipes for new cupcakes to tempt more OAPs into the café."

"Not even warm." Eleanor gently brushed bits of cracker from Daniel's lower lip and smiled at him. "If you must know, we were coming up with some points to raise with the planners about the new development."

"Oh right." Daniel nodded while trying his best to sound casual. "You did say something about this the other day." Eleanor looked at him queerly.

"Remember?" said Erika. "The meditation centre slash theme park that some rock star type is planning to build on the cliffs above town."

"Sure. No, of course I remember now."

"You can't have forgotten – people have talked about little else for days. There's a meeting about it in the parish hall the week after next. Want to come? It should be interesting because – judging by what was in the local paper – the development looks far too big for the site and there may be some opposition." Eleanor picked up her notebook and pen. "Actually, you might be able to help us to come up with more questions."

Daniel shook his head. "I'm sure you can manage without my input. And I think I'll give the meeting a miss, too, if you don't mind."

Erika frowned at Eleanor, surprised by Daniel's lack of interest in what promised to be a controversial development in his own backyard. Eleanor caught her friend's eye across the table and shrugged. She was feeling especially tender towards her lover and knew Daniel spent a lot of time in tedious negotiations with planners as it was. She could see that a night out discussing someone else's building project might not be his idea of fun.

"Okay love. We'll let you know if there's any gossip."

"Yes, if anyone actually exchanges punches, I'd like to know about it." Daniel did his best to smile but he felt a knot of anxiety growing in his gut, knowing as he did exactly what the news from the meeting would be. Freya had kept her name out of the papers and he just had to hope that her team had covered any environmental issues and would present the plan well. If they didn't and Eleanor hated it, he wasn't sure how that would affect their friendship.

He'd offered Freya his help the day before, but now he really hoped that he would never be forced to choose sides. Then again, he was probably worrying about nothing. The plans were stunning, so how could Eleanor not be impressed by them?

"Knowing what local politics is like, I doubt if the meeting will be as eventful as that."

"You're probably right, Erika," said Daniel, laughing a little too heartily. "Pass the Stilton, will you?" Boring and uneventful was the best he could hope for.

Chapter 13: The Secret's Out

Eleanor ended up going to the planning meeting with just Connie and Harold: Erika cried off, saying that she couldn't miss her Pilates class. Jim Rowe was bound to be at the event, which Eleanor suspected was behind Erika's reluctance to attend.

The hall was packed with people hoping to catch a glimpse of Mr Widget and find out more about the development. Rumours had been flying around about a theme park, a water park and a zoo, so everyone was keen to discover the truth.

Eleanor dashed home, eager to share the gossip with Daniel. She had arranged to meet him back at her cottage even though he'd said he could wait until the next morning to hear the outcome.

"Hi, honey, I'm home," she said laughing, as she kicked off her shoes and sank down on the sofa.

"Want a drink?" asked Daniel, heading into the kitchen to fetch a glass.

"Yes please. And make it a large one."

Daniel had run over Freya's sketches in his mind and come to the conclusion that most of what she had suggested was relatively uncontroversial. Yes, there were a few more challenging suggestions, but on the whole the development was going to be a good one. More than likely everything would have gone well at the meeting and there would be nothing to worry about. He sat down opposite Eleanor and forced a smile, deciding to think positive and stay calm. "So how did it go?"

"It was fascinating. There was a team there from Mr Widget's side who showed us the plans for the development. The architects didn't come – instead they sent some underlings to try to baffle us with loads of drawings and captions in tiny writing. You wouldn't believe what they want to do." Eleanor took a sip of wine and patted the space next to her. "Come and sit by me."

"Like what?"

"Oh, like carving up a perfectly nice bit of land, calling it a 'Meditation Zone' and plonking a hideous statue in the middle of it called 'Mother'."

"Installation art." Daniel shrugged. "That doesn't sound too bad."

"Ha, that's what you think! It's going to be a twenty-foot-tall naked figure made out of some awful reconstituted marble. Her enormous, snowy white knockers will be visible for miles around. And get this," said Eleanor, laughing. "There'll be jets laid in a circle all around her sending out puffs of mist in time to music chosen to suit the phases of the moon. You couldn't make it up."

"It certainly sounds, er, original." Alarm bells were going off in Daniel's head. Either Freya hadn't been entirely truthful or her client had made a few major changes to the plans since he had seen them. Whatever the cause, he wasn't sure that he liked the sound of the new direction the development was taking.

"Hideous would be a better word. Oh, and then he

wants to have a kind of cable car collecting people from near the harbour and taking them up the cliff, past Busty Bertha, to an enormous aquarium filled with dolphins, stingray and sharks. Sharks in an aquarium on a cliff top!" She stopped for a glug of wine. "Is that even legal? Mr Widget has obviously got more money than sense and no interest in wildlife. And what can the architects be thinking of?"

"It does seem rather extraordinary." This was not sounding positive at all, but Daniel knew from Freya's sketches that the house she had planned was a beauty. Surely there was nothing anyone could object to there?

"And did you see the model for the house?"

Eleanor nodded. "Yes, and I have to say that the building itself looked very striking: big and open with lots of blue glass and pale wood, then decorated with local slate and copper panels. You know the kind of thing. It would look great in California, or wherever he's flown in from, but probably not here. And the helipad is a no-no."

"There's a helipad?" Daniel suspected that Freya had included the cable car and the helipad to give the planners something to reject, so they would feel they had achieved something and the client would lose a couple of expensive features he didn't particularly want in the first place. "Anything else?" he asked nervously, his chest tightening as he posed the question.

"Oh, there's just so much to tell you." It had puzzled her that Daniel hadn't wanted to go to the meeting, even if he had been busy with his own work. "You really should have come, you know?"

Daniel nodded, but said nothing, apparently gripped by the contents of his wineglass.

Eleanor took another sip of her drink and snuggled into Daniel's shoulder.

"What was the conclusion? Do you think it will go through?"

Eleanor sat up and guffawed. "No chance! One or two misguided people – builders mainly – were in favour, but the majority were dead against it."

"Really?"

"Well yes, of course." She looked at him now in astonishment. "Are you surprised after what I've told you? It's completely the wrong place for a development of that size and the animal-rights people will be up in arms over the sea life."

Daniel shifted uncomfortably in his seat. "Don't you think it could be good for business? I mean, it may bring more people to the area to catch a glimpse of Bill Widget. Or to meditate."

Eleanor huffed. "It's clear that the architects were either very economical with the truth or the press only reported half the story. The dreadful man has far more destructive ideas in mind than meditation." She curled around on the sofa, stretching her legs across Daniel's knees. "For instance, they want to use jet skis to ferry people from the town harbour to a new marina and cable car station around the corner. Can you imagine it? Think what effect that will have on the wildlife, not to mention the tranquil nature of the place."

Daniel was quiet, looking down at his hands resting on Eleanor's knees. The knowledge that he was going to have to confess all was making him feel quite ill.

"Dan, is something wrong? You look grey."

There was no way around it: he was going to have to tell her what he knew and face the music. Putting down his glass, he took her free hand gently in both of his. "There's something I need to tell you."

"God – there's me rattling on when something awful has happened." Eleanor's heart missed a beat, alarmed by his serious tone. "What is it? There's nothing wrong with Emily or Malcolm is there?"

"No, Dad and Emily are both fine."

"Then what is it?"

There was no way of saying this well. "The thing is that I know about it. Or some of it at least."

Eleanor was puzzled. "What do you know, darling?"

"I know all about the cable car, the jet skis and the marina. Though actually they are more like hover-bikes and it's not a marina, it's a pontoon than can be moved, depending on the season and the tides."

"How come you know about this?"

Daniel took a deep breath. "I've seen the plans."

"You have. How?"

"It's Freya who drew them up."

"Freya, as in your wife?"

"Ex-wife."

Eleanor pulled her legs off his, snatched back her hand and sat up straight, staring at him in surprise. "But, how? I don't understand." She narrowed her eyes at him. "Did you recommend her?"

"No, of course not! She can manage quite well without me. No, she met Widget's manager at some do or other and talked her way into the job." Daniel smiled ruefully. "She always was great at networking."

Eleanor was not impressed. "You let me witter on

about the meeting when you already knew about the plans?"

"I didn't know everything. I mean, some elements have clearly been changed or added. The helipad is obviously out of the question and I didn't know about the sculpture, so I reserve my judgement on that."

Eleanor felt herself flush with anger. "How long have you known the parts of it that you do know?" She was trying hard to stay calm until she knew what was what, but failing in her efforts.

Daniel shrugged, "Oh, a fortnight or so I guess."

"A fortnight?" Her determination to stay calm was severely shaken. He smiled weakly.

"Or so."

"And you didn't think to tell me? Even when you knew how I felt about it?"

"I didn't know you were quite so strongly against it." Daniel looked pained. "In fact, I thought you might welcome a new development that would bring more people into town. As I recall, you even said that it might bring more customers to the shop."

There is nothing quite so annoying as having your words quoted back at you in an argument and Eleanor was starting to lose her temper. "As *I* recall, that was before we discovered exactly what that man had planned. A meditation centre didn't sound too bad, but a gigantic naked woman and jet skis are another thing altogether."

Daniel was going to correct her about the jet skis again, then thought better of it and shut up.

Eleanor shook her head in disbelief. "I really can't believe you knew all this and didn't tell me, even when you realised I had concerns about it." What she really wanted to know – but was determined not to ask – was where Daniel had had this conversation with his ex. Had he been to London without telling her or had Freya been to his house? And when exactly had this happened?

"It's a huge commission for Freya," said Daniel, standing and running his hands through his hair. "It could make her name as a ground-breaking, cutting-edge architect – can't you see that?"

"You might be right, but at what price? Think about the pollution and the traffic, and the poor dolphins trapped in a tank on the cliff top."

"There aren't going to be any sharks or dolphins – well, only if they choose to swim into the bay, which is very unlikely." Daniel grinned, hoping to lighten the mood, which only infuriated Eleanor more.

"Ha – yes, especially with all the jet skis slicing off their fins!" She was furious now.

"They're hoverbikes!"

"Oh, so that's all right then."

"El, try to understand. This could lead to some really big, well-paid jobs for Freya and the money would help secure our daughter's future."

Eleanor had been pacing the room, but now she stopped with her hands on her hips and stared at him. "I'm really disappointed in you."

There was something about her fierce expression and the tilt of her body that was so appealing it made Daniel smile. He was filled with tenderness for his lover as she stood there, her cheeks pink with indignation. "Do you know that sometimes you look exactly like your mother?"

If he had slapped her, Eleanor could not have looked more shocked. "Ooooh!"

"What? What have I done now?"

She looked at Daniel as if he had uttered the worst profanity ever. "How *dare* you say that to me!"

"El, I like your mother. You know I do. Connie and I are friends."

Eleanor crossed her arms tightly across her chest, as though protecting herself from blows. "That is *not* the point."

"Look, I'm sorry if I have offended you somehow and I'm really sorry you're disappointed, but please try to understand – I'm caught between wanting my daughter's mother to be successful and not wanting to hurt you."

Eleanor went to the window, brushing her hair from her face with both hands. What had he said? "A fortnight or so"? Had Daniel known about Freya's involvement when they were discussing their romantic mini-break? Or when he had joined her and Erika after supper? She could feel heat rising to her cheeks. "It's late, Daniel. I need to go to bed." The situation and her emotions were rapidly getting out of control.

Daniel walked over and held her gently by the shoulders, trying to look her in the eyes. "I'll be off then, shall I? See you tomorrow?" Surely by then she would have calmed down and realised that Widget's plans were not worth fighting over?

She shrugged, causing his hands to fall away from her. "Maybe. I don't know. I think I need some time to think about this. I'll call you."

"Okay," he said, bending to kiss her lips but catching her cheek as she turned her face away from him.

At the door, he stopped and turned towards her, his voice half-pleading. "Don't be angry, El. Please?"

Was she overreacting? Eleanor recognised that she sounded harsh, but lately she'd felt closer to him than ever before and the fact that Daniel could have been in cahoots with Freya all this time felt like a betrayal.

She leant one hand on the back of a chair to steady herself and spoke very slowly and clearly, wanting him to understand how upset she was: that this was about more than some ridiculous plans.

"I am angry and sad that you didn't feel you could tell me what you knew about the development when you could see how worried I was about it." What she didn't say but felt acutely was jealousy: she was jealous that Daniel had seen Freya and not told her. Worse, that he had secretly sided with her. Eleanor felt sick at the thought that Daniel might never come close to loving her as much as he had loved his ex-wife. And if that was the case – what future did they have together?

Chapter 14: A Shoulder to Cry On

Daniel had got into the habit of visiting his father on the days when Eleanor was tied up in the bookshop or sorting through the endless piles of newspapers and magazines that filled her house. The morning after the planning meeting rumpus, Daniel dug out his running gear and jogged over to his father's place, Crumpet dashing along by his heels. Man and dog were both hot and out of breath by the time they reached the garden of Malcolm's 1930s bungalow.

His father was on his knees weeding as Daniel came up the drive. Malcolm wrestled playfully with the dog for a moment before getting to his feet and greeting his son. "What's the matter, old chap? You look rather serious this morning."

"No offence to our furry friend here, but I'm in the doghouse."

"Oh dear." His father tried to sound sympathetic. "Have you managed to upset my ex-daughter-in-law again?"

"No, not Freya. It's Eleanor I'm in trouble with this time."

"Really? What on earth did you do?"

"Nothing!"

"You must have done something. I mean, Eleanor is a very even-tempered lady."

"Unlike Freya, I know. You don't need to say it."

Daniel wiped his damp brow with the bottom of his T-shirt. "All I did was say that she looked like her mother and she went completely off the rails."

"Ouf!" Malcolm's sharp intake of breath and slow shaking of the head were worrying signs. "Well, there you are."

Daniel stopped and looked at him. "What does 'ouf' mean?"

"You should *never* tell a woman that she resembles her mother in any way, shape or form."

"Why ever not?"

"Hard to say." Malcolm placed a fatherly hand on Daniel's shoulder. "It's like the female species' dislike of carnations. There's no logic to it. It's just one of those things that separates men from women."

Daniel looked gloomy. "I'm hopeless with this relationship business."

Malcolm, feeling that he was about to get out of his depth, asked himself what his late wife would have done. "Shall we go inside and I'll put the kettle on?"

"That would be great, Dad, thanks."

"Good, good. It will all sort itself out, you know?"

This was Malcolm's mantra and Daniel knew he was probably right as they walked into the kitchen, though it didn't feel like it at the moment.

"I'm afraid there was something else."

"Oh? I thought there might be." Malcolm turned away from the sink and looked at his son. "You look very uncomfortable. So, come on. What is it?"

Daniel walked over to the window and breathed out heavily. "I told Eleanor that it was Freya who was behind the development this rock singer is planning for up on the Top."

"Freya's the architect?" Malcolm sat down at the table, shaking his head. "Well, I'm not surprised Eleanor is upset. I have to say I'm rather disappointed that you didn't tell me about it either."

That word again! Was there anyone who wasn't disappointed with him at the moment?

"She asked me not to, Dad. She didn't want to tell me at all, but I winkled it out of her over lunch."

Malcolm's expression was stern. "You had lunch? With Freya? Just the two of you?"

"Don't look at me like that!"

"Like what?"

"Like I've done something wrong. We were married a very long time and we do have our daughter to consider."

"I'm well aware of that, Daniel." Malcolm got up and swished hot water around the teapot thoughtfully. "And did you tell Eleanor you had discussed all this over a meal with Freya?"

"No. Obviously. Because she'd have got the wrong idea."

"Or the right idea, perhaps."

It never failed to amaze Daniel how he could be catapulted back into adolescence by his father's disapproving voice.

"Dad, please."

"Eleanor is a lovely woman. Not that Freya wasn't. I mean isn't."

"Thank you."

"But if you want to build a life with Eleanor, you need to let Freya go."

Daniel was taken aback by Malcolm's comments. They had never discussed his marriage or his relationship with Eleanor. All he could do now was splutter like an enraged teenager. "Well! I think you'll find that Freya was the one who let *me* go."

Malcolm stopped what he was doing and looked levelly at his son. "That is not the same thing at all."

He was right, of course. "I have let her go, Dad. I hadn't seen her for months, as it happens, but she wanted to meet me so we met and she told me about her commission."

"Be careful, Daniel. Freya is a very smart lady. Don't underestimate her."

"What do you mean?"

"I mean that simply because she isn't married to you any more doesn't mean she wouldn't like to have some control over your life."

"That's nonsense!" But was it? Daniel was loath to admit it, even to himself, but he could see that his father had a point. Freya had always liked to have things her own way, and perhaps that included approving his future love affairs.

"I'm only saying how it seems to me, but I've probably got it wrong." Malcolm shrugged and poured the tea. "Right then. Let's have a biscuit with this."

Daniel jumped up and went over to the cabinets, relieved to be back on familiar ground with his father. "Do you have any decent biscuits in this house?"

"Of course. We've some of those posh chocolate and ginger ones over there that Eleanor brought from the shop, and some gravy bones for Crumpet."

"Perfect."

Malcolm looked thoughtful. "Do you know what, Daniel? I think our Eleanor is pretty near perfect, too."

"Okay." Daniel raised his hands in submission. "Point taken!"

"The question is, what are you going to do about it?"

To that he had no answer. He couldn't publicly come out against the development and possibly scupper Freya's chances. On the other hand, if he carried on supporting her, he had the horrible feeling that he risked damaging what he and Eleanor had together.

"I don't know, Dad. I really don't."

Chapter 15: The Morning After

After the argument with Daniel, Eleanor had rather unwisely had a second bucket-sized glass of Chardonnay and woken up dehydrated with a mouth like sandpaper and puffy red eyes from fury and lack of sleep. Despite her thumping head, she had decided to open up early and was restacking their greetings cards display when Erika arrived. Her cheery "Good morning" was met with a grunt.

"I wish it was."

"You look dreadful. What's up? Actually, don't tell me yet." Erika stopped, halfway to the kitchen. "I'll put the kettle on and you can tell me what's wrong."

Coming back a few minutes later with two coffees and a plate of biscuits balanced on top of them, Erika nodded at the cards and frowned.

"I think you might need to check those again."

Looking at the stacker, Eleanor could see that half the cards were upside down and she'd put "In sympathy" cards in the slot labelled "Wedding".

"Darn," she said, getting to her feet and relieving Erika of a fig roll. "I can't concentrate on anything this morning."

Erika beckoned her over to the sofa. It was still early so there was no one in the shop who needed attending to.

"Come and tell your Aunty Erika what happened."

214

Eleanor threw herself on the sofa with a groan. "It's all too awful."

"It can't be so bad that we can't put it right," said Erika, grabbing a custard cream.

"Oh yes it can. Get this: Daniel knew about the development all along and he didn't bother to tell me." Eleanor was expecting a shocked reaction, but all she got was a shrug. She was used to Erika being generally undemonstrative, but this was a disappointment.

"He's an architect. He knows loads of people in the planning department. It's not so surprising really," she said, sipping her coffee. "Although I agree it is a bit odd that he didn't mention it the other week at your house when we were making our list of objections."

"Ha! Exactly. He obviously knew he was in the wrong or he'd have said something then. Not saying anything is bad enough, but there's worse to come: he didn't find out about the development from his cronies at the town hall."

"Maybe he read about it in the architectural press."

"Nope. It hasn't been featured yet."

Erika was tiring of the guessing game. "Does it matter where he heard it?"

"I think it does," Eleanor leant back triumphantly, "when he got it from Freya."

Erika looked puzzled. "Freya, his ex in London? What can she have to do with it?"

"Apparently she's Widget's architect. She has planned out the whole bloody thing. Jet skis, aquarium, Busty Bertha: the lot."

"Shall I take those?" Erika held out her hand for the greetings cards that Eleanor was still gripping under the fig roll, worried she was about to tear them to pieces.

"Sure, sorry. I just feel a bit tense."

Erika cocked her head to one side, smiling. "This really has rattled you, hasn't it?"

"Are you surprised?"

"Honestly? Yes, I am a bit."

"But it's a terrible plan."

"I think we all agree it's not the best development plan ever, but I don't understand why you're quite so upset."

"Let me count the ways." Eleanor started to tick off the effects with her fingers. "It's going to cause untold damage to the cliffs. We'll lose access to the beach, there'll be loads more traffic, then there's the light pollution, not to mention damage to the sea life."

"I know, we listed all the problems the other evening and Combemouth is obviously the wrong place for something that size." Erika looked at Eleanor, hesitating. "And I don't mean to be funny, but since when have you been the great environmental campaigner?"

"Since I found out that that bloody woman was coming here to trash our coastline." She took a mouthful of chocolate biscuit, spluttering through the crumbs. "And since Daniel didn't bother telling me he was still all cosy with her."

"Ah, now we're getting down to it," said Erika, flicking shards of biscuit off the sofa and onto the floor where Bella eagerly hoovered them up. "It seems to me that this is more about Freya and Daniel than it is about the development."

"Nonsense." Eleanor marched over to a row of bookshelves and started to tidy the maps. "I'm cross with him, obviously. But damage to the local environment and the negative impact on businesses along our high street is what matters most."

"If you say so."

"I do say so," she said crossly.

Erika could see that Eleanor was not going to budge. "What do you intend to do about it?"

Eleanor had picked up a box of new books from behind the counter and was snipping the tape around the top with a pair of scissors. "I don't know. What do people normally do in this situation? Cut up the villain's ties?"

"Don't you think you might be overreacting?"

"Possibly. Anyway, I don't think Dan owns any ties worth chopping up."

Erika laughed. "I meant, what are you going to do about the development, not about Daniel."

Eleanor sighed as she ripped back the top of the box and delicately stroked the cover of each book as she took it out and laid it on the counter top.

"I don't suppose there's anything I can do."

"Nonsense. There's lots you can do."

"Sure. I'll write to the local paper again and lodge a complaint with the planning board – yawn – but I don't expect it will make a blind bit of difference."

"That's a very defeatist attitude, if you don't mind me saying so." Erika was amused to see that Eleanor had gone into a sulk. "Don't underestimate your role as local bookseller. You are already a heroine around here and a hub of the community, etc."

"You're pulling my leg, now."

"I'm serious. You are in a really strong position to make a difference to the outcome. If you want to stop the development from going ahead, organise a protest group and fight it."

Eleanor guffawed. "I wouldn't know where to start."

"There's nothing to it: get a few people together for a demo, put up some posters, spread the news on social media." Erika shrugged. "It'll be easy."

"Will you help?"

"There's nothing I enjoy more than a punch-up with the establishment."

"In that case, let's do it!" Eleanor grinned. "Mr Widget is about to have a fight on his hands."

* * *

After sleeping on it, Eleanor was ready to follow Erika's advice to oppose the development with the help of the local community. Over the next few days, posters were designed and put up in all the local shops, at the library, the leisure centre and the church hall. Connie and Harold made sure everyone at their French class and the amateur dramatics group knew what was going on. A call was put out to fellow business owners to meet and discuss how they could tackle Widget's plans.

To Eleanor's slight discomfort, she was elected leader of the group. At the inaugural meeting it was decided that direct action was needed, though no one was quite sure what form this should take. Connie suggested a march through the town and someone else said they should drop leaflets through everyone's doors. When it was pointed out that printing and distributing leaflets would cost money, Connie's proposal won and a day was set for the march.

Jim Rowe attended the meeting in his dual role as

local newshound and friend – having cleared it first with Erika. Eleanor greeted him with a kiss. They had been friends for a long time and she was relieved to see that Jim and Erika seemed to be getting on a little better.

"Thanks for your support, Jim, I appreciate it."

"Happy to help. And we could do with some exciting news for the front page."

"I'm not sure how exciting it will be, but I suppose it will make a change from stories about amusing vegetables."

"Last week's hippo-shaped marrow story was one of my best, I'll have you know," he said with a smile. "Anyway, you'd better make it exciting. I contacted an ex-colleague of mine who's gone up in the world and now works for the local telly and he said he'd try to attend if there was nothing else happening."

"Telly?" said Eleanor. "That would be tremendous. The wider we can spread the word, the better."

Chapter 16: Hitting the Streets

Thanks to everyone's hard work, Eleanor and the team managed to persuade about fifty locals to gather outside the shop on Saturday morning ready to storm the high street.

Eleanor was busy passing out posters (hand-drawn to save money) and getting the crowd to practise their chants when Jim turned up with a big grin on his face.

"Good news. I've heard from my mate Bob at the Beeb and he's bringing a crew to Combemouth this afternoon."

"The BBC? Oh that's great!" said Eleanor, clapping her hands together with glee. "They must think we're newsworthy after all."

Jim shrugged. "Actually, they're coming down to film the annual regatta and duck race at Piggledown, but I promised Bob a beer if he and the boys could drop by on their way back to Bristol."

Eleanor felt slightly deflated to be playing second fiddle to a flock of plastic ducks, but did her best not to show it. "Any publicity we get will be helpful," she said, smiling. "Let's spread the word."

As news got around that a camera crew was going to be there, more people turned up at the shop in the hope of getting their faces on TV. By lunchtime there were about a hundred protestors ready for action.

Eleanor had cleared it with the police for the group to march down the high street and back past the harbour with placards saying "Hands off our Cliffs!", "No Sharks in Combemouth" and "Ban Busty Bertha" to the bafflement of day-trippers.

Connie and Harold held up posters and talked to passers-by, urging them to let the council know how they felt about Bill Widget's plans. It was warm work and quite a few of the protestors gave up after an hour or so and peeled off to the King's Head for a cooling pint. Eleanor was becoming anxious that everyone would drift away before the television people arrived when the welcome news came through that the Beeb was in town.

"There they are!"

Joe had spotted the broadcaster's white van, surrounded by two or three bored technicians who'd come along for the ride. Jim Rowe went over and shook hands with the grey-haired, perma-tanned man everyone recognised as the presenter of the regional TV news programme who was smiling and signing autographs.

"Is that Bob Smart? He's much older than he looks on the telly," said Connie, thoughtfully. "And I reckon he gets his tan done at Beryl's Hair like me. It doesn't half clash with his shirt."

After a while, Bob broke away from his fans and came over to Eleanor's group with his microphone. "Okay guys. I'll ask you a few questions, you tell me what's happening – try and make it sound exciting, love, if you can. We'll film a short sequence and hopefully get it into the evening bulletin. No promises though – that'll be down to our lady Rottweiler producer." He laughed at his witticism, oblivious to Eleanor's irritated expression. "Ready to roll, Phil?"

The cameraman gave him the thumbs up. "Ready when you are, boss."

Mr Smart put on his serious "I'm listening" face and did his introduction to camera before turning to address the group. "So why are you protesting here today?"

The seas parted as everyone suddenly took a step backwards, leaving Eleanor in the limelight. "Well," she said, feeling shy and tongue-tied as Phil zoomed in on her face. She wished she'd combed her hair and worn something less dowdy. "The thing is that Combemouth is an old-fashioned seaside town and we don't think this is the right setting for Mr Widget's theme park."

Heads nodded all around her as the group moved forward again like a flock of timid but inquisitive sheep and turned serious faces towards the camera. "It's not that we're against progress, of course. We just feel this is the wrong place for a development of the proposed size."

Bob Smart tilted his head to one side, trying to convey interest whilst all the time giving the impression of a man who would much rather be sitting in front of a cold pint than doing what he was doing.

Warming to her theme, Eleanor explained the problems of increased traffic, possible pollution and damage to the cliffs. "So we really hope the planning committee will see sense and throw out this proposal. Or, better still, that Mr Widget will have a change of heart himself."

Bob Smart nodded again, ready to end the

interview with a final shot to camera. "That's the state of play here in ..." Before he could finish his summing up of events he saw his colleague's eyes light up as they focused on something happening behind Bob's left shoulder.

"Mate, let's get a shot of this," said Phil, moving away from Eleanor and her flock. "This is more like it."

Miffed to have been interrupted as she was getting into the flow of things, Eleanor turned and to her horror saw Connie lying in the middle of the road. Her heart lurched as she threw down her placard and ran over just in time to see her mother trying to kick a policeman on the shin.

"Mum, are you all right?"

Connie ignored her and began to sing "We shall not, we shall not be moved" as the young PC stood over her with his arms crossed.

Eleanor's son was standing on the sidelines looking embarrassed.

"Joe, what the heck's going on?"

"I think Gran thought she could get herself arrested by sitting down in the road."

Some of the more agile protestors had decided to follow her lead and Connie was now surrounded by a motley collection of laughing teenagers and earnest pensioners.

The policeman tried to encourage her to move. "Madam, will you please get up and go home?"

"This is great," said Bob to his cameraman. "Keep rolling." He patted down his already sleek hair and fixed the camera with an earnest look. "Tensions are running high here in Combemouth as a controversial development by ageing rock star Bill 'Fingers' Widget threatens the tranquillity of this spot. Even pensioners have felt moved to gather here today to make their feelings felt."

As the camera panned from Bob's serious face back to the small crowd, Connie swooned dramatically. "Arrest me, I don't care!" she said, offering the policeman her wrists.

"There's really no need for that," he said, looking aggrieved.

"I'm prepared to give up my liberty to save our town."

"I think you've made your point, madam. Now be sensible and go home."

"Well, really," said Connie, furious that the PC refused to put her in handcuffs and take her to the station. "Is this what we pay our taxes for?"

Pushing past the policeman, Eleanor knelt down by her mother.

"What are you doing?" she hissed under her breath, aware of Bob Smart and Phil who were still filming the event. "I'm so sorry, officer." Smiling ingratiatingly, she grabbed Connie by one arm while Joe took the other. "Come along now, it's time for your tablets."

Connie tried to fight back. "Put me down."

"She can be a little vague sometimes," said Eleanor, between gritted teeth.

"Officer, make these people put me down."

The PC had pulled out his notepad and pen and looked like he meant business. "I suggest that you go with your daughter. Otherwise I'll have to book you for obstructing the public highway."

Eleanor laughed, slightly hysterically. "Mother, get up and stop being silly."

"My democratic rights to protest against this development are being hampered."

"I thought you folk were all on the same side," said the PC wearily.

"We are," said Joe. "Gran just gets a bit carried away sometimes." And with a final heave, he and Eleanor managed to pull Connie onto the pavement and into the bookshop where Harold and Erika were watching events from a safe distance.

Inside, Connie shook off her minders and brushed herself down. "Did they get it?"

"Did who get what?" asked her infuriated daughter.

"Did the Devon telly people film the struggle?"

"Unfortunately, I think they got the whole darned thing," said Eleanor. "The last thing we need is for the public to see us manhandling a demented OAP into the shop." She sank down onto the sofa next to her son, both of them panting from their exertions. "What on earth came over you?"

Connie looked hurt. "I was simply trying to liven things up a bit. Erika says that sex and violence always sell."

"In books, yes, but not in real life." Eleanor hid her head in her hands. "It was very inventive of you, but we don't want to distract attention from the development."

"I'm not sure about that," said Erika, who had been quiet until then. "The media always like grannies behaving badly."

"Perhaps I should have lain down in front of the police van," added Connie. "That might have shown them how strongly we all feel about this threat to our coast."

"I think you were magnificent, love," said Harold, beaming at her. "I'd have been on the ground with you, you know, if it wasn't for my hips."

"I give up." Eleanor was looking at the elderly pair in disbelief. "Will someone keep an eye on Emmeline Pankhurst here? I need to get back to the march and see if I can catch Mr Smart."

"I'll come too," said Joe, getting to his feet. "This is wicked!"

"I think that 'barmy' might be a better word for it."

Erika was standing by the door, where a queue of shoppers had formed, all eager for tea, books and a glimpse of Connie. "There's no such thing as bad publicity, remember that. Can I let them in now?"

"Sure," said Eleanor. "But don't let our local freedom fighter start signing autographs."

"As if I would," said Connie with a grin.

"I suggest we all meet up again in a day or two for a debriefing, so we can assess the situation. What do you think?"

"I think that's a very sensible suggestion, Erika. Come on Joe, let's see where the rest of the march has got to."

Chapter 17: The Debriefing

A couple of days later, Eleanor and her trusty team met up to assess the effects of their protest. Once they all had a mug of tea in their hands, the meeting began.

"I think we can agree that the protest was well attended," said Eleanor. "And it certainly encouraged people here in town to think about the effect Widget's plans might have on them. As for spreading the message further, Jim wrote a report for the local rag, but it wasn't picked up by the nationals. As we know, the telly news featured Mother behaving badly, but it hasn't had any effect on the planning people or on Mr Widget, from what I can tell."

"I knew I should have chained myself to something," said Connie, thoughtfully. "That might have got us some proper publicity."

"I think it's time we invested in professional help," said Erika, in a determined voice.

"Nice idea," said Eleanor, "but we can only just afford to print a few posters. We couldn't afford a real-life PR person, too."

"Fortunately, I know someone who might be prepared to help."

Connie bent forward, intrigued. "Who's that then?"

"My pal Georgie."

"Of course!" said Eleanor. "If she could spare a

weekend to visit and give us some advice, that would be tremendous. Do you think you could give her a call?"

"It's already done."

"Really? And what did she say?"

"She's on her way," said Erika, looking a teeny bit smug. "And Joe has volunteered to drive down and meet her at the station this evening."

Eleanor looked at her son suspiciously. It was not like him to volunteer for anything. "That's very good of you."

Joe raised his eyes from his phone for a second and smiled. "No worries, as they say Down Under." He couldn't wait to see Georgie again. They had met when she came down from London in her role as publicist to help The Reading Room with the launch of a book by her author – and local romantic novelist – Lavinia Threlfall. Georgie had ended up staying the weekend in Combemouth and Joe had spent enough time with her to make him keen to meet up again.

Joe was not Georgie's only fan. She and Erika had bonded over a bottle of Chardonnay after the book launch and become firm friends. Secretly she was also helping Erika to write a memoir about her transformation from Chief Superintendent Eric to Ms Erika Wilmott, bookseller.

"You must all come over for supper tonight and we'll discuss tactics. Joe, bring Georgie, will you?"

"Sure thing, Ma," he said with a salute.

* * *

The women were all in the kitchen chopping veg for salads and watching Eleanor make a gigantic broccoli and blue cheese quiche. Connie finished slicing some cucumber and sat down next to Georgie. "I want to talk to our guest. So how did you end up over here, love?"

"Oh, I did it the usual way. I flew to London from Perth in Western Australia at the tender age of nineteen and talked myself into a bar job. Of course, I travelled quite a bit, too – Thailand, Vietnam, Cambodia – it's a great family tradition. My parents hiked around India before their stint in Earls Court in the late 1980s."

"I remember that – Kangaroo Alley, we used to call it." Eleanor had a vision of the super-efficient young men and women with dazzling smiles who seemed to be in every pub you went to in those days. "Alan and I had friends who lived over there and we loved visiting because it was like being in Oz – without the great weather, of course."

"I wasn't in a bar long. I got a temping job at a publisher's and I was lucky enough to be taken on full time by the publicity department."

"That's not luck, Georgie. They obviously recognised your skill and liked your enthusiasm."

"Ah, that's sweet of you to say, Connie."

"It's true. I saw how well you looked after our very own Barbara Cartland." Georgie had been quite junior when she'd looked after Lavinia Threlfall, but had been promoted since then.

"It won't be long before you're running the department," said Eleanor.

"That would be great. But I'll have to climb over a lot of dead bodies to get there. Those women never seem to retire."

"Maybe you should go freelance."

"Yeah, maybe. I guess I can practise on you guys!"

"If we help your CV, that will make me feel less guilty for not being able to pay you very much."

"Ah, no worries, Eleanor. It's really great to be here and see Erika and ..." She stopped speaking, and glanced out into the garden before concentrating again on cutting up tomatoes. "And everyone."

Right on cue, Joe sloped into the room from the patio where he was supposed to be setting the table. "Any chance of another beer?"

Eleanor and Connie exchanged a smile, noting the sidelong glances that passed between Joe and their guest.

"Help yourself, love. And Georgie, you've done enough. Go and relax outside with Joe."

"Oh well, if you're sure, Eleanor."

"I'm quite sure. Here, take these glasses with you. I'll give Erika a call at the flat and tell her supper is nearly ready."

* * *

After the meal, Joe and Georgie helped to clear up while Eleanor took Connie back to Harold's. On her return, Eleanor found them on the patio chatting to Erika.

"This is all getting a bit girlie for me, so I'm off," said Joe. "Nice to see you, Georgie."

"Nice to see you, too."

"See you tomorrow, maybe?"

"Sure thing." Georgie beamed at Joe while Eleanor and Erika pretended not to notice the buzz in the air.

When Joe had gone, Georgie pulled out a packet of cigarettes. "Do you mind, Eleanor?"

"Of course not."

"Erika said you'd given up, right?"

"Don't tell Daniel, but I do still have a sneaky puff every now and then." Eleanor's face fell as she took the proffered cigarette. "Although I don't know why I'm saying that when we don't seem to be together any more." She hadn't spoken to Daniel for ten days and was feeling gloomy about their prospects.

Georgie patted her arm sympathetically. "I hope you manage to sort things out. From what I've heard, you suit each other really well."

Eleanor harrumphed. "That's what I thought, but obviously I was wrong."

"Nonsense. You'll sort it out, I'm sure you will. Anyway, tell me – how did you get together? When I was here a couple of years ago it looked like you were going to end up with Jim ... oops." Georgie grimaced and looked across at Erika. "I'm really sorry things didn't work out between you."

Erika shrugged. "*Que sera, sera.* It will make an interesting chapter in my coming-of-age novel. Anyway, I'd better be going too." She handed Georgie a key. "You come back whenever you're ready and I'll see you in the morning, boss."

After saying goodbye to Erika, Eleanor and Georgie sat down with a cup of tea.

"If you don't mind me asking – how exactly did you and Daniel link up? Connie said something about him discovering you hiding in the rose bushes?"

"You should never believe a word that woman says." Eleanor laughed. "I was in the camellias. And I wasn't actually hiding."

"No?"

"There was a misunderstanding, that was all."

Georgie tipped her head to one side, smiling. "Okay. Go on."

Eleanor thought back to that eventful evening. "I'd met Daniel a few times – he came to the book launch you helped us with, in fact – but I'd found him a bit cool. Not rude exactly, but a bit dismissive."

The air was fresher on the patio now, and they had put on sweaters over their tops. Eleanor cast her eyes up to the sky, which had taken on a purple hue. What had she felt back then? Two years on, she found it hard to reconcile the warm, loving man she had grown to love with the individual she had first met.

"Anyway, we hadn't hit it off and I didn't particularly want to run into him. So, I was dropping off a cheque for Malcolm at Daniel's house when I thought Dan was out." She remembered herself tiptoeing around the huge garden, peering at the glass walls that faced the sea. "Anyway – horror of horrors – I spotted Daniel through the windows of this amazing home and had to slip behind a bush ..."

"Right," said Georgie, who was clearly not convinced by Eleanor's logic. "But couldn't you have just said hello?"

"Probably. But by then I was in the shrubbery and there didn't seem to be an easy way to explain what I was doing uninvited in his garden. We weren't exactly best friends, you see. He'd been helping out at the shop while I was away and Connie had grown fond of him, but – oh, it's a long story."

Eleanor had come to accept that it was impossible to describe why she'd been hiding – which she had been – without sounding like a fool. And she was foolish, not wanting to bump into Daniel because she thought he was a grumpy so-and-so who didn't like her.

"So you hid in the garden to avoid him?"

"No, well – yes. And once I'd ducked behind the bush I couldn't come out because that was when I saw Daniel in the kitchen with a gorgeous young woman in his arms."

"How exciting!"

"It was a bit. I thought I'd caught him with the 'other woman'. Anyway, it turned out it wasn't anything that scandalous – it was his daughter Emily."

"And she saw you prowling around in her dad's garden?"

Eleanor winced. "Yup – it was pretty embarrassing. I might have got away with it if Bella hadn't trotted over to the window to say hello. As soon as Daniel saw the dog, he knew I must be there somewhere."

Georgie raised a hand to her mouth, trying not to laugh too hard at the ridiculous scene that Eleanor was painting. "Then what?"

Eleanor remembered extracting herself from the camellias and being introduced to Daniel's baffled daughter. "He invited me in, gave me a drink and some supper and that was it really."

"Go girl!"

"Oh, I don't mean it like that – we didn't pounce and rip each other's clothes off then and there."

"Shame."

"We had a drink and he cooked a meal for the three of us and we talked about all kinds of things." Eleanor felt wistful and sad when she thought about the promise of that evening. "And our friendship took off from there."

"Ah, but it's so nice there was a happy ending."

"I hoped we'd have a happy ending, but since he turned into a two-timing, two-faced weasel I'm not sure."

"He's a good guy, Eleanor. Don't write him off yet."

"I'm trying not to, but he's not making it easy. Anyway, that's enough about my love life. How's yours?"

Georgie looked down at her feet and shrugged. "Oh, there's no one special in my life at the moment."

"I'm sure you won't have long to wait."

"I hope you're right," she said with a smile.

Chapter 18: The Path to Romance

When Georgie had gone, Eleanor switched on the TV and curled up in her favourite armchair. She jumped channels, trying to find something to watch that would take her mind off her stalled affair. She tried to concentrate on a historical documentary but gave up and let the images blur in front of her eyes as her mind drifted back to that evening two years before.

After he'd found Eleanor hiding in the flowerbed, Daniel had given her a tour of the cliff-top villa that he and Freya had completely transformed by replacing one whole side of the building with glass so you had stunning views of the sea. He had been charming and welcoming, inviting her to enjoy a glass of wine and watch the sun set over the water.

She had found herself telling him how she had planned and refitted the shop. Despite her complete lack of experience, she'd been determined to make The Reading Room the kind of shop where visitors would feel welcome and everyone would find a book to suit them. She'd made some mistakes at first, and her stories of signings with authors who invited their entire families, drank the place dry and bought nothing made him laugh. Then there was the time when she'd invited the local playgroup and found chocolate fingers down the back of the sofa and sticky fingerprints all over her very expensive art books.

Daniel told her about his sailboat and they discovered a shared love for campervans and picnics. As they compared the things they liked to do and swapped stories about friends and families, Eleanor discovered that they had much more in common than she would ever have thought.

Before they knew it, it was dark and Daniel insisted on walking back down the lane with her and the dog. In the moonlight, they fell silent, listening to the rattle of shingle on the beach below and the occasional call of an owl in the trees that clung to the cliff face. She recalled feeling pleasantly tipsy after the bottle of wine they had shared and distinctly remembered the tingle she had experienced as Daniel's fingers grazed hers before he took her hand to help her over some uneven ground. It had felt nice, so she left it there as they picked their way down the lane.

Soon the path met the lower road, which snaked along the sea front. Here, the last few revellers were finishing off their pints outside the King's Head.

Under the streetlamps, Eleanor had felt a bit self-conscious wandering down the road holding hands with Daniel Pearce. She was relieved and a bit sad when their hands naturally fell apart. "I'm fine from here, really."

"Sorry – I'm the old-fashioned type. I have to see a lady to her door."

"Well, that's very gallant of you!"

As they reached the bottom of the high street, she suddenly felt bad at having made Daniel walk all the way to town only to climb back up the dark path on his own.

"Now I feel guilty at dragging you down here."

"Don't be silly. I quite often used to walk down to the beach with the dog at night. Since Freya took Crumpet away with her, I've not had an excuse to come here."

Eleanor understood exactly what he meant. Sometimes when she couldn't sleep, she would pull a thick pullover and jeans over her pyjamas and walk down to the sea front to breathe in the tangy air and clear her head.

"You could come anyway."

He laughed. "I could, but people would think I was a burglar if they saw me creeping around in the dead of night all on my own."

"True."

"It's a shame, because I love walking by the sea at night. Maybe I should risk arrest and come out anyway."

"Or get another dog?"

"Or find a friend who enjoys nocturnal strolls?"

"Well, that's always an option." She fumbled in her pocket for the key, hesitating before opening the front door to her cottage. The "coffee" moment had arrived and she wasn't quite sure what to do. All they had done that evening was talk, but something had changed between them and Daniel was no longer a customer's rather annoying son. She really liked him, and there was no way to avoid the inevitable question.

"Can I offer you coffee before you hike back up the hill?"

Daniel hesitated, perhaps sensing her slight reluctance. Smiling, he tilted his wrist towards a streetlamp and looked at his watch.

"Another time, perhaps. It's gone midnight and I need my beauty sleep."

"Is it really?" How had that happened? Could they really have been talking for six hours?

"Time flies when you're having fun, as they say."

Eleanor thought back over the evening. "I did have fun, thank you."

"You're very welcome. And you know I was serious about going out on my boat. If you'd like to, that is."

"I would like to, definitely."

"Great. Give me a call when you're free and we can fix something up."

"That would be lovely." She was conscious of grinning like an idiot and tried to sound a bit less eager. "I'll look at my diary and let you know."

And so they stood there half-smiling at each other in the dark, neither of them quite knowing what to do next. Eventually, Daniel bent towards Eleanor. "Well, goodnight then."

She turned her face, thinking that they would kiss each other chastely on the cheek, but Daniel pressed his lips gently against hers.

"Sleep well."

"I will now," she said, stretching up on her toes to kiss him back. They stood there in the dark for what seemed like ages, their lips together as Eleanor wound her arms around Daniel's neck.

Eventually he pulled away, gently stroking her cheeks and smiling. "I hope this means you'd like to see me again?"

"Yes please."

"Good. And you don't need to come via the garden next time."

She squirmed. "Sorry about that."

"All is forgiven," he said, kissing her again. "Call me?"

She nodded eagerly, all thoughts of trying to appear cool and nonchalant blasted away by his kisses. "I will."

* * *

That evening with Daniel seemed like such a long time ago. Finishing her tea, Eleanor sighed. Why were things never straightforward? Everything was going swimmingly until the blasted Widget person had turned up and dragged Freya back into their lives. She guessed that something would have tempted Daniel away from her sooner or later. God, now she was getting really paranoid.

The documentary had finished and the ruffs and codpieces had been replaced by a quiz show featuring lots of people she didn't recognise shouting at each other. Eleanor turned off the TV and headed for bed.

Peering at herself in the bathroom mirror, she was sure the wrinkles were multiplying daily. Her skin was definitely fading and her hair needed more than a little help from Clairol. She pulled at her lips and examined her gums. "Christ, my teeth will start falling out soon. If I was an Eskimo, they'd be putting me out to die in the snow," she muttered.

In the bedroom, her eyes came to rest on a photograph of her and Daniel at the beach that she kept by her bedside. She remembered how he had set the timer on the camera then dashed back to sit beside her. The photo captured their smiling faces against the dense blue of a summer sky.

It was now well over a week since she'd seen him. He had called a couple of times, but she had let the phone go to voicemail as she honestly didn't know what to say. Disappointingly, he hadn't yet left a grovelling message and she certainly had nothing to apologise for. She hadn't done anything wrong, for heaven's sake!

"Ratbag," she muttered to herself. If he was on Widget's side, she couldn't see how they would ever sort things out between them – even after Freya had gone back to London. "Everything is a bit poo, eh dog? Which reminds me."

She padded back downstairs in her jimjams with the dog at her heels and opened the back door so Bella could do a last wee before bed. Above her, the sky was full of stars and she could hear the flapping of sails in the harbour. Despite herself she smiled. The great wheel of fortune must turn in her favour again before too long.

Chapter 19: Unexpected Help

The next day, Connie and Harold were lined up to hold the fort so Eleanor could have a "strategy meeting" with Georgie and Erika in the office at the back of the bookshop.

It was going to be a bit of a crush because Joe had decided that this was the day to tidy up some shelves.

When Eleanor asked him if there was any particular reason why the spring-cleaning urge had come over him that morning, he just shrugged. "Nothing to do with Georgie being here, then?" It seemed clear that her son was smitten.

"I've got some time on my hands. That's all."

"If you say so, love."

At 11am, the team trooped in. Georgie had been on the phone and had already managed to fix up an interview for Eleanor with the eponymous DJ on "Chubby Jo's Breakfast Show" on the local radio. "I think it could be really useful."

"I'm sure, but does it have to be me?"

"Well, they really wanted Connie – since her TV appearance, I mean – but ..."

"But she's not to be trusted."

Georgie shrugged and smiled. "I'm not saying a word."

"Breakfast show. Does that mean I'll have to get up at 7am?"

"More like 6am, I'm afraid. They want to put it out early to catch the farmers and fishermen who are likely to be affected by the development."

Eleanor grimaced. "So long as I don't have to sit in a claustrophobic studio with that smoothie Bob Smart, I guess it will be okay. Do we have anything else lined up?"

"That's pretty much it at the moment, but it's early days."

"You're so upbeat, Georgie. Are you secretly wishing you hadn't taken this on?" asked Erika.

"No, not at all. I enjoy coming up with new campaigns. Although it would be nice if there was something a bit more ..." She waved her hands in the air.

"Newsworthy and exciting?"

"Yes, I guess that's it. We need something eye-catching and fun that the press can get excited about." She chewed the top of her pen thoughtfully. "Ideally something visual that will work on social media. You know, an item we can Tweet about and that people will want to share."

"What do you suggest?"

"Oh, I don't know. It needs to be original. Preferably with a big name attached, but that isn't essential."

Eleanor wracked her brain for useful contacts, but couldn't come up with anyone apart from a few authors who were interesting but didn't really come into the category of "fun".

There was a polite knock then Harold, who had just finished a storytelling session in the shop, put his head around the door. "Sorry to bother you, ladies, but I wonder if I could get to the kettle. I'm parched and Connie won't abandon her post at the counter."

"Sure, Harold, help yourself. If you can squeeze past us all."

"And how is the meeting going, may I ask?"

Eleanor sighed. "I'm afraid our protest hasn't had quite the impact we hoped for. In fact, I'm not sure whether 'Fingers' Widget even noticed it was happening. And we don't have anything quite sensational enough to ignite public interest."

"Never mind," said Georgie. "We've got the radio interview and something is bound to come to us if we bounce a few ideas around. It's a matter of being inventive. People love stuff that's funny or different in some way. Think about all those cat videos on YouTube and people doing mad things or falling over. Quirky beats celebrity every time."

Harold chuckled as he put tea bags into two mugs. "And what about the young lady with a beard who won the singing competition a few years back? She was exceedingly quirky."

Georgie nodded encouragingly. "Yes, that's an excellent example, but I'm not sure where we could find a bearded lady around here."

"Oh, you'd be surprised," said Erika, laughing.

"Failing that, Eleanor, do you have any local characters, rare flora and fauna? That kind of thing?"

"Well, my mother's dramatics caught the media's interest for a nanosecond, but I'm not sure there's much mileage in repeating it. I could ask our local diva Lavinia Threlfall to help, but she tends to be more interested in promoting her books and leading punters on vampire walks than anything else."

"There are vampire bats in Devon? I could do something with that."

"No, Georgie, I'm afraid not. It's all a figment of Ms Threlfall's fertile imagination."

"Shame. What about other wildlife?"

"Apart from the goats on the cliff walk?" said Eleanor.

"There's always Joe's mysterious reptile," said Harold.

Joe had been quiet until now and they all turned to where he was sitting on a pile of boxes, stroking the dog who had come in behind Harold.

"What's that, Joe?"

"Oh, it's just this thing I came across the other day."

Sometimes it seemed to Eleanor that her grown-up son was almost as inarticulate as his thirteen-year-old self had been. "Which was?"

"A lizardy-looking thing I saw when I was out with the dog. I mentioned it to Harold."

Georgie looked at Joe with a glint in her eye.

"Wildlife is good. I don't suppose there's any chance it was a rare or endangered species?"

"Probably both," said Joe, laughing. "Bella thought it was one of her squeaky toys and chased it. Luckily it shot under a rock at the edge of a pond or she'd have brought it home."

"Ah, yes," said Harold, thoughtfully. "I was going to do a bit of research into that. Remind me what it looked like, will you?"

"Well, I don't know much about newts and lizards and stuff, but I've never seen anything like it before."

"That doesn't matter," said Harold, encouragingly. "If it likes water, it's more likely to be a newt than a lizard – I'm a bit of an amateur herpetologist, you know. Can you tell us what you remember: size, colour, distinctive markings, that sort of thing?"

Joe thought for a moment. "It was about ten centimetres long …"

"That's about four inches in old money," said Eleanor, translating.

"And it had this thing like a fan on its head."

"That's what we call a crest. Do go on," said Harold. "Green or brown?"

"Neither. That's what was so odd. It was red. Oh, and it had these weird whiskers." Joe shook his head, caressing his own fuzzy chin. "And I hadn't been smoking, before anyone asks," he added with a grin.

Almost before Joe had finished speaking, Harold had abandoned his tea-making duty and was heading back into the shop. "This sounds most promising, but I must check something."

"Wow, it must be important for Harold not to finish making tea," said Eleanor, with a smile. "Mother will have his guts for garters."

After a few minutes, Harold came back into the office carrying one of Eleanor's second-hand treasures from the natural history shelves: a book on British wildlife published in the 1930s. Joe and Georgie exchanged amused glances.

"It may look ancient to you young things, but – if I'm right – you won't find anything about the newt you described in recent books."

"And why's that then, Mr Greaves?" asked Georgie.

"Because the particular species that I have in mind has almost completely disappeared from our shores."

Erika stood so Harold could sit down and rest the heavy book on his knees. He carefully turned the pages. "Minnow, moth, navelwort. Ah, here we are. Newt. So, do any of these chaps look familiar?"

Joe frowned as Harold turned the book around so he could study the illustrations. "They're all in black and white, so it's a bit difficult to tell."

"The young have no imagination these days," said Harold. "What about the body shape? And the tail?"

Joe pointed at one of the drawings. "I think it was that one there with the headgear and the whiskers, but it would really help to see it in colour."

"Good, good." Harold examined the illustration and read out the caption.

"Here we are. *'Triturus ibericus*, commonly known as the Iberian bearded newt. Once found in abundance in the south-western counties of England, but becoming rare.' And that was in 1937."

Meanwhile Joe had taken out his phone and was searching for images. "Got it! This is definitely what I saw, Harold. Do you see the funny beard thing?"

Erika, Eleanor and Georgie all crowded around the screen. Harold peered over his glasses. "What does it say?"

"Okay," said Joe, clicking onto a page about European wildlife. "It says 'Iberian bearded newt: so-called because it originated in the Balearic Islands.' Blah, blah. 'Thought to have been introduced into England by the Romans. Now found in small colonies in Mallorca, Menorca. Formerly common along the south-west coast of England, but now rare.'" Joe stopped reading and looked up. "Cool."

"Wow," said Georgie, peering over his shoulder. "It says that this thing is an endangered species."

Eleanor clapped her hands together with glee. "Harold, you're a genius."

"Thank you, my dear. I like to be useful."

"What about me?"

Eleanor ruffled her son's hair, making him squirm. "You are a hero."

"That's better," said Joe, with a grin.

"I'll call the council tomorrow and tell them what you saw. They'll have to stop the development now." Eleanor felt fired up and full of hope. "Oh, this is great. Don't you think so, Georgie?"

"Absolutely. Whatever happens, it could be the focus of a new publicity campaign to embarrass Mr Widget away."

Erika was standing by Harold's side looking pensive. "There's one slight problem."

They all turned and looked at her.

"Oh dear, really? What's that?" asked Eleanor, knowing that Erika was rarely wrong about anything.

"You don't have any hard evidence that this creature actually lives here." All of their faces fell. "I don't want to be negative, people, but I think that the environmental folk would take this more seriously if Joe had a photograph." She was, of course, right. As an ex-policeman, Erika knew a thing or two about evidence.

She turned to Joe, who shrugged. "Sorry to disappoint guys, but I didn't have time to take a picture before Bella scared the thing off."

"Never mind," said Harold, patting Joe on the back. "If you report the sighting and describe what you saw, I'm sure they'll take you seriously."

"Sorry, but I doubt that very much." Erika frowned. "The best thing would be for Joe to go back, find it and take some photos."

"I guess I could try."

Eleanor laughed. "It's a rare newt, love. You can't just go up there and expect to find it."

"Well, that's not entirely true," said Harold. "The *Triturus ibericus* is a creature of habit. If you can remember where you saw it, Joe, there's a possibility you might spot it again." He looked at his watch. "The male will be coming out to feed soon."

"But I've got plans this evening," said Joe, looking across at Georgie who smiled shyly.

"I don't mind going on a newt hunt," she said. "It will give me an appetite for the burger you promised me."

"If you youngsters are busy, I could go on my own," said Harold, nobly, "but it would help to know the precise spot where you saw the newt."

Eleanor stepped in before Joe could wriggle out of it. "We'll all go. That way we're more likely to spot something."

Sensing that a walk was in the offing, Bella stood and stretched. "Hmm, I'm not sure you should come," said her owner.

Harold frowned. "I'm afraid I have to disagree, Eleanor. I think we need her to take us to the exact same pond."

"Okay, but let's keep her on the lead."

"Splendid. But I must finish making that tea or Connie will be withdrawing my privileges."

"Ugh – too much information Granddad, I mean Harold."

"You can call me Granddad if you wish," he said, positively beaming. "In fact, that would make me very happy." He loved Connie and wanted nothing more than to be part of her family.

"Okay, Pops," said Eleanor. "Give Connie a cuppa then let's go."

And so Eleanor, Joe, Harold and Georgie trooped off up the hill. It was decided that Erika should stay to help Connie and close the shop.

On the cliff top, they spread out in a wide circle around the area identified by Joe – and Bella – as the likely place. They wandered around for a while, peering into ponds and under the heather, and lifting stones in search of the elusive newt. To begin with it was quite fun – like being on a nature walk at junior school – but after nearly two hours, their enthusiasm was fading.

"This is hopeless," said Joe. "The thing has obviously gone off somewhere." Reluctantly, Eleanor had to agree.

"You might be right. What do the rest of you think?"

Turning she saw that Harold was holding Bella's lead and that they were both totally focused on something a few feet ahead of them.

"No sharp movements," he hissed. "Camera, quick!"

Georgie tiptoed up behind Harold, hardly daring to breathe.

"Wow, I can see it!" She raised her phone slowly and clicked. "Got it!"

Joe and Eleanor had moved over and now they all crouched down, staring at the tiny red creature on the damp peaty patch of ground. After a few moments, a second smaller newt moved into the sunlight.

"A female!" exclaimed Harold. Georgie managed to grab another couple of pictures before a high-pitched yelp from Bella startled the newts, which shot off into the undergrowth.

"Never mind," said Eleanor, getting to her feet and brushing moss from her knees. "We now have our photographic evidence. Let's celebrate! You two don't mind if we join you in the King's Head, do you?"

"No, that would be cool," said Georgie, taking Joe's hand. "Wouldn't it?"

"Sure," said Joe, who could think of better ways to spend his evening than in a pub with his mother.

On the way to the King's Head they collected Connie and Erika, so they could share the news.

Once the drinks were in, they huddled in a group in one of the side rooms. "Best keep this under our hats for a day or two," said Erika.

Georgie nodded. "You're right. It'll give us time to come up with some new ideas for the campaign."

Eleanor described the moment of discovery to Connie. "I don't know who was more excited, Bella or Harold."

Harold scratched the dog behind her ears. "She's a splendid huntress, aren't you?" Bella gazed up at him adoringly, revelling in the praise.

Eleanor gave Harold a hug. "You and Joe are rather splendid, too. There's no way the development can go through now we have proof of endangered wildlife in the area."

"I'll drink to that," said Joe. "Cheers."

Chapter 20: Strategy Meeting

Georgie was at the head of the table with her notepad, all fired up by the discovery. "Okay guys. We need to decide on our strategy. I think we're all agreed that we have to talk about the environmental impact, the newt's role in maintaining balance in the local habitat, etc., but I'm worried the wildlife thing alone won't get us much coverage."

"Hmm. You're probably right," said Eleanor. "So what do you suggest?"

"I think we should sex it up a bit."

"Really?" asked Eleanor, nervously.

"Sure, why not? The newt thing is a good-news story, let's have some fun with it. But you're the campaign leader. What do you say?"

"I'm not sure how you're planning to make newts sexy, but if you can think of a way I'm happy to back you."

"Well, I think we need to organise a protest march for this Saturday with loads of people in newt costumes," said Georgie. "Oh, and false beards and anything Spanish to link in with the Iberian bit."

"Like what?" asked Joe.

"I don't know – fans, flamenco costumes, tortillas."

"I think you mean mantillas," said Erika.

"Sure, whatever."

Eleanor chewed her lip thoughtfully. "I'm not sure how many locals I'll be able to persuade to dress up like reptiles. We need people who don't mind making a bit of a show of themselves."

"I'll give our friends in the amateur dramatics club a call," said Connie, helpfully.

"Thanks, Mum," said Eleanor, thinking that some of the newts might be rather small and tubby. She turned to her son. "Do you have any mates who might help out?"

Joe gave his mother a look of pure horror. "Er, no!"

"Ah, come on," said Georgie, grabbing his arm and giving him a squeeze. "It'll be fun!"

"Okay, I'll ask them," said Joe, melting under Georgie's gaze. "But I'm not promising anything."

Eleanor looked across at her colleague. "What about you, Erika? Do you think any of your friends might be persuaded to join in?"

"Actually, there's a big gay and trans event in Barton at the weekend that a few of them are coming over for, so they'll be in a party mood. And possibly hung-over, but you can't have everything."

"I'm not entirely sure how the connection between gender rights and conservation is going to work," said Eleanor, nervously.

"Darling, you have to think outside the box," said Georgie.

"Exactly. Anyway, those gatherings tend to be more about fun and partying than politics – certainly for my mates, who'll turn up for anything so long as it involves beer and frocks."

"The more outrageous we can make this thing, the wider coverage we'll get."

Eleanor looked from Georgie to Erika. "I don't want to take advantage of you and your friends."

"Are you kidding?" said Erika. "You know what my crew are like – they're always looking for an excuse to glam up and misbehave. Half of them spend their working lives in suits, toeing the line and pretending to be ever so 'normal' – whatever the hell that means. Our march will give them a chance to let their hair down a bit."

"Well, in that case, give them a call and invite them to join the fun." Eleanor was beginning to feel quite optimistic about their event. "Let's tell everyone to meet in the village hall at 9am on Saturday with their flamenco gear or lizard costumes – or a wild combination of the two."

"I can't wait to see this. It's going to be awesome," said Georgie, gleefully.

* * *

Once word of Joe's discovery spread, the whole town went newt crazy. Eleanor and Georgie worked hard to get the high street traders involved: the bakery and teashop offered marzipan newts and cupcakes with sugar newts on top. The hardware store put out extra fishing nets and buckets – slightly confusing the conservation message, as Erika pointed out.

At The Reading Room, the window display featured all kinds of local wildlife and birds and two slightly wonky lizards knitted by Connie. Eleanor's café also had a range of newt cakes topped with lurid red and green icing to appeal to the kids.

Thanks to Jim, the *Combemouth Chronicle* was running a "Name our Newts" competition for the local children with "Wilma and Walter" and "Chico and Rita" the joint favourites at the bookies.

Eleanor had ordered in more books on British

wildlife and put a "Pin the Tail on the Newt" game at the front of the shop. She stood back to admire her work. "I think we've done as much as we can at this stage."

"Yup." Georgie smiled her approval. "Local awareness is growing. Let's hope the Newt Walk will spread the message even further afield."

"Do you think spreading the message will make any difference to Widget's plans?" So far, he had steered clear of the place and Eleanor wondered whether he was even aware of their campaign.

"Sure. Mr Widget is more likely to pull out of this project if it looks like spoiling his reputation nationally."

"But this is a man who built his career on being nasty. Will he really care?"

Erika nodded sagely. "At this stage in their career, old rockers like him want to get involved with kiddies' charities, pick up an OBE, open a kitten sanctuary – you know the kind of thing. Damaging the environment won't win him any friends."

Eleanor frowned. "Yes, what would his guru say about all the havoc his builders are about to cause?"

"Never mind his guru," said Erika. "It's what the Tryll Spigot fans and our planners think that really matters, and the photographic evidence is irrefutable. Combemouth has newts and that's going to throw a serious spanner in the works."

"I think we deserve a coffee and a bun," said Eleanor. She was heading for the office when Connie burst into the shop, blew kisses at everyone and sat down on the sofa with a satisfied look on her face.

"You look like the cat that got the cream."

"Something like that."

"Well, what is it?"

Connie opened her bag, pulled out a black and white photograph, and slapped it down on the table. "Barry Charm."

Eleanor picked up the photo and examined it. "A singer from the dark ages. So what?"

"Look again."

"It's signed to 'Connie with love'. Is it valuable? I've never heard of him."

"Look at that weak chin, the piggy eyes and the kink in the nose."

The assembled company studied the photo more closely.

"Mother, what are you getting at?"

Connie picked up the picture and waggled it in the air. "It's him!"

"It's who?"

"You can be dim sometimes." Connie sighed. "Why, our Mr Widget, of course. And I'm sure he'd prefer it if no one knew."

Erika picked up the photo and peered at it through her varifocals. "You're right. My wife was quite a fan of his back in the day. But it's not actually a crime to be a cheesy crooner, I'm afraid."

"That's true," said Eleanor, distracted by the unexpected mention of a wife.

"No, it's not a crime to wear pastel suits and sing ballads but it won't help his rock-and-roll image, either."

"I still don't see how this can help our cause, Mum."

Connie smiled and looked wicked.

"You're not suggesting blackmail, I hope?"

"Good heavens, no. How dramatic you are, Eleanor. I've thought of something much better."

"Oh dear."

"We'll show it to Bob Smart when he comes to town on Saturday and embarrass Mr Widget into submission."

Eleanor and Erika exchanged glances. "What do you think, Georgie?"

"I don't suppose it can do any harm. I'll dig into Barry Charm's background a bit and see what I can come up with."

"Why don't you leave it to me," said Erika. "I enjoy a little light detective work now and again. It's always nice to keep your hand in." With that, she headed off to the office computer.

"And I'll make the coffee," said Georgie following her.

Once the two of them were out of earshot, Connie turned to her daughter and whispered. "Did Erika say 'wife'? Did you know she'd been married?"

Eleanor shook her head a little sadly. "No. She's never mentioned it before." She thought she knew everything about her friend but now it came to her that she had never once asked Erika if she had been married or had children. "And I never thought to ask."

Chapter 21: Walking the Walk

It was Saturday morning and Daniel had a thumping headache. Tentatively drawing back the curtains in the bedroom, he peered down at the street, screwing up his eyes against the sunlight that bounced off the sea and pierced his aching brain.

Standing by the window, he saw a gaudily clad figure wiggle past who was joined by another who appeared from the bus stop. The street seemed to be filling up with striking individuals in skin-hugging dresses whose sea-green and blue sequins flashed in the light. More and more people appeared, some of them in long flouncy dresses wafting Spanish fans.

Daniel wiped his eyes blearily with the back of his hand, trying to focus on the unexpected sight. "Well, I'll be ..." He couldn't help smiling as he surveyed the scene. He'd seen the notices up in town about the Newt Walk, but he'd never imagined the campaigners would come up with anything as extraordinary as this.

He rubbed his chin, realising that he hadn't shaved for three days. With Eleanor no longer in his life, he was beginning to let things slide.

He pottered down to the kitchen and switched on the coffee machine, grimacing as he saw the overflowing sink, discarded takeaway containers and empty beer bottles.

"Damn," he said, sweeping his fringe from his eyes. "Got to get a grip." It wasn't like him to let things slip out of control: he was a man who needed order in his life. He dug under the sink for a bin bag, the act of bending down making his brain shift uncomfortably in his skull. He closed his eyes then focused on the mess around him, half-heartedly throwing tins into the bag.

He'd only managed three beer cans when there was a knock at the door. Probably the local Bible bashers. He ignored it, focusing instead on the comforting smell of his macchiato which was nearly ready. The bell rang followed by another sharp tap.

Sighing, Daniel threw down the bin bag and went to the door.

"Hello old chap. Coming out to watch the fun?"

His father was silhouetted against the bright white road, making Daniel squint. "Maybe not, Dad. I'm enemy number one around here at the moment."

"Don't exaggerate. I think the Widget rascal is number one." Malcolm looked thoughtful. "Having said that, I don't think you have many fans at The Reading Room. So, are you going to invite me in?"

Daniel shrugged and turned back to the kitchen, leaving his father to close the door behind him.

"It looks like you've had quite a party. Did you have a few friends round? Good for you."

Daniel felt a rush of affection for his father. Malcolm was no fool and it was pretty obvious that the mess in the kitchen was all Dan's and had built up over several days.

"Something like that," he said, knocking back the scalding-hot coffee in two gulps.

"You get yourself dressed and I'll see what I can do here."

"There's no need, really."

Malcolm had picked up the bin bag and was gingerly throwing rubbish into it. "Nonsense. I'll have it shipshape in no time. Go and put some clothes on."

Daniel was going to protest then looked down at his boxer shorts and sweaty T-shirt and closed his mouth. "I'll jump in the shower."

When he emerged freshly dressed, he found the dishwasher on, the surfaces clean and a pot of tea on the kitchen table. Several thick slices of mushroom were sizzling on the hob and Malcolm was buttering slabs of fresh bread.

Silently Daniel brought over a couple of plates and a bottle of brown sauce.

"Good timing," said his father. "Pour the tea, will you?"

They went out to the back of the house and climbed up a few steps to the sunny patio that gave them a view of the sea between the trees and sat together, eating on their laps. It's hard to be depressed for long when you have a pile of fluffy scrambled eggs and juicy field mushrooms on your plate and a mug of strong tea in your hand. Daniel felt his stomach relax, his head clear and his mood lift.

He knew that his father would never say how worried he was about his son – he didn't need to. Malcolm didn't make a habit of calling round and making him breakfast. The fact he had come over today was his way of showing concern.

"How do you fancy seeing the show?"

The thought of seeing Eleanor and not being able

to get close to her was unbearable. "I don't think so, Dad."

"What about a spot of fishing, then?"

Usually Daniel loved to go fishing with Malcolm, letting his mind wander as his eyes focused on the silvery flash of mackerel beneath their boat. They always threw the little ones back into the water and took a couple of fat fish back to barbecue in Malcolm's garden.

"Maybe tomorrow, eh? I think I need to stay in and sort things out here today."

Malcolm nodded. "Very well. You get yourself organised."

Later, when his father was leaving, Daniel gave him a brief hug. It wasn't their habit to embrace each other "like Italian footballers", as Malcolm would say. But Daniel was full of affection for the man who had taught him to sail and to fish, and today a handshake and a manly slap on the back were just not enough.

* * *

In the town, visitors and locals waved and cheered as a conga line of demonstrators progressed along the promenade. Georgie had arranged for a carefully choreographed "flash mob" to spring up between the high street and the sea front singing and dancing to Tryll Spigot's number one hit, "Thrash Love". It was quite a sight.

Joe, Jim Rowe and other supporters were in place and ready to capture highlights that were immediately uploaded onto YouTube and Twitter. Nearly everyone had made an effort to dress up, including Erika and two of her friends, who were especially eye-catching in their flamboyant outfits.

"Wow, you look the mutt's nuts." Joe reddened, and looked down at his feet. "Christ, sorry. That's probably not the best description in the circumstances."

Erika's friends guffawed and one of them – an impressive figure going by the name of Cherry who wore a blue beehive decorated with miniature bejewelled lizards – slapped Joe on the shoulder with a hefty arm.

"We've been called much worse than that in our time, don't you worry mate."

Across the road, Connie and her friends were in long red frocks with crests sewn down the back. As she turned around, Connie revealed a bushy beard. "What do you think of the outfit, Joe?" she asked, giving him a twirl.

"I'm liking the crest. Not sure about the face furniture."

Connie did look like an enraged gnome under the mass of terracotta fuzz. "I dyed it myself."

"If that doesn't keep the developers away, Gran, I don't know what will."

Just then the music started up again and all the protestors started to bob and weave like newts.

"Oh, I love this one," said Cherry. "It's from the Spigot's first album, *Verruca Patch*."

Georgie came over, looking gleeful. "This is perfect, guys. Keep doing what you're doing while I find Mr Smart from the telly."

Bob Smart thought that he had drawn the short straw having to attend Combemouth for a second demo, but his look of weariness disappeared when he saw the sinuous group of emerald- and ruby red-clad demonstrators headbanging to the music.

"Mr Smart, thanks so much for coming. We're sure it will be worth your while," said Georgie, flashing him her best and brightest Aussie smile. "We've got an exclusive story for you today."

"An exclusive? I doubt that when everyone with a mobile phone can broadcast their own version of events." The thought that, before too long, news presenters would be as endangered as the newts plunged him into gloom.

"Oh, this is a genuine exclusive, I can promise you that. Wait till you see the Charmettes!"

At that moment a group of women with identical black bobs wearing two-tone minidresses and shades appeared around the corner and began dancing to a catchy pop tune. They were followed by another group of people, each holding a large black and white photograph of Barry Charm on a stick. The woman leading the dancers went up to Bob Smart and his cameraman and smiled.

"Thanks for coming, gentlemen." Eleanor – for it was she – pointed at one of the photos. "Were you aware that Barry Charm is coming to live in Combemouth?"

"Phil, film this will you pal?" said Bob, slapping his colleague on the shoulder.

"Sure thing. Whenever you're ready."

Eleanor turned her apricot-coloured lips to the camera and pouted. "Everyone was so excited to have a genuine pop star moving in until we discovered that Mr Charm was none other than … Bill 'Fingers' Widget: wrecker of cliff paths and newt murderer!"

Behind the camera, Phil grinned. "Good stuff, love. This might actually get us onto the national news."

* * *

A little way from the excitement was a matte black Jeep with tinted windscreens that had been chosen to foil the paparazzi. One of the windows was wound down, and a pale figure in dark glasses could be seen staring out to sea. The chauffeur had pulled up under a tree at the entrance to a park, hoping that a nearby ice-cream van would distract passers-by from their presence. In fact, it had quite the opposite effect and people gawped at the ungainly vehicle as they scoffed Cornettos and 99s.

"Look Daddy, a tank," one small child was heard to remark before the window smoothly rolled shut.

In the back of the car were three people, one of whom was Bill Widget. What he wanted most of all was to stay hidden in the vehicle's dark interior, but his wife had other ideas.

"You have to go out there and face them."

Bill looked aghast. "You must be mad. They'll pull me limb from limb."

"Are you a man or a mouse?" Brenda Widget sighed, flicking back her immaculate red hair. She would have frowned, but her latest nip and tuck had made the display of emotion difficult. She began tapping at her phone, searching for photographs and news of the demo.

"You see?" On the brightly lit screen held out by his wife, Bill could see a protester holding up a placard. On it, was a picture of a newt with a red cross scrawled over it. Underneath, the text read "Widget = no wildlife".

"It doesn't look good, Brenda. They've got me down as a killer."

Sometimes she found her husband exasperating. "Remember who you are: you're a gold-plated, platinum-disc-selling celebrity and people love celebs. They'll be all over you."

Widget shifted uncomfortably in the back of the car. "You say that, duck, but I don't think I'm flavour of the month in Combemouth at the moment. Speaking of which, do either of you ladies fancy a choc ice?"

If he had offered his wife a plate of raw tripe, she couldn't have looked more disgusted.

"I'll take that as a 'no' then, shall I? What about you, Freda?"

My name's not bloody Freda was what she wanted to say but instead Freya gave Bill a tight smile. "That's very kind, but I'm on a diet."

"Suit yourselves. Vince, fetch me one will you? Or a raspberry mivvie if they don't have any choc ices. And one for yourself."

"Thank you, sir." The chauffeur tipped his hat and went off to Mr Whippy where his dark suit and peaked cap made him appear rather incongruous in a queue of people wearing shorts and flip-flops.

Freya had her phone out and was also looking for pictures of the protest. At the photo of a sign saying "No to Busty Bertha" she wrinkled her nose in disgust. "They are an ignorant bunch of yokels with no appreciation of art or design. And to think that I lived among these people for nearly twenty years."

There was silence in the car. Looking around, she realised that she was criticising the place her client had set his heart on and changed her tune. "But that lack of sophistication is all part of its rural charm, of course."

Brenda Widget rolled her eyes. She recognised Freya's skills as an architect, but she didn't like the woman one bit and was looking forward to getting the development built so they could get rid of her.

She turned back to her husband. "Judging by the stuff coming through on Twitter, this so-called demo is nothing more than an assortment of loons dressed up as amphibians and flamenco dancers. I suggest we go down there, you sign a few autographs, explain how much you're looking forward to living here, etc., etc. They'll be putty in your hands."

Bill leant across to his wife and kissed her taut skin, which reminded him more and more of his favourite snare drum. "You know I never say no to my manager."

"I should think not," she said, gently patting his wizened cheek. "But eat your choc ice first. We don't want you being papped with vanilla ice cream all down your front.

"Yes boss."

"And eat it outside – I've only just had this leather upholstery cleaned."

"Whatever you say, duck."

The women sat together in frosty silence for what seemed like ages while Bill and Vince lounged under a tree enjoying their ice creams and chatting about their days on the road in a beaten-up transit van. Brenda dozed while Freya checked her phone. How odd, she thought. There seemed to be a 1960s event going on in Combemouth today as well. She sighed and dropped the phone into her bag.

Bill had finished his choc ice and was wiping his

sticky hands on his trousers. Brenda emerged from the vehicle and handed him a wet wipe.

"Stand up straight and don't forget to scowl now and again. We want to win them over but we don't want people thinking you've gone completely soft." She gave his chin a quick wipe and looked him up and down. "Right. Let's do it."

The time had come for Bill to face the music.

Vince dropped the three of them at the top of the high street so they could walk down to the waterfront. Around them, people took photos and waved sugared newts in the air. Bill waved back and signed some newt posters, but largely obeyed orders and did his best to look menacing.

As they progressed, Brenda was getting increasingly annoyed by the number of people giggling, pointing and humming an annoying melody. "What the heck is that awful tune?"

"I don't know, but it does sound very familiar."

Approaching the prom, they caught sight of a glitzy gaggle of Newt Walkers just as Bob Smart spotted the trio and made a beeline for Bill.

"Give them a bit of a smile now," whispered Brenda, "and tell them how delighted we are to be here."

"Welcome to Combemouth, Mr Widget." Bob Smart thrust a microphone under Bill's nose. "Or would you prefer me to call you Barry?" With that he swept back his arm and the Charmettes hopped and twisted towards them.

The expression on Bill's face was one of stunned surprise as Bob Smart held up one of the Barry Charm photos to Phil's camera. Bill Widget's dark secret was out and Tryll Spigot's fans were about to discover that the band's leader had had an early career as a crooner. But after ten years of driving teenage girls wild with his boyish grin and cheeky smile, that career had ground to a halt. Times change and his brand of sentimental music had fallen out of fashion.

Fortunately for him, his manager (the third and current Mrs Widget) was not quite ready to throw in the towel. After "resting" for a year or so, Barry Charm the crooner was reinvented as Bill Widget, bass player and gravelly voiced front man of Tryll Spigot.

The band didn't have much impact until Brenda decided that they needed something to make them stand out from the crowd: snakes and bats had been taken by other groups, so the Spigot's gimmick became reptiles, which occasionally got them into trouble.

One particular show in Birmingham became notorious when a giant lizard escaped and took a chunk out of two of the ground staff. No one could ever explain how Kevin the iguana had managed to open the door to his own cage, but he was allowed to retire soon afterwards and Bill was forced to go on national television to apologise. Or rather, he stood silently in the background in his trademark dark glasses, snarling and looking distinctly unrepentant, while his manager explained that he was too upset to speak to the press.

After this unfortunate incident, the band's notoriety was guaranteed, stadiums were filled and every boy in the country – including Eleanor's son Joe – had a Trull Spigot poster on his bedroom wall.

In recent years, the band had been taking it easy.

Bill was spending more time in the States but his finances were starting to dwindle and his knees were going, so his advisors had suggested a move back to the UK for the benefit of his bank balance and his health. The plan was to get onto the festival circuit and Brenda had been spreading rumours that the band was being courted for Glastonbury.

So now Bill's heart sank as he saw his reputation as the hard man of rock set to crumble. Around him, newt protesters, Charmettes in minidresses and amused members of the public were all twisting and singing along to the tune they had heard earlier: Barry Charm's 1963 hit, "Be My Beach Baby, Baby".

As Bill's entire career flashed through his mind, Freya whispered to Brenda. "Why doesn't he say something?"

Pulling herself together, Brenda leapt into action to save her man. Fixing Bob Smart with a steely gaze she smiled. "That was all a very long time ago, don't you agree? What we're interested in talking about here today is the fabulous development that we're building and the huge benefit this will be to everyone in the area."

"Perhaps good for 'everyone'," said Bob, putting on his quizzical face. "But not so good for our wildlife, according to the inhabitants of Combemouth who have come out to protest today in such impressive numbers."

Brenda laughed and batted Bob coquettishly on the chest. "Your newts are not in any danger from us, and here's the architect to tell you why."

And with that she shoved Freya into the spotlight. "You'd better make it convincing," hissed Brenda. "We've got a lot riding on this."

Chapter 22: Sisterly Advice

After the protest, Eleanor crashed out in her front room with the family. Joe was hunched over his phone, scrolling through messages. Along with Phoebe in Canada and Georgie at home, he had done his best to spread the word about the march on social media. "This is good, Ma. The Newt Walk and the unexpected appearance of Barry Charm and the Charmettes have got us masses of hits."

"Really, Joe?" Eleanor peered myopically at the screen.

"Yes, really," said Joe. "The flash mob dancing is getting loads of views on YouTube and we've had people tweeting links from across Europe, the States and even Australia."

"Well done, that man," said Harold. "As I'm sure you know, Tryll Spigot have quite a following in the Antipodes."

"How do you know that, then?"

"Connie and I have been doing our research."

"This is interesting," said Joe, turning towards his mother. "Some guy in Sydney has asked us for your email address. Says he's got a question for you."

"It's probably spam," said Connie, who knew about these things. "Ask him to DM you instead."

Eleanor raised her eyebrows. "Does anyone know what she's talking about?"

"DM means 'Direct Message' in Twitter," said Harold, who had been on the same social media course as Connie.

"I'm glad you young folk have got to grips with all this twittering lark," said Eleanor, sardonically.

"Good idea, Gran," said Joe. "We don't want too many nutters emailing the shop."

"No, we've got plenty of those already. So, who's staying for supper?"

"Not us, love. We're going to the cinema," said Connie, taking Harold's hand. Eleanor gave her mother a kiss. "You kids have fun."

"We will. What are your plans?"

"Supper and an early night, I think. I'm shattered."

"Joe, you stay and help your mother, won't you?"

"Will do, Gran." He was always happy to enjoy some home cooking. "Hey, that Australian guy has got back to us already. He wants to know more about our newts."

Eleanor went over and sat by her son. "Let me see."

Reading over the short message, it didn't seem too mad. "Okay. Give him that email address of mine I never use, and we'll see what he comes back with."

"You could do this yourself, you know," said Joe, tapping away on his phone.

"No I couldn't. I was born too early in the twentieth century to develop the necessary thumbs."

Joe looked at his mother, not sure whether the thumb thing was a serious fact or not. "Okay. That's sent. Can we have supper now, I'm starved?"

"Sure. Now you've warmed up your digits, you can chop some onions for the spag bol. If you're not heading off to meet Georgie, that is."

"Nah. Maybe later."

"Okay. It's just you and me, then."

After the meal, Joe helped stack the dishwasher then headed out to the pub to meet his mates. Erika and Georgie had gone clubbing with Cherry, Lola and the gang, so Eleanor had the place to herself.

She filled her glass and went into the living room. Home alone with half a bottle of Rioja and a house full of books – bliss. She selected a slim hardback and curled herself up on the sofa. "Bliss," she said out loud. "Isn't it, dog?" Bella lazily wagged her tail in response.

Eleanor ran a finger over the jacket. "Very nice. And proper head and tail bands, too," she noted, examining the spine.

After ten minutes of reading, she glanced up at the clock. Nine o'clock. What would Daniel be doing? Damn it. Why did thoughts of that man have to creep into her head and spoil her mood? She was darned sure he wouldn't be thinking about her. She smoothed back the pages and tried to concentrate again. After a few more minutes, she carefully closed the book before less carefully tossing it onto an armchair.

It wasn't fair: the Newt Walk had gone far better than she had dared to hope and the last thing she wanted to think about now was her faltering relationship. Unable to concentrate on her book, Eleanor grabbed her laptop from its usual place on the floor and slumped back onto the sofa.

Once it had cranked into life, she scrolled through news pages and was gratified to see that their newts and the "Fingers" Widget/Barry Charm controversy were getting loads of coverage. Restless again, she shut off the machine and grabbed her phone. She really wanted to speak to Daniel, but he had to call and apologise first. Instead she called Jenna.

"Hi Sis, it's me."

"Hello. What's up?"

"I'm recovering from today's Newt Walk."

"It sounds like things are getting rather exciting in Trumpton." Jenna was a dyed-in-the-wool Londoner, and the fact that both her sister and her mother had actually chosen to live somewhere beyond the tarmac embrace of the M25 still baffled and amused her.

Eleanor, who was used to this, ignored Jenna's jibe. "If you're referring to our campaign, you're absolutely right. We're getting quite a lot of attention."

"You can say that again. I nearly choked on my Pinot Grigio when I saw you all on TV. Especially Mother in her ridiculous outfit. I mean, what was she wearing? She seemed to have half a deceased guinea pig glued to her face."

"She made it herself out of fun fur."

"Why does that not surprise me?"

"Our embarrassing parent is being interviewed by *Saga* next week, I've been on local breakfast radio and we've had the media camped on our doorstep all afternoon." Eleanor sighed. "It's been quite exhausting, but I think we're winning the battle."

"But that's great."

"It is, really it is."

"So ... ?"

"So, what?"

"So why are you sounding so miserable?"

"I'm not miserable. It's just ... Oh, I guess everything is a bit of an anticlimax after this morning."

Jenna knew her sister well and could tell she wasn't happy. "Anything else?"

"And I've decided that I'm crap at relationships."

"Wow – hang on. I think I need a top up before we carry on with this conversation."

Eleanor lay back on the sofa, listening to the sound of her sister pouring a generous quantity of wine into her glass.

"Okay, I'm ready. Tell all."

"Is it just me, do you think?"

"Is it just you what?"

"Who can't keep hold of a man. What's wrong with me?"

"Well, apart from being slightly pissed and feeling sorry for yourself, there's nothing dramatically wrong with you."

One of the reasons for ringing Jenna was that she never pulled her punches.

"That's sweet of you to say …"

"You're welcome."

"… but Daniel seems to have gone back to his wife and Alan got so bored that he had to leave."

"The Daniel situation is complicated, but Alan didn't simply get bored of you. There had to be someone else."

"Oh, I'm not sure Jenna."

"Listen: no man leaves a loving wife, two gorgeous kids and a perfectly okay marriage unless he has something ten times better already lined up."

"Thanks a lot! You make me feel really special."

"I don't mean it like that. Just better in his tiny, blokey mind. Not better in reality, obviously."

Eleanor pursed her lips, but before she could

answer Jenna continued. "Believe me. It doesn't happen. Men sit tight and put up with all the dull stuff until they're sure they've got a nice comfy landing lined up."

"And how exactly do you – Mrs Happily Married Forever – know all this?"

Jenna shrugged. "I am wise beyond my years. And I have seen an awful lot of my friends go through it."

"I guess by your mid-fifties you will have achieved some kind of wisdom." It seemed only right that there should be some compensation for getting old.

She could hear Jenna take a slurp of wine. "Think about it. Who do we know who's been dumped by a husband who didn't have a gorgeous young woman waiting in the wings? Anybody?"

Eleanor frowned. It was true that examples of couples separating simply because they had "grown apart" were as rare as hens' teeth, but there had to be some.

"What about Anne and Pete?"

"You think it was a coincidence that Pete married the exact same Latvian girl who had been their au pair six months before?"

"Okay. Fair point." Eleanor searched her memory, flicking through all the divorced couples she could think of.

"June and Trevor?"

"Hmm, I think she went off with his best friend."

"Ouch, nasty. Okay, I've got one: Audrey and Richard. I don't think he left her for a younger woman."

"True, but Richard very quickly found himself a boyfriend and they're getting married. So it's the same deal, really."

"I must send them a card." Eleanor sighed, unwilling to admit defeat. "However, I still don't believe Alan was seeing somebody else for the simple fact that he would probably have told me all about her. You know how straightforward he is about everything."

Jenna grimaced. "Yes, emotional intelligence is not one of his strong points."

"You're being unkind, Sis."

"I may be wrong," said Jenna, with a shrug. "I'm only saying what I think." They were both quiet for a moment, pondering the mystery of men.

"And what about Daniel cosying up with his ex?" asked Eleanor.

"From what you've said he hasn't gone back to her, El. They had lunch and she told him some stuff that he didn't share with you. End of."

"You're really not much use for a rant tonight."

"I enjoy a rant as much as the next woman but, in this case, I think you're perhaps overreacting."

"That's what Erika said."

"And she's right."

"Rubbish! Dan has been a complete weasel, backing that woman instead of me." Eleanor paused to top up her glass. "And did I tell you that she actually had the bloody nerve to turn up here?"

"What? Cruella returned to the scene of the crime?"

Eleanor couldn't help giggling over their nickname for Freya, earned when she had first taken Daniel's dog away and then dumped the terrier back with him when she couldn't fit poor Crumpet into her London life.

"Yes, she turned up with the dreadful Widget man and his terrifying wife and talked a load of rubbish about the eco-credentials of the development and how it won't damage the environment, blah, blah. And did I also tell you that bloody Daniel took her to the Lighthouse? My favourite restaurant? With two Michelin stars? I mean, can you believe it?"

"You did tell me – several times – and, yes, I can believe it. They were married for donkey's years, El, and they do have a daughter ..."

"And a super-stressed Border terrier ..."

"I can see that it might seem a little insensitive for him to back his ex-wife in the circumstances, but I'm sure Daniel will see sense eventually."

"Why are you being so understanding about all this when I want a proper moan?"

"Because I don't want you getting overwrought. And my ear is getting hot and the wine's run out."

Eleanor looked at the empty bottle by her feet. "Mine too. It was a bad day when Joe grew out of Ribena and discovered Rioja."

Jenna chuckled. "That's kids for you. So, feeling any better now?"

Eleanor didn't know why, but things tended to look a bit less glum after a conversation with her sister.

"I guess I'll survive to fight another day."

"You will. Now get your beauty sleep. You never know what gorgeous hunk might cross your path tomorrow."

"True. And I wouldn't want to run him over in the campervan."

"Night Sis."

"Goodnight Jenna. And thank you."

"You're welcome. Look, I'll call you in a couple of days to see how you're feeling."

276

"Oh, I'll be fine."

"I'm sure you will, but I'll call anyway. That's what big sisters are there for."

* * *

Eleanor was pleased that the next day was a Sunday and her day off. The effects of the Newt Walk and an excess of red wine had left her feeling a bit dull around the edges. She decided to have a sorting-out day at home. Since the campaign has started, she'd had hardly any time to herself. In a way it was a blessing because it distracted her from Daniel.

She set to with the piles of paper on the kitchen table and even dusted some of her books. After an hour of domestic duties, she made a cup of tea and went out into the garden with her laptop and a sneaky fag. Erika made sure they kept on top of work stuff, but Eleanor had been neglecting her own private emails.

One of the new messages made her laugh out loud. It had to be a joke. She picked up the phone and rang her son.

"Joe, you know the Australian guy you gave my email address to last night? The one interested in our newt."

"Oh yeah. What about him?"

"He's sent me a message," she scrolled down the screen. "He's a herpetologist and wants us to go to a conference."

"Say that again?"

"He wants us to talk about your critter to a load of newt experts."

"You're having me on."

"No I'm not." She clicked on a link at the end of the

message which took her to the conference website. "This looks super impressive. I think we should go."

"We? Both of us?"

"Well, he says me, but you're the person who discovered the thing."

"No way! Attend a conference? I couldn't face it, Ma. I had enough trouble with exams at school. I'd be scared sh ..."

"Joe!"

"Sorry. I mean I'd be scared to death if I had to stand up and talk to a load of beardy academic types."

Eleanor laughed. "Beardy academics and beardy newts."

"But you should go."

"Me? Oh, I don't know."

"Why not?"

"Because I know nothing about newts either."

"I guess the Aussie guy knows that. Would they pay your fare?"

Eleanor nodded. "Yes, it says here that they would pay my fare and two nights' accommodation."

"Wow, Australia's a long way to go for two nights!"

"It would be Joe, but that's not where the conference is being held."

"Right. Don't tell me – London."

"Nope, a bit further afield than that."

Eleanor looked at the description of the conference venue and smiled. "Actually I think I might go after all."

Chapter 23: Time for a Trip

A day or two later, Eleanor had a call from Jenna who wanted to check on her sister's state of mind after all the excitement of the Newt Walk had died down a little. "I've thought of something to cheer you up," she said.

"I don't need cheering up, Jenna. We're leaving the planners to mull things over for a few days, but the word on the street is that they're bringing in more experts to advise them on the wildlife conservation aspect of Widget's nutty scheme."

"That's exciting news for the local reptile population, but I think a break would do you good. We haven't been away since our mission to France to find Christophe, and we promised each other then that we'd have another holiday together. And now that Mother has got Harold in her life – who just happens to have a daughter with a bijou hotel – I thought we could invite ourselves down there."

One of the many things that their mother and Harold had in common was offspring who had fled England for France although, unlike Eleanor, Rachel Thompson – Harold's daughter – had stayed put and made a life for herself there. It had all sounded rather blissful until the husband dumped her for the kids' dance teacher. Rachel had coped by turning the family home into a guesthouse complete with chickens, olive trees and an assortment of eccentric guests. Apparently, she now had a new man in her life and everything was going swimmingly again.

Jenna continued. "I gather that as extended members of Harold's family we have an open invitation – assuming there's room. From the photos I've seen, it looks very bijou and charming, and handily close to Monsieur Rumpy Pumpy, too, I gather."

"Yes, Pelette isn't far from Christophe and Rosanne's place," said Eleanor, ignoring Jenna's alternative name for her long-lost boyfriend.

"That's if Rosanne hasn't seen sense, dumped him and gone off on her own. The man was obviously a five-star love rat."

Eleanor smiled guiltily as she remembered the illicit kiss she had shared with her ex-lover after she and Jenna had tracked him down to the restaurant he ran with his wife in Chevandier two years before.

Once he'd recovered from the shock of meeting them, Christophe had invited the sisters to visit the family vineyard where they had enjoyed a memorable lunch with the Vauban clan. After a delicious meal, Christophe and Eleanor had gone for a walk on the hillside above the farmhouse. And, despite the fact he was married to Rosanne, Eleanor had let him kiss her. More than that, she had returned his kiss with the deep emotion which had been reawakened in the days since she had decided to find him again.

It was a mad thing to have done: to sit, kissing under a tree like a couple of teenagers. But it had been rather wonderful.

Eleanor sighed dreamily. "You may not approve, but *je ne regrette rien*."

"Slapper."

"It was one kiss, Jenna, and I blame you entirely!"

"Me? Why do I get the blame – you were on your own with him under that tree."

"I might have been, but we only met because you dragged me into his restaurant in Chevandier. I would have been happy to see Christophe from afar, just to know he was okay."

"Oh pleeeeze!" Jenna snorted down the phone. "What a load of nonsense. We weren't going to travel all the way across France so you could spy on the man from across the road. You wanted to speak to him – all you needed was a bit of a shove in the right direction."

"I rest my case."

"Yes, okay El. I suppose I was guilty in encouraging you to speak to him …"

"Thank you. "

"But I didn't *make* you kiss him." Eleanor was going to protest but Jenna continued before she could get a word in. "The man is gorgeous and I might have succumbed to a cheeky snog myself in those circumstances, but he's obviously not to be trusted. You only have to look at the way he behaved with you. Just think – if I hadn't dragged you away, you could still be on that vineyard drinking vin rouge and getting plump on foie gras and stinky cheese."

"Yup, it would have been horrible."

"So what do you think? Fancy another trip to the Rhônes-Alpes to see how the Vaubans are getting on? It would make up for a forthcoming break with my husband that I'm not particularly looking forward to."

"Why on earth wouldn't you want to go away with Keith?"

"Because Kiff has planned one of his birdwatching tours. I've said I'll go, of course, but I don't really fancy traipsing around for days in search of lesser-spotted snipe or whatever it is twitchers get up to."

"So how are things with you and Keith, anyway?"

"We're absolutely fine – and we've got proper hols organised for later in the year before you ask – but never mind that. What do you think about you and me catching the TGV south again? It would take my mind off warblers and yours off newts."

"I'd love to, but I have to go to a conference in Spain."

"You *have* to go to Spain? Poor thing. Spill the beans: it sounds rather exciting."

"I'm not sure that exciting is the right word. It feels scary to me." The thought of addressing a room full of academics was pretty daunting and, by the time she had given Jenna a run down of what was involved, Eleanor was in two minds about going at all. "I'm not sure I can face it. I mean, what do I know about reptiles?"

"Don't worry so much. They know you're not an expert – that's what they're all there for. I would guess that they simply want to hear how Joe discovered the little blighters and see some photos of the local ladyboys in their sequins and flamenco gear. Then they'll take you to dinner somewhere Spanish and marvellous and wave you a fond farewell. What's not to like?"

"Oh, I don't know. Mallorca is supposed to be beautiful, but I can't say I'm really looking forward to it. I just wish someone was coming with me."

She had hoped that Erika might join her, but she had been reluctant to go for reasons Eleanor hadn't yet fathomed.

"Mallorca, you say?"

"Yes. The conference is at some amazing-looking *parador* in the centre of the island."

"Well, I might be able to help you out."

"You don't say. And how's that exactly?"

Jenna laughed. "As luck would have it, Mallorca is where Kiff is going birdwatching. So if you're on the island as well, I could leave hubby with his buddies for a few days and join you. If you'd like me to, that is."

"That would be great – if you're sure. I'm only going for a couple of nights and I won't have much time during the day."

"So stay a few more days. I can do some twitching with Kiff while you do your thing, then we can have dinner and maybe do some shopping and sunbathing when you're free."

"Apart from the shopping that sounds like a great plan. But what about Keith?"

"The darling man will be delighted to have some time with the other bird enthusiasts, believe me."

"Well, if you're sure he wouldn't mind being left to his own devices …"

"Of course not. It'll be fun to stay somewhere gorgeous and live *la vida loca* without the men folk. And it will do you good to get away from this business with Daniel."

"Ha, you're right there." Eleanor ran through the practicalities in her head. "I guess I could ask Mother to help Erika in the shop for a bit longer."

"She'll love it. You know she will."

"Okay. Let me check with my backup team, but in theory we're on."

* * *

Later that afternoon, Eleanor popped round to see her mother. Over tea and warm scones, she told Connie she had a favour to ask. "Could you and Harold help Erika with the shop for a few days? Jenna wants to meet me in Spain after the conference and have a bit of a break."

"Shouldn't you be having a holiday with Daniel?"

"With that Judas!" Eleanor harrumphed and banged her cup down on the saucer, causing the dog to lift an ear. "I'm not going anywhere with that man. In fact, I'm shocked you would even suggest it after everything that's happened recently."

"I'm as concerned about the newt situation as anyone, but you can't let a few lizards come between you and true love."

"Says the 'Newt Queen' herself."

Connie tutted modestly, pleased at the reference to her new persona in the *Chronicle*. "I was – I am – happy to help you fight this development, but you mustn't let it permanently damage your love life. I would hate to see you on your own."

The words "again" and "at your age" hung unspoken in the air, but Eleanor was aware of her mother's fears that she would end up alone and unloved in her dotage.

"It's his decision. If Daniel wants to back this ridiculous scheme, that's up to him. Anyway, could you do a few more shifts in the shop?"

"Of course I can." Connie smiled sadly and patted

her daughter's hand. "Just make sure you think about things while you're away. One of you has to figure out how to get your lives back on track, whichever way the planning decision goes."

"I don't intend to give that man, his ex-wife or their ridiculous scheme any thought at all while I'm away." Seeing her mother's worried expression, she softened. "Okay, okay. I might give it a little bit of thought."

"Good girl. And if I see Daniel, I'll give him a piece of my mind. It's time for him to decide who and what he wants."

Chapter 24: Off to Spain

Eleanor couldn't remember the last time she'd caught a plane on her own. It was ridiculous really, but for years she'd gone everywhere with Alan and the kids. Since then, when she'd travelled abroad it had been with her sister or other friends. She felt a wave of sadness wash over her and decided to push Daniel to the back of her mind. As for her sister, Jenna was already in Mallorca and they had arranged to meet up in a couple of days' time.

She looked at her fellow passengers in the busy departure lounge, trying to spot other newt people but there were no obvious candidates. She felt a tad guilty watching the young couples with infants struggling with buggies and hoped they wouldn't sit directly behind her.

Shuffling onto the plane, Eleanor was surprised and pleased to get two whole seats to herself, which she soon covered with her bag and coat. Once airborne she took out her notebook and pen, intending to go over her notes for the talk.

"Can I get you anything from the trolley, madam?" A young woman with lank hair and a bored expression parked her chariot next to Eleanor's seat. Growing up, she had thought that being an air hostess must be the most glamorous job in the world, but things were not what they used to be.

Was it too early in the day for a G&T, she asked herself. Of course not. "I'll have a gin and tonic and a Sunburst Bagel, please."

"Euros or sterling?"

"How much in sterling?"

"That will be £13.85."

"Good grief," muttered Eleanor under her breath as she gritted her teeth and handed over the cash. "Any chance of ice and a slice, Amanda?"

Amanda looked affronted that anyone would actually address her by the name on the badge affixed to her nylon-clad chest.

"Raymond – the passenger wants ice and a slice," she said, tapping the figures into her calculator and sighing wearily.

The steward at the other end of the trolley gave Eleanor a tight smile as he handed over a bag of scalding hot bread and a lukewarm tonic with one tiny ice cube. "I'm afraid the citrus garnish is really for business class passengers only, but I'll see what I can do."

"Very kind. And my change?" asked Eleanor as the trolley disappeared up the aisle at speed.

Sighing, she decided to have a quick look at her notes as she waited for the bagel to cool enough to eat without it removing the skin from the inside of her mouth. She looked around the plane to see what other people were doing: there were a few passengers who looked as though they were travelling on business like her. On business! That sounded very grown-up, she thought, taking a sip of the clear tangy liquid in its plastic cup. It might not have been chilled to perfection, but there was still something quite decadent about a G&T mid-morning.

"Citrus garnish?"

Raymond had returned and was holding out a polystyrene plate with one paper-thin slice of lemon on it. It's the thought that counts and Eleanor thanked him extravagantly. She managed to squeeze two reluctant drops out of the fruit and dropped the mangled slice into what remained of her drink. No change from her £15 had yet appeared, but you can't have everything.

Flying was grim. The last time she had been abroad was when she and Jenna had taken the train to the southeast of France because Eleanor had been over-whelmed by an urge to find out what had happened to her first love. Thinking back, it had been a slightly mad venture. She tried to remember her emotions at that time: it was before she had got together with Daniel and, although the shop was going well and everything was basically okay with her life, she had felt there was something missing. She had needed to answer some "what-ifs".

She knew it was ridiculous: she and Christophe had only been together for a few months, but it was a passionate affair that had helped to make her the person she was today. And what was it Rod Stewart said – "The first cut is the deepest"? Except that she hadn't been cut. She had upped and left France with barely a backward glance, little knowing that she wouldn't feel anything like the pure uncomplicated love she had felt for Christophe until the birth of her children.

Glancing through the streaky plastic window at the clouds below her, she smiled at the recollection of the journey with Jenna. Although they had found

Christophe – and his German wife and gorgeous family – the visit hadn't answered the big question: would they have survived as a couple if she hadn't made the decision to go back to England? Who knew? There was no denying that she had found the grown-up Christophe just as appealing as he had been in his twenties and it was gratifying to discover that he still found her attractive, but she couldn't regret her life with Alan and the twins.

Harold's daughter Rachel and her children had been to Combemouth the previous summer before they went north to see their other grandparents in Yorkshire. Hearing about Rachel's life running the guesthouse in Pelette had briefly set off the "what -ifs" again in Eleanor's head. But by then she was in an exciting relationship with Daniel, which meant she could safely file Christophe under "Things I did in another life" where he belonged.

"Damn it." The thought of Daniel and the mess things had got into dented her good mood, which was not improved by the rubbery cellophaned mass that masqueraded as food. Peeling back the plastic, she managed to chew her way through about half of the bagel before giving up and closing her eyes for a brief gin-induced snooze.

Before she knew it, Amanda and Raymond were bustling up and down the aisle, prodding sleeping travellers into upright positions, folding up tables and whisking away rubbish. Eleanor yawned and stretched, suddenly nervous again at the thought of what lay ahead.

Down on the ground, she collected her case and exited customs, intrigued by the holiday-makers around her. It was her first visit to Mallorca and she wasn't quite sure what to expect. Milling around was a group of chubby lads in *Tarzan* costumes and another lot dressed like something from *The Flintstones*. There also seemed to be rather a lot of buxom women in tutus and pink hot pants. Everyone was either pale and pasty or looked as though they had just escaped from a pressure cooker, depending on whether they were arriving or departing.

She wheeled her way to the information desk where she had arranged to meet Dr Mitcham from Sydney. She was expecting a Crocodile Dundee looka-like, so she was a tad disappointed to be met not by a strapping Australian, but by a little stocky chap. At least he had an open, friendly expression and was wearing khaki shorts.

"Dr Mitcham?" she asked, unnecessarily, to the man holding a board with her name on it.

"Call me Steve." His smile was warm and welcoming, making Eleanor feel immediately at ease. "G'day and welcome to Mallorca. Let me help you with the suitcase."

"Okay, thanks."

As they walked to the car, they chatted about her trip. Eleanor had worried that a newt expert might be hard to talk to, so she was relieved to find that Steve was easy company.

"So where exactly are we going?"

"Ah, you'll love it." Steve handed her a map and stabbed at a spot in the middle of the island. "Our conference is being held in this old place at the edge of a dinky town up in the mountains. It's a great venue."

Nowhere near the beach, then, thought Eleanor, who had actually bought a brand-new swimming costume specially for the trip.

As if reading her mind, Steve traced his finger down the coastline. "The great thing about this island is that it is really small and easy to get around. The beaches along here are pretty good." He grinned at her. "It's not Bondi, of course, but it's a nice enough place to get a tan."

"That will do me just fine."

As Steve drove out of the airport towards the city, they fell silent. The windows were rolled down and the air was warm as it bustled around the car. For a while they drove alongside the ocean and Eleanor breathed in the tangy aroma of the sea.

Once in the city, they drove up wide tree-lined avenues and Eleanor gazed at the brightly lit shops and busy pavement cafés. It all felt wonderfully continental and alive. After a few minutes, Steve spoke again. "It's an interesting place. I hope you have a chance to look around after the conference."

"I will – I've got someone joining me for a few days afterwards."

"Your husband?"

"My sister, actually."

Steve looked at her with a smile. "Sorry. Scientists are inquisitive by nature. And Aussie scientists are the worst."

"That's okay," she said, laughing. "What about you? Isn't it a long way to come for a few days?"

"Yeah, it would be, but I've got other things lined up in Europe before I head back Down Under. Meetings, libraries – that kind of thing."

After journeying through the centre of the city then the suburbs, Eleanor noticed that the buildings began to get fewer and fewer as they crossed a broad plain and headed towards the mountains.

Steve still had both the windows wound down. "I hope you don't mind, but I can't stand air-conditioning in cars."

"Me neither. I much prefer 'real' air and this scenery is divine."

"It gets even better in a minute."

As the road climbed, they passed groves of gnarled olive trees, and fields of almond and fruit trees. Eleanor closed her eyes, enjoying the wafts of pine coming from the trees as they went further into the hills.

Eventually they left the main road and drove towards what looked like an overgrown village perched on a hill top. An even narrower track wound around the hillside, suddenly ending in front of what could only be described as a palace.

"Not bad, eh?"

"Wow! I thought academics spent their whole time in libraries – not that libraries aren't nice places, you understand. But this is …" she was speechless for a moment, searching for a word that would sum it up. "Stunning."

Steve smiled. "Yeah, they've done damn well this year. We've had the conference in some shitty places to be honest, but this one is quite something."

He was a gentleman and insisted on carrying Eleanor's embarrassingly tatty suitcase into the palace's cool marble hall. He left her gawping at the chandeliers and high ceilings as he checked her in, then took his guest up to her room and handed her its heavy old-fashioned key.

"I'll leave you here to prepare for your talk this evening." He cocked his head to one side and smiled. "You okay?"

Eleanor chewed her lip nervously. "I am anxious about the talk, to be honest."

"Ah, don't be."

"I've made a few notes." She opened her handbag and rummaged around in it, failing to find the notebook that she knew for sure was in there somewhere. "Sorry – this is a bit out of my comfort zone, as they say. I've not had much to do with academics before. I'm a bookseller so I've met them at literary events, of course, but I've never spoken at a conference." Fearing that she was burbling, Eleanor decided to shut up.

Steve shrugged. "You'll be fine – it's only a research symposium anyway."

"Which means?"

"Which means it's a group of us newt freaks who get together once a year to discuss what's happening in the world of amphibians, bitch about the colleagues who aren't here, present new work to each other and have a few beers in a decent venue."

"I suppose that doesn't sound too threatening."

"It really isn't, you know? And to be honest we've invited you as light relief – if that doesn't sound too patronising." Seeing Eleanor grimace slightly, he checked himself. "What I should have said is that you're our 'treat' at the end of the conference. All the serious work has been done and you're our final speaker. The idea is that I'll ask you questions about your photos and you'll tell me how your son discovered the newts and the impact the discovery has had on your community. No pressure. Then we'll have a couple of drinks, go to dinner and generally have a nice time. Okay?"

She nodded, feeling encouraged by this. "It doesn't sound too scary put like that. Thank you."

"Right. Good." Steve looked at his watch. "The delegates are all out on a field trip at the moment – have you eaten?"

"Only a nasty bagel."

"I've got to join the others, but order anything you like in the restaurant, have a wander around, make yourself comfortable and I'll come and find you at 7pm for your session. How does that sound?"

"Perfect, thanks."

"And have a decent lunch. Things get started late here, so we'll have drinks at 9pm and dinner about midnight."

"Thanks for the warning. I'll make sure I have pudding."

"Good stuff. Well, *hasta la vista*."

"Bye Steve."

Chapter 25: The Combemouth Two

After Steve left her, Eleanor unlocked the door to her room and thought there must have been a mistake: as well as two enormous double beds, there was a separate sitting room and a huge bathroom. Best of all were the glass doors that opened onto a slender balcony overlooking a central courtyard containing full-grown palm trees.

"Wow!" A low whistle escaped her lips: this was quite something. "Not bad at all."

She had a quick shower and lunch, then looked around the small hill town where it seemed that everyone was asleep: all the green wooden doors and shutters were tightly closed against the heat and there were no cars on the narrow roads.

After walking up and down a few deserted streets, Eleanor decided to join the rest of the population in a siesta and headed back to her elegant suite. Stretched out on the bed, she grabbed the conference pack that had been left out for her. Leafing through it she experienced a childish thrill from seeing her own name printed in the programme as Guest Speaker under an item entitled "The Combemouth Two: the latest discovery of Iberian bearded newts (*Triturus ibericus*) in the southwest of England". She was less thrilled by the list of delegates, which contained an alarming number of professors. She'd been okay talking to her new friend that morning, but she felt slightly sick at the thought of being grilled by actual professors.

In the end, she needn't have worried. Steve was as good as his word and led her gently through the facts of Joe's discovery. They then had a conversation as he asked her questions about the photographs and the video that Georgie had managed to capture on her phone the afternoon of the newt hunt. Steve had also got hold of some images from the Newt Walk, which raised a few eyebrows and led to a lively discussion about innovative ways to engage the community in campaigns to preserve wildlife.

When Steve brought the session to an end, Eleanor was buzzing and would have happily gone on for another hour.

"I hope you'll join me in thanking our speaker. I'm sure she'll be happy to answer any further questions you might have in the bar." When the applause had died down, Steve gently took her by the elbow. "The talk was great, Eleanor."

She beamed at him. "Really? Do you mean it?"

"Absolutely. I wouldn't say so otherwise. Everyone loved it. Now, are you ready for the bar? I'll introduce you to everyone properly, then you'll know who's who when they ask the difficult questions they've been saving up."

A look of terror passed over Eleanor's face. "They won't, will they?"

"Jeez, only joking!"

She laughed, slightly hysterically. "Sorry – I think I'm overexcited."

"Why don't you take a breather and come down in ten minutes?"

"Yes, good idea. I'll do that."

Back in the room, Eleanor brushed her teeth, swigged some water and slapped on some lipstick. Her talk had been a success! She was ready for anything tonight.

* * *

Steve smiled a greeting as she entered the bar area, her sandals tip-tapping across the marble floor.

"Everyone, I'd like you to give another warm welcome to Eleanor Mace, our special guest from England."

Clustered around the courtyard bar in wicker chairs was an assortment of people in small groups who all nodded and smiled or waved across. Steve led her towards the table nearest the courtyard, which was occupied by a bear of a man in a cream linen suit, a younger man with a mass of floppy hair and wire-rimmed glasses, and a pale woman in jeans and a green shirt. During her talk, Eleanor had barely dared to look at the audience, concentrating instead on Steve's comforting presence as he sat opposite her at the front of the room.

The man in the linen suit stood and rearranged the seating, pulling another chair into the group. "Have a seat, Eleanor, please." He extended his hand, "I'm Mike. What would you like to drink? Sherry, beer?"

"Sherry, please."

"Excellent choice. *Jorge, un otro fino, por favor.*"

Eleanor associated sherry with the warm Bristol Cream that Connie used to inflict on guests at Christmas, but what she held in her hand was a small glass of icy cold liquid with a dry, almost biscuity flavour.

"*Salud*! And congratulations on a very entertaining talk."

Eleanor nodded her thanks. "This is delicious," she said, taking far too big a sip from the tiny vessel.

"Try it with one of these," said the young woman, passing over a bowl filled with fresh green olives.

The Sunburst Bagel and her salad lunch had clearly contained no calories because Eleanor was starving again. At home, she was used to eating at about 7pm and the sherry had gone straight to her head. She grabbed an olive gratefully and stuck it straight into her mouth.

"Mind the stone."

Eleanor nodded wordlessly as she extracted the olive and tried to nibble it delicately around the edge.

"I'm Lily, by the way."

When she could speak again, Eleanor wiped her hand on her trouser leg and shook Lily's hand.

"I really enjoyed your presentation," said the young man, who introduced himself as Gunter.

Eleanor couldn't help pulling a face. "It wasn't really a talk. More of a picture show with captions."

"That's even better," said Mike. "There's nothing worse than people banging on for ages without pictures."

"You're not referring to me, I hope," said Steve with a smile. "I was let down by the technology."

Mike guffawed. "Ah, yes. Who could forget your keynote speech in Warsaw last year?"

At this the others joined in, as though this was the funniest thing they had ever heard. Eleanor looked at her feet, feeling distinctly out of place.

Once the hilarity had died down, Lily turned to

Eleanor. "I'm sorry the guys are being very rude and not including you in the joke, and it actually wasn't all that funny."

"What my colleague is trying to say," said Mike, "is that you had to be there to appreciate the exquisite comedy of the moment." Eleanor had a half-smile fixed to her face to show willing. "Have a nut."

This was another world, she thought, helping herself to the salted almonds and finishing off the sherry.

"Jorge – more of your finest *fino* for our speaker, when you're ready."

After the second sherry, Eleanor relaxed and was delighted to discover that newt experts were just like everyone else and enjoyed a drink and a chat. By the time they were all sitting down to dinner, she felt completely at ease and chatted to her companions about the bookshop and life in Devon.

Steve was sitting opposite her in the dark, wood-lined restaurant. He leant across the table so he could be heard over the lively chatter. "Are you having fun? Not finding these guys too terrifying?"

"No, not at all. Everyone has made me feel very welcome."

"I'm pleased," he said, smiling and raising his glass to her. "And you're welcome back to our symposium any time."

"Thanks, Steve. If we make any more discoveries in Combemouth, I'll be sure to let you know."

Chapter 26: A Chance Encounter

When Eleanor met her sister the next morning, she was still basking in the success of the previous evening and had a satisfied grin on her face when Jenna stepped down from the bus.

"You look well, *chica*," said Jenna, kissing her on both cheeks. "How did it go yesterday?"

"Steve said it was a great success and that I'd be welcome back any time."

"And Steve would be?"

"Dr Stephen Mitcham – the Australian newt expert who invited me over here."

Jenna noticed the sparkle in Eleanor's eyes and smelled a rat. "And so you and Dr Mitcham hit it off, did you?"

"He's a nice guy, and he may come and stay in Combemouth next year so he can check on our newts, but that's all."

"Hmm. He's certainly put a bounce in your step. I haven't seen you looking so perky for ages."

"Oh, that's not about Steve. Well, not directly anyway. I got a real kick from doing the talk and being made welcome by all those people with their massive intellects."

"And am I going to meet Doc Steve and the others?"

"Nope, I'm afraid not. They all left before daybreak for one of their field trips. Fancy a coffee?"

"When did I ever say no to coffee?"

After dropping off Jenna's case at the hotel, Eleanor led the way to a local café that she had spotted the day before.

"How's Keith getting on?" Eleanor asked, once they had two big cups of coffee and a basket filled with fresh *churros*.

Keith had offered to drive Jenna to the hotel, but there was a birdwatching trip into the Tramuntana mountain range leaving at 5am, which his wife knew he didn't want to miss, so she had offered to get the bus.

"Kiff sends his love and tells us to have fun, which I said was pretty much guaranteed. He's having a marvellous time counting *Milvus milvus*."

"The what?"

"It's a big brown bird. Rare." Jenna shrugged. "So what are the plans? I hope this jolly lives up to the last one. I enjoyed creeping around the back streets of Chevandier looking for your ex-lover. Have you heard from him recently?"

"No." When Eleanor had returned from their French trip two years before, Christophe had sent her a few texts but communication had gradually petered out – largely because she hadn't wanted to encourage him.

"'No' as in nothing at all?"

"Oh, I had a Christmas card – obviously written by Rosanne – but that's all."

"Shame."

"Hang on – I thought you disapproved of me keeping in touch with him at all?"

"I did, but no harm can come of you and Christophe being 'pen pals'."

"It was lovely to see him again, but we have our own lives now."

"Hmm." Jenna was still not convinced that Eleanor didn't occasionally pine for her first love.

"Anyway, never mind France. Let's enjoy Spain while we're here."

"Agreed, though it's always nice to have other trips lined up," said Jenna, brushing sugar and bits of crispy batter from her lips. "So what delights do you have lined up for me?"

"I thought we could look around town today and I've been recommended a good place to have lunch."

"Sounds great, although you missed out the shopping."

Eleanor grimaced. "I don't mind shops with crafts and gifts, but I draw the line at clothes and shoe shops. I might leave you to it and check out an extra church."

"I don't *have* to look at clothes, El. As long as there are plenty of coffee breaks in the schedule, I can do churches, too."

"Well, that's very grown-up."

"You know, you should take up tour-guiding as your next career."

"Hopefully the bookshop will keep me busy for a few years yet, but thanks for the suggestion."

After coffee, Eleanor managed to lure her sister into a couple of churches and an art gallery as well as several more cafés before a late lunch and a siesta.

Afterwards, they meandered down the shady side streets and walked up the broad bank of steps to a chapel on a rise just outside the town. They walked slowly, but it was fairly hard work.

The crickets sawed away all around them and small invisible creatures rustled in the dry foliage. It was late afternoon, but the dust felt warm beneath their feet.

Jenna removed her wide straw hat and brushed damp strands of hair from her face. "It's too hot for all this activity."

"Maybe," said Eleanor, taking a swig from her bottle of water. "But we're not here for long and I want to see as much as I can."

"Don't let me hold you back. I've seen plenty so I'm quite happy to sit under a tree while you yomp up to the next monument."

"You're not getting out of it that easily," said Eleanor laughing. "We're on this trip together, so come on. Hoik yourself off the wall and let's get going. It's not far now and the view will be worth it, I'm sure."

"I hope you're right."

"Of course I'm right. And you know that the very best thing about a dusty walk in a heat wave is having a cool shower afterwards, followed shortly thereafter by a glass of chilled white wine."

"You are a mind-reader, Eleanor Mace. I would race you to the minibar now, but it's too hot."

"History and culture first, minibar next. Come on."

* * *

Back at the hotel, the marble floor in their room was pleasantly cool underfoot. Collapsed on the bed with her arms outstretched under the old-fashioned ceiling fan, Eleanor smiled. "Maybe I could make a living travelling around Europe, talking about 'The Combemouth Two' and getting paid for it."

"That sounds like an excellent idea. And I'd be

happy to carry your bags." Jenna looked around. "If this is typical of the academic lifestyle, I think you should go for it. I could happily move in here."

"And you haven't even seen the roof terrace yet. There's a fantastic view of the town from up there."

"I'm sure it's super," said Jenna, rubbing her calf muscles. "But I've seen plenty of views of the town and I'm not sure I can manage any more climbing. Can't we chill out in the courtyard? The walk to the chapel has done me in."

"Ah, wait till you see it. And bring your binoculars. You might spot some interesting bird life to report back to Keith."

Jenna wrinkled her nose. "Okay."

Freshly showered and dressed in cool cotton dresses, the sisters grabbed glasses and the bottle of wine they'd left chilling in the minibar and Eleanor led the way to the top of the *parador*.

"Ta dah!" she said, swinging back the door with a flourish. Jenna gazed around, approvingly. "You were right. This is quite something."

The roof terrace was arranged like a walled garden with tubs of lemon and orange trees, and blue-glazed pots packed with flowers and cacti. Masses of bougainvillaea stretched along the top of the white wall, covering it with papery purple leaves. Mosaic-topped tables were arranged across the terrace and the sisters pulled up a couple of chairs and clinked glasses.

"It's a gorgeous spot, so where is everyone, El?"

"Most of the people from the conference have left and the ordinary guests haven't arrived yet. So we've got the place almost entirely to ourselves this evening."

"I'm not complaining."

Eleanor stood and went to look over the edge of the balcony at the roofs of the houses that surrounded them. At the edge of the small town were hills covered in clumps of olive groves. Among these were numerous stone buildings and what looked like much newer villas.

"Wow, look at those places." Jenna, who had wandered over to join her sister, now took out her bird-watching binoculars and leant over the edge of the bougainvillaea to get a better view of the buildings.

"You're so nosy!"

"Excuse me – it was you who said I should bring the binoculars up here."

"Yes, to look at the birds. Not the neighbours."

"I'm interested in wildlife more generally."

Eleanor pursed her lips and tried to look disapproving.

"Oh, come on El. I just want a closer look at those mansions." Jenna scanned the surrounding hills. "Wouldn't you like to know who those fabulous villas belong to?"

"Not really." Eleanor took her glass and retreated to the table. "Come and sit down."

"Don't be so po-faced, El. Some of these places must be worth millions. There's a villa over there that's got one of those infinity pools and a divine terrace with palm trees and everything. Oh! Good heavens. That is amazing." She stepped back. "El, I think you should have a look."

"Thanks, but I can see well enough from where I am."

"Rubbish, you're far too low to see anything. Get off your backside and come and have a look at this."

Ignoring her sister, Eleanor leant back in the chair and closed her eyes. "I'm quite happy sitting here."

"For goodness' sake." Jenna walked over and tugged at her arm. "El, believe me: you need to see this one."

"Ow, that hurt!"

"Sorry, but I really think you should look." Jenna's tone surprised her, so Eleanor put down her glass of wine and walked over to the low wall at the back of the hotel. "This had better be good. I don't want my wine getting warm for nothing."

"It's good, believe me."

Eleanor took the binoculars and raised them to her eyes. "Okay, so where am I looking?"

Jenna waggled a hand towards a striking three-storey building set into the hillside a short distance from where they stood.

"I hope no one is watching us." Eleanor followed the direction of her sister's arm and focused on the villa. "This is really naughty – there's actually some-one in the pool."

Jenna nodded. "Exactly. Look again."

Sighing, Eleanor scanned the terrace and the pool, then stared at her sister. "Oh!" Wiping her eyes she turned again to the villa, sharpening the focus to be sure of what she was seeing. "It can't be! He lives in France and we're in the Balearics."

"If it's not him, it's a double. Or does he have an identical twin brother?"

"No. Just a younger sister." Eleanor looked again. "I really don't believe it."

"But I'm right, aren't I?"

Eleanor shook her head, not in denial but in

astonishment. There was no mistake: the man doing a slow backstroke in the clear water was Christophe Vauban. "It's him."

"Ha! I knew it." Jenna clapped her hands in triumph. "So, we need to find out from reception who the villa belongs to, then go over and say hello."

"No way, Jenna. The guy will think I'm stalking him or something."

"Don't be ridiculous, El. Seeing him twice in twenty years hardly qualifies as stalking. And now you're just 'pen pals', it can't do any harm."

"I'm not sure the long-suffering Rosanne would be quite so understanding."

"Oh, that's a point. Give me those binnies." Jenna took the binoculars and scanned the patio surrounding the swimming pool. "Where's wifey, do you think? And the kids?"

"The kids, as you put it, are in their twenties and far too old to go on holiday with their parents and Rosanne is probably slaving away in the kitchen. Poor woman."

Jenna was looking at the road that led up to the villa. "It doesn't look too far to walk over there, not if we go right after breakfast when it's cool."

"I'm not going to pester Christophe when he's in the middle of a family holiday. It wouldn't be right."

"You are a coward," said Jenna, pouting. "And no fun. Never mind seeing your ex-boyfriend – don't you want to see the villa? I certainly do. Oh hang on. Someone else has come out of the house."

Despite herself, Eleanor couldn't help being intrigued. "Is it Rosanne?"

"Nope. It's a little chubby bloke in a Hawaiian shirt."

Eleanor grabbed the binoculars, thinking for a moment that it might be her new friend, Steve, but she didn't recognise the man in a floral shirt and baggy red shorts standing by the pool.

"Maybe you get a butler when you rent those places. Unless the villa actually belongs to Christophe."

"I think it's unlikely, Jenna. Where would he get the money from?"

"We could grab a taxi, go over there right away and ask him."

"No, we could not!" Eleanor knew her sister well enough to recognise that Jenna was actually serious.

"Well, if we're not going to do that, shall we have dinner?"

"It's far too early to eat. Top me up and pass the nuts."

Chapter 27: Guten Tag, Mi Amigo

After breakfast the next morning, Jenna insisted on heading up to the roof terrace again to check out "Christophe's villa", as it had become known. Eleanor refused to go with her, preferring to stay in the courtyard with coffee and warm *ensaïmadas*. Her sister wasn't gone long.

Eleanor put down her cup, trying and failing to look uninterested. "So?"

"I thought you weren't bothered."

Her sister could be annoying. "Did you see anything or not?"

"Unfortunately, there were new people up on our roof having breakfast, so I couldn't be too obvious about it."

"But?"

"But, I did manage a quick glance and the swimming pool was empty and I couldn't see anyone on the terrace either."

Eleanor couldn't help a wave of disappointment sweeping over her. "Oh well, never mind. Maybe they've already left."

"We can still wander over there and peer over the fence."

"I don't think so. It was nice to catch a glimpse of Christophe again, but I guess that will have to keep me going for a few more years."

"Rubbish! If he and Rosanne are here on the island, we ought to go and say hello. It would be rude not to."

Eleanor laughed. "Well, if you put it like that maybe we will. But not today. Today we're getting a bus down to the seaside, so get your cossie on."

"Sounds fabulous – let's go."

In the hillside town where they were staying, there were a few tourists but most of the people they met were Spaniards, with a smattering of visitors from other parts of the world. Arriving at the coast was quite a surprise. They'd been expecting "Kiss Me Quick" hats, Irish pubs and caffs selling full-English breakfasts, but what they found was a little bit of Munich.

After getting off the bus they wandered along the main street, puzzling over the menus and unable to understand a word. It seemed that every bar was packed with young Germans drinking beer and eating curry wurst to a soundtrack of Europop.

"This is amazing," whispered Jenna. "It feels so foreign to see everything written in German."

"You mean instead of English?"

"Yes, exactly."

Eleanor laughed. "English is foreign, too, you know?"

"I know it is, but not in the same way. I mean, we're used to people using English all over the world."

"Which doesn't mean that it's not foreign."

"Lordy, you can be pedantic sometimes."

"Okay – I know what you mean. Anyway, I think it's fun – it's like two holidays in one. I've always wanted to visit Germany, but now I don't have to."

Jenna's tummy rumbled at they passed yet another

sausage vendor. "I might be up for a beer and a brat-wurst after a swim."

"You're on."

They slung their beach bags over their shoulders and Eleanor led the way along the road to the edge of the resort. A path ran through an area of wood-land and across a bank of dunes then opened up onto an exquisite bay with sand the colour of ground almonds.

"Wow!" said Jenna. "This looks like photos of the Caribbean. The sea is actually turquoise."

Eleanor nodded, smiling. "You're right. We don't need to go there now either. Think of the money we're saving on this trip."

Once down on the beach, they tiptoed through a smattering of other holiday-makers, pulled up a couple of loungers and parked themselves under a wide straw parasol.

"This is bliss," said Jenna. "I think you should defi-nitely pursue this new academic career of yours."

"I'll see what I can do."

They spent the afternoon sunbathing and making occasional sallies into the crystal clear water for a reviving dip, aware that they were pale and pasty compared to the bronzed bodies surrounding them.

"So, are you going topless?" asked Eleanor, slather-ing suntan lotion on her belly.

"At my age? You have got to be joking. Anyway, I don't want my bits burnt to a crisp." Jenna lifted her sunglasses and looked around, wincing. "Those women over there have boobs the colour and texture of overdone roast potatoes."

"Ouch. That looks painful."

"What about you?"

"No chance. I prefer to preserve my modesty. And if I take my top off, my chest will sink to my knees, which is not a good look."

Jenna chuckled. "You exaggerate."

"Only slightly. Is it time for a beer yet?"

"Any time is beer time – we're on our hols."

* * *

They had put away a beer and a sausage in a bun, and were walking along the busy street peering into shop windows when Jenna grabbed Eleanor's arm.

"Isn't that Christophe over there? The one talking to the blond bloke in the green trousers and pink shirt?"

"What?" Eleanor looked in the direction indicated by Jenna. "Damn it. Let's hide," she said, stepping behind a stacker full of brightly coloured postcards. "I don't want him to see me looking like this."

"Like what?"

"Like a drowned rat. With my hair all awry, no make-up on and covered in sand." She tried to re-arrange the wrap she had tied around her waist to cover her legs. "God, I look terrible."

"Don't be ridiculous." Jenna – who would look elegant in a bin bag – tutted as she tried to brush her sister's hair back from her face at the same time as extracting her from the safety of the gift shop. "You look sun-kissed and delectable. Just remember that."

As she spoke, they watched Christophe wave goodbye to his companion and amble over in their direction. He moved with the same loose stride he had used in his twenties and, in his pale blue shirt and white shorts, he didn't look much older. Eleanor's heart leapt the way it had when she had seen him in France.

As he approached, his slight frown turned into a broad grin as he realised it was them. He removed his sunglasses, ran his hand through his hair and smiled. "Ella and Jenna! What a pleasant surprise."

He kissed them both twice on the cheek then turned to Eleanor. "I was hoping to run into you while you were in Mallorca."

"You were? But how did you know I was here?" She was trying to stay calm and not stare too hard at the patch of coffee-coloured skin under the open collar of his shirt. "I mean, you don't seem very surprised at all."

He shrugged. "You are famous, Ella. For the lizard, you know?" He spoke English with the kind of Gallic accent that was guaranteed to make grown women swoon. "Please, let me invite you for a coffee. Or perhaps afternoon tea for my English ladies?"

Jenna watched as Eleanor laughed girlishly at Christophe's cheesy invitation, aware that neither of them was paying any attention to her. Christophe ushered them to a table under an awning by the sea and ordered the drinks.

"How do you know about the newt business?" asked Jenna, rather more sharply than was perhaps necessary. The tone of her voice caught Christophe's attention and he tore his glance from Eleanor and fixed it on her sister, who was less susceptible to his charms.

"It is a Spanish creature that was found, so everyone was very excited," he said with a shrug, as though the answer was obvious. "It was on the television and the newspapers here had your picture in them." He had turned his gaze back to Eleanor, who was smiling modestly. "I saw that you were coming to speak to those professors, so I knew it was only a matter of time before we saw each other again. If not, I would have come to the *parador* to find you. I am staying nearby, you know?"

"Gosh, really? What a coincidence." Eleanor shot her sister a look, hoping she would stay quiet about spying on him from the rooftops. "We had no idea, did we Jenna?"

"None at all." After a moment or two, Jenna noticed that the conversation had stopped and her sister was gazing at Christophe like a lovesick schoolgirl. "And how are Rosanne and the family? It will be very nice to see them all again, won't it El."

Eleanor looked around, her sister's words reminding her of the other members of Christophe's family. "Yes, indeed. Are they here?"

A cloud passed over Christophe's face. "No."

What did just "no" mean, wondered Eleanor. Perhaps recognising that he had piqued the women's curiosity, he smiled. "The children are in France. Rosanne was here, but she has gone now."

Jenna nodded slowly. "So you are having a few extra days' holiday? How nice."

"No, it's work. I am here to check on the business."

"You have a restaurant in Mallorca, Christophe? I didn't know," said Eleanor.

"It is a brand new venture – something I am developing with a friend of my *beau-frère*. Oh, what do you call that?"

"Your brother-in-law?"

"*C'est ça.* That's right. A friend of my brosser-in-law who has a little money to invest, you know?"

Jenna watched her sister nod and smile, the soppy look still fixed on Eleanor's face.

"You must meet him while you are here."

"Isn't he in Germany?"

"No, he is on his boat in the marina. If you have finished your tea, I will take you over there and introduce you to him. He is always happy to meet beautiful women."

Jenna had wrung every last trace of tea from her tiny tea bag and was ready to go, but Eleanor hesitated.

"Perhaps we should meet your friend when we are properly dressed?"

Christophe shrugged, sliding his eyes up and down her body in a way that made her blush. "You are perfectly dressed but, if you prefer, I will collect you later when you have had – how do you say? – a wash and brush-up. Correct?"

Eleanor laughed. "Correct."

"You taught me well all those years ago, Ella."

Her chest contracted at Christophe's mention of their past and she gazed down at the ground, not having an answer.

"That sounds like a much better plan," said Jenna, breaking the tension. "You come and get us about 8pm and we'll be ready for you, won't we Sis?"

"We will."

"Perfect. I look forward to seeing you both this evening."

Chapter 28: Party Time

"Well, what do you know – a date with the love rat."

"It is not a date, Jenna. And we only have circumstantial evidence that he is actually a love rat anyway."

"Like the famous kiss, you mean?"

Eleanor sighs. "Which hardly counts as full-blown adultery."

"People might argue with you about that, but the point is you've been invited to spend an evening with Monsieur Rumpy Pumpy, who just happens to be the love of your life."

"*We* have been invited and he is not the love of my life."

Jenna raised her eyebrows in disbelief and carried on. "An evening on a posh boat sounds rather exciting. And – perish the thought – there could be more snogging opportunities."

"There won't be any snogging."

"So you say."

"Firstly, Christophe is married …"

"Which he was last time."

"Secondly, I am with Daniel now."

"Really? You keep telling me that you've dumped him and it's all over between you two."

"I haven't 'dumped him'. He has separated himself from me by being a two-faced, money-grabbing weasel."

"I thought that Freya was going to put all of Widget's lolly towards their daughter's dowry or something."

"Okay," said Eleanor, shiftily. "Dan isn't profiting from the deal financially, but he's still involved."

"It doesn't sound to me like you're together."

"Well, we are. I think." Eleanor sighed. "Oh, I don't know. It's complicated. However, the fact remains that I am not going on a date with Christophe and there won't be any snogging."

Jenna crossed her arms across her chest and made an attempt at looking fierce. "You're right there because I shall be keeping a very close eye on you both."

"You don't need to worry about me – I shall be very well behaved."

* * *

The women were ready and waiting when Christophe came to collect them from the palace and usher them to his car. It was dark as they headed down the hill and in the distance they could see lights twinkling on boats moored out at sea. On reaching the coastal town, they drove past countless bars and sea-front restaurants leading to the wide promenade. Beyond the end of the main strip, they came to a halt in a small bay packed with huge yachts.

"We are nearly there now," said Christophe, opening the car door and leading the sisters down some steps to a pontoon with numerous fingers that stretched into the sea with gleaming white boats on each side.

Towards the end of the main walkway, Christophe stopped and whistled. A man dressed in red shorts, his skin the colour of walnuts, looked down from one of the biggest boats there and waved at him.

Christophe jumped onto the boat, hugged him and exchanged a few words in German.

On the pontoon, Jenna shoved her elbow into her sister's ribs. "It's the butler we saw by Christophe's pool last night," she whispered.

"Shh! They might hear us. And judging by the size of the boat and the amount of gold he's concealing in that hairy chest, I don't think he's the butler."

Christophe turned to the women and extended an arm. "Señoras, Herr Rutger invites you to join him on his yacht."

"Too kind," said Jenna, shoving her sister onto the gangplank.

"Welcome, ladies, welcome." Herr Rutger greeted the women as Christophe helped them on board. "I believe that you are old friends of Monsieur Vauban?"

"We are indeed, Herr Rutger," said Jenna, flashing a winning smile as their host raised her hand to his lips.

"Call me Klaus, please."

Eleanor thought it was a bit a rich of Jenna to claim to be an "old friend" given that she had only met Christophe twice, but said nothing as Klaus greeted her in turn. "What a gorgeous boat," she said, her mind straying to how much Daniel would enjoy sailing in such a vessel, even if there were no sails. The yacht was sleek and white and at least the size of her cottage.

"Yes, she is a pretty English boat. And I have a pretty Mallorcan villa to go with her." As he laughed, the soft folds of his belly shuddered as though hit by a mild earthquake. "It is too warm to stay below, so let's go up onto the top deck. We will have champagne and a few little things to eat up there while we wait for the other guests. What do you say?"

Eleanor had no need to check what Jenna thought about the invitation. "That sounds wonderful, thank you."

So they chatted and sipped champagne served by staff in crisp white uniforms, feeling like extras in a Bond movie. Gradually the four of them were joined by other guests who spoke in a variety of languages, but switched to immaculate English when talking to the sisters.

Christophe was sweet and attentive, but Eleanor could tell that hers were not the only eyes following him as he moved around the boat. He was charming to all the women there, but when he looked at Eleanor anyone could see there was "history" between them. She felt the warm glow of possession, the memory of every curve of his body flashing through her mind. She might not have lain naked in his arms for two decades, but the sweet intensity of those nights was not something she would ever forget.

He came across and whispered to her. "You look beautiful tonight, Ella."

"Thank you." She felt herself sway towards him as his warm brown eyes seemed to embrace her and draw her in. She could easily have stood there gazing at him all evening had Jenna not appeared at her side and broken the spell.

"Dinner," she said, tugging her away.

"That is not to be missed," said Christophe, smiling. "Klaus always provides excellent food."

The "few little things to eat" promised by Klaus were delicious canapés including tasty slices of char-grilled chicken, chunks of spicy lamb and plump scallops, all laid out on long tables under the stars.

As they ate and talked and drank more champagne, the low murmur of voices and music drifted over from the harbour-side bars and restaurants. Behind them the only sound was of the sea and the rhythmic clanking of ropes against tall masts.

"This is the life, Sis. Maybe you should have clung on to Christophe after all. He certainly has some very smart friends."

"Don't tempt me," said Eleanor, who was now feeling pleasantly tipsy.

After a while, Jenna excused herself and went to find the ladies. Returning to Eleanor, she could barely stop giggling. "You've got to go 'below', El. It's like Stringfellows down there."

"What do you mean?"

"Wall-to-wall animal print and gold tassels, that's what I mean." She looked down at the leopardskin pumps she had chosen to wear that evening. "I thought my feet had disappeared when I sat on the loo – they're an exact match for the carpet."

Eleanor looked around, embarrassed. "Shush, Jenna. You shouldn't laugh at other people's taste."

At that moment, their host tapped a silver teaspoon against his champagne glass.

"Ladies and gentlemen, if I may have your attention, please." Klaus looked around at his guests and smiled. "Thank you all for joining us this evening – and especially our English friends, Eleanor and Jenna."

The sisters smiled and raised their glasses in acknowledgement, trying their best not to appear quite as squiffy as they were.

Klaus stretched up and put an arm across Christophe's shoulders. "We are here to celebrate the launch of our new venture – Bratwurst Bonanza – a chain of restaurants that we hope will put sausages on the map in Spain."

Eleanor became aware of Jenna choking with laughter and whacked her smartly on the back as a dozen heads turned towards them. "Don't worry," she said, through gritted teeth. "Her champagne has gone down the wrong way."

"Jenna – behave," she hissed. "What's so funny?"

Tears were starting to form in her sister's eyes as she fought to subdue her giggles. "Did he say Bratwurst Bonanza? Sorry El. It's the thought that all this glamour is based on flogging sausages at the beach that has set me off."

Frowning, Christophe extracted himself from a crowd of admirers and advanced towards them with a glass of water. "Are you okay?"

"She's fine, really. The bubbles have gone to her head, that's all."

Jenna was struggling to speak and simply waved a hand in the air as if it was nothing.

"Perhaps I should take you both home."

Eleanor couldn't help looking at the glass in his hand and wondering if he had downed as much fizz as she had. "Are you sure?"

"Klaus will lend us his car and a driver," he said with a smile.

And so they said farewell to their host and thanked

him effusively for his generosity. Jenna sat in the front of Klaus's vintage Mercedes, knowing that Eleanor would want to spend a little more time with Christophe.

Sitting side by side in the car, she looked at his dark curly hair and elegant profile and smiled. Feeling her gaze on him, he turned and gently took her hand. Eleanor closed her eyes and let her head loll against the seat rest as the car climbed from the harbour, up through the pine trees towards the *parador*.

After a few moments, she opened her eyes and looked down towards the ocean where myriad lights twinkled on countless yachts, reminding her of the less glamorous waterfront in Combemouth. Christophe's hand felt comfortable in hers but, to her surprise, the face she saw in her mind's eye was Daniel's.

When they arrived at the palace, Christophe asked the driver to wait while he escorted the sisters into the hotel. In the foyer, Jenna kissed him goodnight and turned to her sister. "Don't be long," she said, her warning message clear.

Eleanor nodded then turned to Christophe, smiling. "Well, I guess it's goodnight then."

"I can't say goodnight yet, Ella – will you sit with me for a while?"

"Okay. But just for a minute." She led the way up the wide marble staircase and opened the big old door onto the roof terrace. There was no one else up there and nothing much to see except the stars above their heads. They stood, leaning against the low wall that ran around the terrace and Christophe took her in his arms the way he had so many times before.

"To find you here has been like a little miracle, you know?" He raised her face to his with his fingertips and gazed into her eyes.

Eleanor nodded, her emotions in turmoil. She felt charmed and seduced by Christophe's attentions, the way she always had, but the boat and the champagne and the starlight had made her think of somebody else.

"We are tied together, Ella. I think we always will be." His face moved towards her and his lips brushed her cheek. "I want to kiss you more than anything in the world, but I won't." He stepped back, then held her against his chest one more time. "You have a man in your life who you love and who loves you – and no, Jenna didn't say anything. I can tell by the way you move and the way you look. So, to kiss you now wouldn't be right." He laughed a little sadly, taking her hands and holding her at arm's length. "I have not always been a good man, but I would never do anything to cause you pain, Ella."

Standing on tiptoes, Eleanor took his face in her hands and pressed her lips to his, holding them there for three long seconds. When she closed her eyes, the familiar scent of his skin and the sound of his voice sent her brain into a spin. With him, she had discovered sex and good food; she had learned how to play *pétanque* and speak French with a southern accent. She had developed a love of Françoise Hardy and *bandes dessinés* that had never left her. The months she had spent locked in his loving, playful embrace had helped to make her the woman she was today and she couldn't imagine the person she would be if they hadn't spent that time together.

She looked at his strong, handsome face in the moonlight and caressed his cheek as she pulled away. "I will always love you, Christophe. But now you should go home."

Chapter 29: Return to Combemouth

The next morning, Jenna looked at Eleanor quizzically but didn't ask what had happened in the few short minutes before Eleanor had come to the room and silently climbed into bed. She seemed calm but a little sad as they packed their bags and left the palace. It was their final day on the island, so Jenna had suggested that they head into Palma for one last lunch before she rejoined her husband and Eleanor flew home.

They were settled in the corner of a cosy restaurant in a quiet square before she cracked. "So spill the beans – what happened?"

"I kissed him goodnight and sent him home – that was all."

By the serious tone of Eleanor's voice, Jenna could tell that her sister was telling the truth. "Well done for resisting his charms. I wasn't at all sure that you would manage it after the gallons of Bollinger we'd knocked back."

Eleanor smiled. "I've come to realise that the tricky thing about relationships is timing. It's not about finding 'the one' – it is more about finding the right person at the right stage of your life."

Jenna nodded, happy to turn her attention to the

bowl of *albóndigas* now that a potential romantic crisis had been averted.

"I mean, look at me and Alan. He was what I needed in my mid-twenties, but if I met him now I know for sure that I'd never consider marrying him. Or even dating him, for that matter."

"I wouldn't argue with that."

"You see, it's different with you and Keith. Neither of you seems to have changed at all."

"Are you saying I was born middle-aged?"

"No, silly. What I mean is that because you met when you were a bit older and Keith had already been married and had the kids and everything, you both knew what you really wanted. Your interests have kept pace with each other, but you're not afraid of having different hobbies and friends either."

"So, you've finally accepted that Christophe isn't right for you?"

"Oh, I don't know." Eleanor got a misty look in her eyes only half-fuelled by Rioja. "Perhaps it is meant to be. After all, serendipity has thrown us together again."

Jenna scoffed. "It wasn't serendipity, El, it was a combination of newts and Bratwurst Bonanza. Which gives me an idea. You're both good at selling things. Maybe you could set up a new business in Mallorca – 'Bangers and Books: We have a savoury snack and a slim volume of poetry for every occasion'."

"Very funny. Pass the *chorizo al vino* will you?"

"I know I was keen for us to see him and last night was fun, but Christophe is a lothario and a player. You know that, El. And we've both witnessed the effect of being with someone like him in the long term. It's not fun."

Eleanor took a sip of wine and looked pensive again. "Shatter my dreams, why don't you. And it is just a dream, honestly." Looking her sister straight in the eye she smiled. "Don't worry, Jenna. I love him because of all the experiences we shared and I won't apologise for that. But I know you can't go backwards in relationships."

"Amen, sister." Jenna tapped her glass against Eleanor's. "Leave the past alone and concentrate on the here and now – and the future."

"You mean Daniel?"

"Daniel is perfect for you."

"Correction: Daniel *was* perfect for me. Or so I believed."

"And he can be again. If not, find yourself someone else who is."

Eleanor felt a pang at the thought that perhaps it really might be over with Dan. "Oh, I'm too old to start again from scratch," she said, patting her lips with a napkin.

"Rubbish. You've probably got a few more years left in you yet. Are you going to finish that last bit of *pulpo*?"

Eleanor dunked her bread in the garlicky sauce before passing the dish to her sister. "You do realise that I've been on this earth for half a century? It's no wonder that I look and feel knackered most of the time."

Jenna snorted. "Well, I can think of at least two handsome men who would disagree with you about that and one of them is waiting for you at home."

"I'm not sure he is any more."

"You'll find out soon enough," said Jenna, looking at her watch. "We need to get you over to the airport, pronto."

Chapter 30: What Next?

By the time Eleanor got back from the airport, it was late and the house was empty. Bella was with Erika, who had offered to bring the dog into work with her the next morning. Eleanor enjoyed her own company, but that evening the place was uncomfortably quiet. The last few days with Jenna had been fun and she'd enjoyed her time with Steve and the other academics. Now, back in the cottage, the reality of the situation with Daniel hit home and she went to bed with a heavy heart.

She slept badly, besieged by odd dreams and awoke early the next morning. At 6am she decided to get up and have a quiet read, thinking that she could go into the shop to check on stock. Looking at the kitchen clock after breakfast, she was surprised to hear a knock on the door. Opening it, she saw an enormous bunch of flowers and behind it was Daniel.

"Peace offering," he said, with a tentative smile on his face. "May I come in?"

"Yes, of course," said Eleanor, stepping back into the hallway. Her heart leapt and she felt shy and a little tongue-tied by Dan's sudden appearance. "Come into the kitchen while I find a vase for these." She buried her nose in the roses and peonies. "These are gorgeous – thank you."

"I'm glad you like them," he said, acutely aware

that he hadn't been in the house for several weeks. He leant uneasily against the counter, watching Eleanor as she extracted a couple of vases from the pantry and began unwrapping the flowers.

Her heart was pounding and she felt ridiculously nervous, wondering why Daniel had come and what he was going to say to her. She didn't feel angry any more – just sad that their lovely, easy affair had been mucked up. What she wanted to say was "Do you still want to be with me?" Instead she asked him how he had been.

Daniel had turned up with no fixed plan of what he was going to say. He simply wanted to find out if she'd forgiven him and if they still had a future together. How had he been? That was easy to answer.

"If you want to know how I have been, I'd say bad-tempered and miserable. Oh, and lonely. And I've been kicking myself for getting involved with Freya and her bloody bonkers scheme."

Eleanor was stunned by this admission and she turned towards him in surprise. "Really? You have?"

He nodded. "I have. And how have you been?"

"I've been cross and frustrated by the situation. And saddened that you chose Freya over me." She sighed. "And I don't know what to do about it."

Daniel put his hands on his hips and shook his head sadly, but there was a hint of exasperation in his voice. "It was never about choosing Freya over you and if that's what you think I don't see how we can get over this."

Eleanor's heart sank. "I'm sorry. I'm just telling you how it seemed to me."

"I don't want to go over all that again." Daniel

raised his hands in defeat, but when he spoke again it was more gently. "We aren't going to agree on what happened over the development, but I do have some news that I hope will make things better."

"You have?" Eleanor looked at him quizzically, hoping for the best. "Tell me more."

"A few days ago, Freya rang and told me that her client was having one or two doubts about the scheme and wanted to speak to someone who knew the terrain – she told him about our connection, of course. Anyway, I agreed to meet Widget and we talked for quite a long time about the area and the impact his plans might have on the community."

Eleanor was listening intently. "Go on."

"He said he had come to the conclusion that perhaps Combemouth wasn't the best place for his project after all. Freya had hoped I could change his mind, but I couldn't."

Eleanor's mouth tightened. "I see."

"What I mean is that I couldn't because I thought Widget was right and Freya was wrong. I looked through all the environmental stuff again and the plans for the buildings, the access, etc., and I came to the conclusion that Widget – and you – had made valid points. Combemouth is not the right location for the type of complex he had imagined sitting in his villa in LA."

Eleanor had been half-heartedly trimming and arranging the flowers, but now she put down the scissors in amazement. "So you convinced him not to go ahead?"

"I think Bill had already made his mind up and just wanted someone else to tell his wife and Freya.

Anyway, plans for the water park, the aquarium, Busty Bertha, etc. are off, and what's even better is that he's planning to start a fund to help protect your newts. Turns out that he became rather fond of lizards and their cousins when they were part of his stage act." Daniel smiled. "He's basically a really nice guy who wants everyone to like him and the last thing he needs at this stage in his career is aggravation – and he could tell from the demonstrations that he was in for a lot of aggravation if he went ahead with Busty Bertha and the rest."

"You make it sound like we were intending to send the boys round to duff him up."

"Well, you can't say he was given the warmest of welcomes."

Despite herself, Eleanor felt a pang of sympathy for Widget and his hopes for a brand-new life by the sea. "Are you saying that he's calling the whole thing off and going back to the States?"

"Not exactly. He's had enough of the States and wants to settle back in his homeland. And he still wants Freya to build him the house on the cliff top, but the plans for the meditation centre have been modified – and a lot of the nuttier elements are being dropped altogether. He's hoping to get the go-ahead for a revised water park on the northeast coast – Northumbria somewhere. I gather that Brenda is not best pleased, but he told me he's tired of being bossed about by his manager and if she doesn't like it, she can lump it."

"So Freya's not entirely out of a job?"

"No, not at all. She'll set the house build in motion here, but Bill really wants her to work on the project

in Northumbria. Of course, she's furious about it."
Daniel grimaced. "Coming back to the southwest was
bad enough, but working that far north of London is
her idea of hell."

Eleanor felt herself smirking in an unsympathetic
manner. "So she'll still be getting her hands on
Widget's cash, but she won't be around here quite so
much?"

"Correct." The garden doors were open and Daniel
was gazing at the rough white walls of the patio,
which were gradually turning pink in the morning
sun. "At the moment she's pretty fed up with me, as
you can imagine, but she'll get over it. And yes, I'll
still see her from time to time, before you ask," he
said, turning to face Eleanor. "She'll always be a part
of my life, the same way as Alan will always be a part
of yours. The question is whether you can deal with
that."

Eleanor nodded, feeling chastened – how could
she object after her recent close encounter with
Christophe? "Of course I can deal with her being a
part of your life – so long as she's not the most important part."

"She's certainly not that." Daniel grinned. "So am
I forgiven?"

"Yes, of course you are," said Eleanor, crossing the
room to hug him.

"And does that mean you still want to come away
with me on Friday?"

Eleanor looked puzzled. "Friday? Why, what's
happening?"

Daniel half-turned and tapped on the calendar,
which was hanging from the edge of a dresser behind

him. Someone had scribbled a huge heart over the date in red felt-tipped pen with "2nd" in the centre.

"Our anniversary treat! I'm so sorry – I'd completely forgotten."

"Well, I hadn't, so you'd better get the backup crew lined up again because I'll be whisking you away next weekend."

Eleanor wrapped her arms around Daniel's neck as he grasped her waist and pulled her to him. His hair was still slightly damp from his morning shower and his skin smelt fresh and clean. She breathed it all in and smiled. "I can't wait."

Chapter 31: Time for Romance

A few days later, Eleanor opened the front door to find Daniel standing there with a big smile on his face. "Your carriage awaits, madam," he said, opening the door to his car, which had been specially cleaned for the occasion. Eleanor climbed in and they drove south through the afternoon, arriving at their destination as the sun was turning orange.

Eleanor couldn't believe her eyes when Daniel stopped the car a few hundred yards from a mound that she could see was about to be surrounded by the sea. "How are we going to get over there? I mean, is it safe to drive across the sand?"

"It is at the moment," he said, having checked the times on the board. "Let's go." Daniel drove across the causeway then gradually climbed to the centre of what was fast becoming an island and pulled up outside a stunning Art-Deco building.

Eleanor couldn't help smiling at the venue, its pure white walls gleaming against the blue-green sea that surrounded them. "What a gorgeous place, Dan. How on earth did you find it?"

"I looked it up online after reading about it in one of Dad's Sunday supplements. Apparently it belonged to an artistic couple – she was famous for writing passionate love stories while the husband made a living painting dark and stormy seascapes much loved by

Hollywood types. Anyway, after they died, it turned out that he had been the romantic novelist and she was the painter. I thought you'd appreciate the history." He put his arm around her waist and smiled. "Have I done well?"

"You certainly have," she said. "I can't wait to see inside." As they approached the hotel, a doorman in a smart uniform greeted them and carried their bags through the panelled foyer and up to their suite.

Eleanor smiled as she looked around the bedroom with its round walls and 1930s detailing. "This must have cost a fortune."

"It did," said Daniel, laughing. "But you're worth every penny. Correction: we're worth every penny. I'm just so relieved we're here together." His expression was serious for a minute. "I thought for a while that we'd never make it."

"I'm so glad we came here – I'd have hated to miss all this." She walked across the room and patted the quilted coverlet on the bed. "Look – they've folded the towels into swans. I didn't think anyone really did that!"

"It's all part of the period charm."

"Where's the bathroom?" She opened the door and turned back to him with a huge grin on her face. In the centre of the room was a massive freestanding bathtub with gold fittings. "Wowza!"

Daniel came up behind her and put his arms around her waist, resting his chin on her shoulder. "How do you fancy a luxurious soak with a glass of bubbly, just like in the adverts?"

"Only if you join me."

"Love to," he said, kissing her cheek.

Ten minutes later they were both up to their chests in bubbles, sipping champers from proper champagne coupes.

"I feel like a movie star," said Eleanor, who had pushed her hair into the pink silk shower cap provided.

Daniel laughed. "And very glamorous you look, too." He smiled and raised his glass to hers so they clinked together over the bubbles.

They lay back and closed their eyes, both smiling at the sheer decadence of it all. After a while, Daniel grabbed her foot and gently but firmly rubbed her warm sole with his thumb. "Fancy a massage before dinner?"

Eleanor opened her eyes and smiled seductively. "That sounds divine. I'll do you if you do me."

"Deal!"

* * *

After an hour rolling around on their super-kingsize bed, it was time to dress for dinner. Eleanor looked through the clothes that she and Erika had carefully put together all those weeks before and frowned. "I don't think I've brought anything quite glamorous enough for this venue."

Daniel picked up some hotel literature from the old-fashioned dressing table and started to read it. "It says here that guests are invited to wear 1920s- or 1930s-style clothes on Friday and Saturday evenings."

Eleanor's face fell. "Oh what a shame – I wish we'd known. It would have been such fun to dress up as gangsters or Fred and Ginger, but never mind. My tunic top and trousers will have to do."

Daniel grinned. "Actually, I might be able to help

you out." From his suitcase he withdrew a large box wrapped up with a silver ribbon and handed it to Eleanor.

"For me? But what is it?"

"I think you should open it and see, don't you?"

Inside the box was a second box and a bag containing something silky wrapped in tissue paper. Lifting out the tissue paper parcel, Eleanor gasped. "This is gorgeous."

"I know you say that you aren't terribly interested in clothes, but I hope you like it."

Eleanor whooped with delight as she held up an ankle-length dress in eau-de-nil with a matching fascinator trimmed with peacock blue feathers. "Ordinary clothes are boring, but this is an authentic vintage dress!" In the box was a pair of high-heeled shoes embellished with diamante ankle straps. "These are wonderful," she said, slipping them on.

"There's this as well," he said, handing her a long string of pearls.

"Dan, this is amazing."

"It's just a bit of fun, really."

"But what are you wearing?"

He smiled, looking pleased with himself. "Something casual. You know – white bow tie, a dinner jacket and spats."

She dropped the dress on the bed and threw her arms around him. "You're going to look so handsome."

"Or like an idiot."

She shook her head slowly. "Never that, darling."

Once dressed in their finery, they wandered downstairs for cocktails and dinner. The meal was to be served in the ballroom, the walls of which were decorated with frescos of beach scenes and lit by lamps shaped like flames. A pianist played a white piano and other suitably attired guests sipped side-cars and martinis. It was all rather kitsch and fun, and just the thing for a celebratory weekend.

Daniel and Eleanor ate at a table overlooking the sea, which had crept in around them until their island was cut off from the mainland by a shimmering band of silver. It was magical and gave them both the sensation of being on an ocean liner, far out at sea.

After the meal, they took two globes of cognac and went to stand on the terrace in the moonlight.

"Happy anniversary," said Daniel, raising his glass to Eleanor's. "And thank you for making my life so much better than it has been for years."

She clinked her glass to his and smiled. "Ah, you'll make me cry."

Daniel laughed. "I hope not! The idea is to make you happy, the way you make me happy."

Her heart leapt. Was he going to propose? Secretly, Eleanor had thought that he might for a long time, but what would she say if he asked now? She loved him, but did she want to marry him? Did she want to marry anybody after going through the trauma of her divorce from Alan? Could she bear to give up the freedom of living alone? She tried to calm down – her imagination was running riot. Daniel had never shown any sign of wanting to marry her.

The wind had changed direction and was blowing in off the sea, flicking up the edge of her shawl and giving her goose pimples.

"You're cold." Daniel saw her shiver and opened

his arms to wrap his jacket around her. "Let's get you back inside."

"I'm fine, really. Let's stay a bit longer." She nestled against him, unwilling to break the spell and wanting time to think. "We're the only people out here, you know."

"With the stars above our heads and the sea on all sides." He laughed, hugging her to his chest as they peered over the wall that protected the hotel from the waves below. "It's like being on a ship without leaving terra firma."

"It's fantastic, Daniel. I couldn't have wished for anything more."

He bent to kiss her, sending a warm feeling through her body that had nothing to do with the cognac or the moonlight. "I missed you so much when you weren't around. There were so many times when I wanted to talk to you, so many things I wanted to tell you."

She smiled now, intrigued. "Like?"

"Well, let me think." He leant back, his eyes drifting up to the stars. "Like how the blackbird chicks in my garden had fledged safely. Like the fact Emily has a new boyfriend who might be 'the one'." He kissed her again. "And all the little things: that I'd read the novel you recommended and hated it …" He placed a finger gently on her lips before she could protest. "And I've discovered a new gallery in Waterborough, which I know you'll love. But the thing I really want to say is that being apart has made me realise that the most important person in my life at the moment is you, Eleanor."

"At the moment? That doesn't sound great!" She laughed nervously, but Daniel's tone was serious.

"I'm not great at expressing my feelings, El. You must know that by now." Eleanor nodded, caught up by the intensity in Daniel's voice as he struggled to find the right words. She reached up to stroke his cheek, breathing in the warm, spicy scent of his aftershave. "Sorry Dan. Go on."

He took her hands gently in his, frowning. "What I'm trying to say is that Freya is important to me but you are the woman I love here and now. The woman I want to spend the rest of my life with, in fact." His expression in the moonlight flickered from serious to scared to hopeful as he dropped to one knee.

"Eleanor Mace – will you marry me?"

Chapter 32: Three Months Later ...

Eleanor awoke alone. After years of marriage to Alan, she could only ever sleep on the left-hand side of the bed. It had taken her years to begin using the entire bed without feeling uncomfortable and then Daniel had entered her life and she was back clinging to "her" side again. But today the sheet beside her was crisp and smooth, and the place where Daniel's body should have been was empty and cold.

She pulled the unused pillow across and curled herself around it, burying her nose in the cool cotton hoping to find a trace of his scent there but getting only a waft of clean linen.

The curtains were tightly closed, but Eleanor could tell by the dim light and familiar sounds that the sun hadn't quite risen. Everything was quiet apart from the gulls and terns who sounded shrill and expectant in the autumn air. She squinted at the clock – it was still early – then rolled over again and clamped her eyes shut. She wasn't ready to face the world quite yet.

Where was Daniel now, she wondered, and what would he be doing? Was he thinking of her or lost in his plans for the day?

"Wakey, wakey. Rise and shine." The cheery voice was accompanied by a sharp tap on the bedroom door. "Are you decent?"

"That's a matter of opinion." Eleanor smiled lazily as her daughter came into the room bearing a bright blue mug. "It's very kind of you, darling, but it is rather early."

"Don't thank me, thank Gran."

"Your gran's here already?" She sniffed the air. "And is that bacon I can smell?"

"Bacon, eggs, sausage – the works."

"Good grief. Anyone would think it was my birthday."

Phoebe went to the window and drew back the curtains, allowing the watery sun to enter the room. "It's going to be a beautiful day," she said, turning to her mother who had propped the spare pillow behind her and was sipping the hot tea. "Shall I open the window?"

"If you must," said Eleanor, tucking the duvet around her. "But I imagine it's a bit fresh out there."

"Ah, it's good for you." The air blowing through the window was cool and invigorating. Phoebe took a deep breath, filling her lungs and throwing her arms apart before exhaling loudly. "You don't get that smell in Toronto."

"And what smell is that, love?"

Phoebe took in another lungful and smiled. "A delicious combination of seaweed and chips."

"Phoebe, is your mother up yet?" Connie's voice came from downstairs. "I don't want everything getting overcooked."

"We're coming." She took down Eleanor's fluffy dressing gown from behind the door and held it out to her mother. "You'd better get a move on. Gran's in a bossy mood."

"Okay love. Tell her I'll be down in a second." As soon as Phoebe was out of the room Eleanor grabbed her phone, suddenly desperate to speak to Daniel. Her fingers hovered over the screen for a second – what harm would it do to give him a call, just to see how he was? To find out what he was doing and whether he was missing her as much as she was missing him? "Damn it," she muttered to herself. "I mustn't."

She turned off the phone and opened a drawer to throw it in. Nestled amongst her undies was her favourite photo of them together, which she'd put away the night before. Picking it up, she raised it to her lips and kissed it, then rubbed the tea-damp smudge away with her thumb. She must try to put him out of her mind for the next few hours at least.

"*El-a-norrr!*"

"Okay, okay. I'm coming!" She dashed into the bathroom and had a speed wash then ran downstairs. She hadn't heard her mother use that singsong call since she was a schoolgirl and it made her feel about fifteen again.

Eleanor's nose twitched at the delicious savoury smell as she entered the kitchen.

"Good morning, love. I hope you're hungry. I've made your favourite."

"Thank you, Mum," she said, giving her a hug. "Could I ask why you're wearing my shower cap in the kitchen?"

"I'd have thought that was obvious," said Connie, tucking a stray curl under the floral cap. "I don't want to get the smell of breakfast in my hair when I've just had it done. We both want to smell fresh and lovely, don't we Bella?"

Eleanor's spaniel cocked her head to one side, hoping to receive a bit of sausage. She had been to Purrfect Paws for a de-dogging and was as clean and fragrant as she had been since puppyhood.

"Sit down, love. It'll be ready in a minute."

"You didn't need to do all this, you know? I'd have been happy with my usual yoghurt and a bit of fruit."

Connie was busy at the stove but the back of her head managed to convey disapproval. "You need a proper breakfast inside you on a chilly morning like this. And you've got a long day ahead of you." She moved deftly from toaster to pan, poking mushrooms and stirring eggs. After a few minutes, she was ready and carefully arranged the food on three warm plates, which her granddaughter carried over to the table.

"Here you go, Mum. A Gran special."

"You've made fried bread!" A wave of nostalgia swept over Eleanor as she took a bite from the hot crispy slice. "Mmm, yum." She leant across and squeezed her mother's hand affectionately. "The last time we had fried bread together was the morning of Dad's funeral. Do you remember?"

"Did we?" Connie put down her knife and fork and gazed at Eleanor in surprise. "No, I can't say I do. That day was all a bit of a blur. I think I just automatically did what Jack and I had always done at moments of crisis, which was have a proper breakfast and drink tea."

"With a tot of whisky in it, I seem to remember."

"Gran used to give you whisky in your tea? For breakfast? That's pretty hardcore," said Phoebe, clearly impressed. "No wonder everyone drinks like fishes in this family."

"We didn't have whisky every time, love. The tot of whisky was medicinal – Jack always said it was the thing to have when you'd suffered a nasty shock, you see. Or when you had just come in from a long walk on a cold day and needed warming up."

Eleanor laughed. "Anyway, that could explain why you don't remember the fried bread before Dad's send-off. Jenna and I were sure he would have approved."

"He would," said Connie, softly. "He definitely would." Her eyes filled with tears. "I do so wish he was here today."

"So do I, Mum, really I do." Eleanor felt tears spring into her own eyes as Phoebe handed out squares of kitchen paper.

"Thank you, love."

Phoebe looked from one to the other of them. "You're a fine pair. This is supposed to be a happy day, not one for tears."

"I am happy, sweetheart, really I am," said Connie, dabbing her eye with the corner of a tea towel. "I'm just a bit emotional that Jack isn't with us to see Eleanor get married."

"Well, thank goodness I'm here to keep an eye on you both. Now I'm going to run you a bath, Ma." Phoebe looked at the clock. "Erika will be here in an hour to do your hair and make-up. And before you ask – yes, you do have to have your face done."

Eleanor raised her hands in submission. "It's okay, we've had a practice run and tried out a few things from Erika's box of tricks. I had rather fancied the Lily Savage look, but we decided to go for something more natural in the end."

"Very funny," said Phoebe, collecting the dishes. "Does your outfit need ironing or are you good to go? Oh, and where are your shoes?"

"Everything's ready, darling." She laughed. "I have done this before you know? You just help your gran with the dishes. Oh, and if you could take Bella out for a scamper, that would be great." The dog sat up at the sound of her name, her tail swishing across the stone floor. "And it would be a bonus if you could bring her back not reeking of seaweed and dead fish."

Phoebe bent down and gave Bella a sniff. "Sorry old girl, but you're not allowed to smell like a proper dog until after the ceremony. We don't want people fainting from the pong."

After her bath, Eleanor put on some ivory silk underwear and wrapped herself in the dressing gown again. She stroked the clothes hanging on the wardrobe door and smiled. The choice of posh frocks in Combemouth was limited to say the least, so Eleanor had travelled to London to get some help from her sister. Jenna had been only too happy to raid Knightsbridge and trawl up and down Bond Street looking for something suitable, and on day two they found the perfect outfit: a copper-coloured suit with emerald flecks in the fabric that set off Eleanor's auburn hair and hazel eyes to perfection.

She wanted to put it on now, but had been given instructions to get her make-up and hair done first. Thinking back, it had been much more of a palaver when she married Alan in 1988. Just getting into her frock had been quite a performance because of the underskirt, tiara and veil. She had adored her dress with its sweetheart neckline and puffed sleeves. The day came back to her now in flashes, like scenes from a film. Had Alan really worn a lavender suit?

Her musings were interrupted by the sound of the front door opening. A couple of minutes later, Erika put her head into the bedroom and waggled a bottle of champagne.

"I thought you might be ready for some Bolly."

"What a lovely idea! I think we could all do with a bit of fizz this morning, so long as it won't make your hand wobble too much when you're transforming me into a thing of beauty."

"Don't worry about that – no one has a steadier hand when it comes to applying eyeliner."

"Marvellous. Let's grab some glasses."

A couple of hours later, Eleanor and her entourage were all dolled up and ready to go.

Connie started to well up again when she saw her daughter in her wedding outfit. "Oh, you do look beautiful!"

"Thanks, Mum. Don't let me ruin all of Erika's hard work by making me cry." She looked out of the front window. "Where's the transport that Joe was organising?" She had been slightly nervous designating a task to her son, but he had been determined to take part in the day. As she spoke, the campervan hove into view. "He's not taking me in that?" Eleanor had visions of the interior of her van, full of empty cardboard boxes, biscuit packets and dog paraphernalia.

"It'll be fine," said Connie. "I made him promise he'd clear it out."

In fact, Joe had done a thorough job and the lime-green van looked at its sparkling best both inside and out. Georgie had helped with the decorations so there were white ribbons strewn along the side of the vehicle.

"She looks fabulous, Joe. Thank you."

"You don't look too bad yourself, Ma," he replied, grinning.

Connie and Phoebe clambered in the back with the dog, and Joe drove them the short distance to the country house hotel where Harold, Georgie, Erika and the rest of the gang were waiting.

Daniel had chosen the venue because the room used for the ceremony was the library and books rose up on every side of them to a domed ceiling. The autumn sunlight flooded in through the tall windows, casting a warm glow on the faces of all their friends and family.

As Eleanor entered the room on her son's arm, the best man – Dan's brother – smiled and nudged the groom. Daniel turned to look at his bride and everything seemed to happen in slow motion as Eleanor moved towards him, wanting to capture every detail in her mind and hold it there. Daniel's smile was shy and tentative at first, but it soon spread and filled his face with pride as Eleanor walked towards him.

Daniel grinned and whispered hello as she reached his side.

"Hello my love." Eleanor felt the joy build inside her and wanted to laugh out loud, but instead she stood next to her husband-to-be, entranced by his loving gaze. And when they exchanged rings and promised to love each other forever, neither of them had any doubts that they had made the right choice.

Epilogue

It was the week before Christmas and The Reading Room was busy with shoppers looking for last-minute gifts when Eleanor saw a vaguely familiar figure enter the shop. It was Bill Widget, without his trademark dark glasses and with his jet-black hair now salt-and-pepper grey and cropped short. Daniel had come in to help Eleanor with the festive rush and it was he who stepped forward to greet their visitor.

"I hope you don't mind me turning up like this," said Bill, "but I heard you'd got wed and I wanted to wish you both every happiness for the future."

"Thanks, Bill. That's very decent of you," said Daniel, shaking his hand. "Isn't it, Eleanor?"

"Very kind." Eleanor still held Widget partly responsible for the rocky summer they'd all had and her tone was cool.

Connie had left her post in the caff and came over to see who the attractive older man was, smiling in recognition.

"I also wanted to say thanks to you and your mother."

"Whatever for?" said Eleanor.

"After you 'outed' me as Barry Charm, 'Be My Beach Baby, Baby' stormed the charts and my record company was so pleased that they're releasing a collection of Barry Charm's greatest hits in the spring.

There's also a tour lined up – just small venues, mind. I can't be doing Wembley and the like, not with my knees."

"Mother will be thrilled. She was a big fan of Barry Charm."

"What do you mean I 'was' a fan? I still am," said Connie, looking up at Bill. "I've got all your records."

"That's lovely, duck," he said, taking her hand and giving her a peck on the cheek. "You must all come to the Christmas show at the Waterborough Hippodrome as my guests – but only if you'd like to."

Connie beamed. "We definitely would. Wouldn't we?"

Eleanor nodded, deciding that Widget perhaps wasn't so bad after all.

"That's a very generous offer, Bill," said Daniel, shaking his hand again.

Widget smiled and turned to leave, then stopped. "Oh, there was one other thing. I've had a strong word with my manager and it's been arranged that profits from the shows will go into protecting The Combemouth Two and their pals." He smiled at Eleanor, shyly. "I hope you'll call off the Charmettes now?"

Eleanor laughed. "Don't worry, I can guarantee that you'll never see those girls again."

After Widget had left, Daniel put his arms around his wife's waist and pulled her close. "I'm so proud of you."

"And why's that?" she asked, caressing his shoulders and smiling.

"Not only have you saved the newts, you've also given Barry Charm a whole new career."

"Does that mean I deserve a kiss?"
"You certainly do, my darling."

THE END

If you enjoyed *A Summer of Surprises and An Unexpected Affair* you might also enjoy *The Bookshop Detective*.